The *Luck* of a SISTER

SALLY M. RUSSELL

authorHOUSE®

AuthorHouse™
1663 Liberty Drive
Bloomington, IN 47403
www.authorhouse.com
Phone: 1 (800) 839-8640

Published by AuthorHouse 07/07/2016

ISBN: 978-1-5246-1790-5 (sc)
ISBN: 978-1-5246-1789-9 (e)

Library of Congress Control Number: 2016911116

Print information available on the last page.

THIS BOOK IS DEDICATED
to the memory of my sister, Mary,
with whom I shared dreams, secrets,
and a wonderful sense of ESP.

Books by Sally M. Russell

An Escape For Joanna
*Finding A Path To Happiness
*Dr. Wilder's Only True Love
*Josh and The Mysterious Princess
*A Summer's Adventure
A Surprise Awaits Back Home
#The Attorney and the Untamed Tigress
#Magic in the Bride's Bouquet
^ Rewards of Faith
^ Luck of a Sister

*Haven of Rest Ranch Series
#Sequel
^ Sequel

CHAPTER ONE

*W*ell, here I am, Jill Marie Hale. I just attended my younger sister's graduation from UNC which is also my alma mater since I graduated just three years ago. I am so envious of her because she not only graduated with a Baccalaureate Degree with two majors, Business and Education, but she also has this extremely handsome guy watching over her like a God-sent guardian angel.

The first time Jessica was rescued by him was when she had to escape from her then wannabe boyfriend. He'd talked her into going to the beach over spring break, got a two bedroom suite to appease her rule of abstinence until marriage, but then proceeded to inform her that he didn't intend to abide by that rule when they'd gotten to the suite. She'd been able to lock herself in her room until early morning, when she was pretty sure he'd be asleep, and then she'd gone to the bus station to go back to campus. The bus, however, wasn't going to leave until late afternoon so she'd decided to walk along the beach. After several hours of wading in the water to keep her feet cool, she had gotten so hungry and exhausted that she conveniently fainted into the arms of this C.J. Peterson.

Well, his family had been so anxious to meet Jessica that they invited our whole clan to have dinner at their beautiful home last night here in Chapel Hill. Of course, C.J. hadn't told Jessica that he had gone to UNC and that this was his home town. He came to get us in a big limousine, of all things, and can you believe that there was a slightly older version of C.J. standing with his parents to welcome us when we reached their home?

My heart was doing all sorts of jumps and thumps because it was beating so hard as he introduced himself as T.J. (what is with all these initials, anyway?) With a head full of sandy-colored hair, brown eyes, and a nice athletic 6' build, who could not take notice?

Since we were the only two unattached members of the group, he'd remarked "two loners always have to stick together" and proceeded to become my escort, so to speak. I was in seventh heaven and floating on a cloud all evening with the attention he gave me. Actually, my luck with men hasn't been all that good, being from a small town and just a little shy when it comes to taking the initiative to get acquainted with people. So, when the evening was over and his only remark was that he hoped to see me again, I thought it had probably been one really nice time during which he'd shown good manners, but it would go nowhere.

❧

After the graduation was over, we had a great lunch, thanks to C.J., so I guess my parents, my pregnant older sister, her husband and I will be heading back home pretty shortly. I so wish I could see T.J. again, but that seems to be the story of my life--to meet and then to lose. Well, not exactly that bad, I suppose, since I've only had one or two boy-friends in my life and they were more like very good friends in high school, not one of those romantic situations. I had a few blind dates in college, but I realize now that I'd hit the books pretty hard except during my senior year when Jessica had been a freshman. We had so much fun together that year that we didn't need anyone else, male or female, to share our lives.

Jessica and her handsome guardian angel have been talking to my parents and now they're heading this way to say goodbye, I suppose. Jessica has to clean out her room at the sorority before she comes home. C.J. had asked if she would come back to the beach with him, (I would've jumped at the chance), but our dad asked if we could have her at home for a few days. C.J. readily agreed, when he discovered Jessica had a car of her own, but it wasn't like she didn't have a say in the matter. She definitely wanted to be home for a few days with her family, too, since it had been quite a while since she'd been there.

What is she saying to me? "Jill, would you like to stay here tonight and then I'll have you as company on the way home tomorrow? Mom says it'll be no problem at the bank, and C.J. says he'll call T.J. and we can go on a double date tonight. Would you be willing to do that for me, please?"

Would I be willing to do that? she asks. OK, just play it cool, Girl, and remember it's probably only for tonight. T.J. had said he'd like to see me again, but would he want it to be this soon? "Well, I could probably stay and do that, Jess, but how do we know T.J. will want to go along?"

C.J. can't contain his sheepish grin, which irritates Jessica a little, and she isn't long in telling him that she doesn't know now whether he really wants a date with her or he is just doing it for T.J. I can tell my sister isn't as mad as she wants it to sound, and C.J. just gave her the cutest smile and patted her cheek, so he doesn't believe she's too upset either.

I don't know what to expect when T.J. and his father come home from golfing, but I am dumbfounded when he looks at me, smiles and heads right toward me. Oh, what is he going to do in front of his family and right here in his parent's kitchen? His arms are going around me; he's kissing my forehead, my cheek, and now my lips. Oh, Wow!

"Hello, Jill. I'm really glad we get to see each other again," he says as he backs away so he can look down at me. "Are you going to give me the pleasure of escorting you someplace tonight?"

Everyone is laughing at something C.J. has said about the bashful doctor, but my mind is only on those kisses I'd just received. "Um.....I think so," as I barely manage to get the words out of my mouth.

After visiting with his parents for awhile, it's mentioned that there's a concert in the park that we could attend, so we soon take off. According to the guys, we have to stop at a drive-thru, though, before we go to the concert. Otherwise, T.J.'s stomach will be growling and disrupting everyone nearby who will be trying to listen to the beautiful music. He must apparently like to eat his meals at definite times, and I'm hearing a small rumble while C.J. is teasing him about our waiting until after the concert to eat. We do get a little snack, though, that does the trick for T.J. and tastes good to me, too.

The park is really pretty with some of the trees still in bloom, lush flowering shrubs and gorgeous flowers. The concert is great, especially with T.J.'s arm around me and an occasional kiss on the top of my head or a sweet whisper in my ear. Afterwards, we go to a very nice restaurant with very good food, very interesting conversation, and also a dance floor which we take advantage of. It is wonderful being held in his arms, except it ends too soon. We return to their parents' home where Jessica and I have been invited to spend the night. T.J. asks for my address and telephone number, but then, after a quick goodnight kiss, he's gone. I wonder if he'll ever use that information.

Jessica's car has a very low tire the next morning, and even though she tries to convince C.J. that it has a slow leak and will be all right after she gets some air in it, he insists that he follow us home. He'll cut across country to get back to the beach and his Beachside Resort only after he sees we're home safely. Well, the tire holds up fine, but we have a rather disturbing welcome home by Jessica's ex-boyfriend, Todd Olsen, who even has a gun which goes off and hits C.J. in the left leg. The ER doctor urges him not to drive for at least 24 hours so he stays at our house Monday night.

A hearing is held Tuesday morning, the Judge puts the ex-boyfriend in his parents' custody with orders to get him some help. C.J. takes off for the beach and then everything quiets down again. I go back to the bank, but all week I'm in some sort of a dream world since I can't get T.J. out of my thoughts. I do, however, balance up correctly each day, so I guess I'm functioning all right with the bank's money.

I don't know what I'm expecting, since we live about 35 miles apart, but when the phone rings Thursday night and it's T.J., I'm thrilled. He wants to drive down here Friday evening and take our whole family to dinner and then to a movie, which sounds so sweet until he says he wants to get to know Jessica better before she goes away to the beach. Maybe I hear it wrong, but I'm stunned, totally hurt, and then infuriated. Isn't C.J. old enough to make his own decisions about the friends he wants to have? And why do I think T.J. sounds so distant to me now when he'd been so attentive last Sunday night? Is it my imagination or is he going to make a play for Jessica when his brother is already involved?

Well, to be expected, my self-esteem plummets at least 50%, and all I want to do is hang up the phone and run to my room and cry. Wanting to be the protector of my baby sister, however, I have to consider Jessica's relationship with C.J. which I suspect is a little more than a friendship. If watching them together at graduation last weekend and his insistence to follow us home on Monday wasn't enough evidence, then the courage he portrayed in subduing Todd, when he was waving that gun around, was far beyond mere friendship in my estimation. A glance at that smile on his face, whenever he looked at her, and the kisses I just happened to observe, doesn't sway my beliefs either.

So, of course, I force excitement in my voice as I accept his invitation and give him directions to the house. I have no idea how I'm going to get through the evening as I expect to be ignored as he devotes all his attention toward my little sister with her long silky blond hair that has a soft natural wave, her beautiful blue eyes, and her great figure. How can I possibly compete with my ordinary medium brown hair which has slight natural waves at the ends? Maybe I should think about bleaching it, or I could dye it and become a perky redhead. I do have a few freckles across my nose to go with that. People remark about my pretty brown eyes that are like Dad's, and my figure isn't too bad, I guess, but there's just something about Jessica that makes people take notice of her whenever she's around.

❧

The whole family is so excited about getting to see T.J. again, and everyone has been ready for over an hour, including Jodi and Richard who arrived about 30 minutes ago. I was so lucky today that it was exceptionally busy at the bank, because it kept me from dwelling on my dilemma about tonight.

However, the doorbell is chiming away now and they are all waiting for me to go and invite him in. I'm so glad we have a foyer that separates the entrance from the living room. Maybe I can encourage him to go back home, and then I can tell the family it was a messenger he'd sent to let us know he couldn't make it. *Oh, come on, Jill, you know you're stuck for the evening so you might as well go to the door and face the music.*

"Hi, T.J., you're right on time," I greet him rather coolly. "Come on in, the family is waiting in the living room and they're all so anxious to see you again."

"I'm looking forward to seeing all of them again, too, Jill, but since we have a little privacy right here, I'd really like a special welcome from you. It's been a long week." He pulls me into his arms and the kiss is unbelievable, but I push him away.

"Wha--what was th--that for?" I stammer. "I tha-thought yu-you wan-wanted to see Jess--i--ca to--tonight."

"Jill, Jill, Jill,--Jessica has my brother acting like he did several years ago when he was in love with his high school sweetheart. When she died, he became a lost soul. He got through each day, even completed his college courses with very good grades, but he never was the same happy-go-lucky C.J. that I'd known before. It's wonderful seeing him in such good spirits so, of course, I want to get to know Jessica better, and this will probably be the only chance I have before she leaves to go to the beach. But, Sweetie, it's you I have come to see, and I don't want to be pushed away when I kiss you this time."

"Oooooh" I mumble as his lips are quickly playing havoc with my nerves. As he is quite firmly holding me and continuing the kiss, I hear a soft "Oops" and a little giggle that tells me my nosey sister has at least quickly glanced into the foyer to see what is holding up the party.

"I'm sorry, I must've gotten carried away," he chuckles and gives me that grin which is almost identical to the one I'd seen C.J. give to Jessica, and at that moment I understand why she is so willing to go back to the beach. Of course, C.J. had told us that he also has a plan for her to have the pre-school of her dreams. "I guess we'd better go and join the rest of your family," he continues, "so we can go eat before everyone is starved."

"Especially you," I laugh as I remember last weekend when we had to eat before we went to the concert. Taking his hand, we go into the living room, and the greetings begin.

It wasn't long before he remarked, "I made reservations at the Club for 6:30, so I guess we'd better be on our way. Would it be all right if Jessica rides with Jill and me, and we'll meet the rest of you there? I probably should have hired a limo like my little brother did last week, but I wasn't sure if you had that service here." His grin was adorable.

"That's no problem, T.J., we'll see you there in a few minutes," Richard speaks up. "My car is right out front so we'll follow you in it."

The evening is exceptional. T.J. does talk to Jessica quite a bit, but he doesn't forget me or the rest of the family. I chide myself for the rather bad day I'd spent because of my inhibitions to his remark about wanting to learn more about Jessica. I hadn't been aware of my apparent inferiority complex, but it had certainly shown its ugly head today.

There is a message on the answering machine waiting for Jessica when we arrive back at the house, so she excuses herself and goes to her room while the rest of us tell T.J. goodnight. I walk with him to his car and, of course, I get a wonderful kiss or two or three before he leaves. He also promises to call me again soon as he slips into his car.

I watch as he blinks the lights and then waves when he reaches the street, but I can only imagine that my fantasy bubble will burst any day now. How could I possibly be so lucky as to have a guy like T.J. interested in me?

CHAPTER TWO

*T*he following week moves along pretty fast. Everyone is working while our happy moving girl continues sorting through her belongings to see what she wants to take with her, what can be thrown away, and what can be given to the church's rummage sale. We are all trying to help her in the evenings until Wednesday night when she throws up her hands and more or less tells us to get out of her room so she can concentrate.

C.J. has called two or three times with all kinds of exciting news he has come up with about the pre-school possibilities. Of course, we are all excited, but Jessica is ecstatic. She decides to spend the weekend with us and then take off Monday on her new venture. Finally packed and ready to go, we have a wonderful weekend together, but it is hard to say goodbye before leaving for work Monday morning.

✍

I hadn't heard from T.J. all last week, and now I'm coming home from work on Monday realizing Jessica is truly gone. I'm a little sad and choked up so I decide to go to my room right after dinner. I don't know exactly what I'm going to do, but I've just thrown myself across the bed when the phone begins ringing. Thinking it's probably Jessica just calling to let us know she's gotten there safely, I let Dad answer downstairs. I'm a little surprised when he quickly calls up the stairs saying that I have a phone call.

"This is Jill Hale," I say, not knowing who to expect with all the telemarketers and other organizations calling almost every night asking for money. I wonder how they are so efficient at getting everyone's name and phone number, especially when I don't have mine listed in the phone book separate from the folks. I suppose I've given my name and number to some company who sells their lists.

"You sound very businesslike tonight, Jill. Were you expecting a call about a big investment you want to make, or maybe you were just getting ready to tell a certain someone, who is calling for a date, that you're not interested and you're going to hang up."

I hear a chuckle as I recognize T.J.'s voice and am at a loss for words for just a few seconds. "Jill, this is T.J. if you don't recognize my voice. I talked to C.J. and I understand

Jessica was going to the beach today, so I thought I'd just call to see if you're missing her as much as I missed C.J. the day he left after he bought the Beachside Resort. I was lost and wished I had someone to talk to, so I'm here if you'd just like to talk, but I don't want to intrude if you'd rather be left alone."

"Oh, T.J., that's so sweet. I'd just come up to my room not knowing what to do with myself, and then the phone rings. Thank you so much. I really do need someone to talk to, but I wish you were here."

"I was hoping you'd say that because I'm about four minutes from your house. I had thought about just showing up, but then decided I'd better call to find out if you wanted to see me. That way I could've turned around and gone back home if you'd preferred to be alone. You wouldn't have had to feel sorry about my driving down here for nothing."

"You're almost here? I can't believe you'd understand how I feel tonight and want to be with me. How close are you now?"

"Just a minute or so before I turn into your drive. Will you meet me at the door?"

"You'd better believe I will. Goodbye for one minute!" I quickly glance at myself in the mirror, brush my teeth, and run down the stairs. "Mom, Dad," I call, "I can't believe T.J. is turning into the driveway."

They come to welcome him, but then excuse themselves to go to the den where they spend many an evening together since we girls have grown up. Dad sometimes works on his insurance papers and Mom either writes letters or reads. They always explain that it's the togetherness that counts, and we're always welcome to join them anytime we'd like, but unless we need something, we usually let them have their evenings together.

"Well, you look lovely, Jill, as usual," he says as we stand awkwardly in the middle of the living room looking at each other. He gives me that devastating smile and I notice a dimple appear in his cheek. I hadn't noticed it before and it caused me to wonder what had caused it to appear now. His voice, however, brought me back to reality, at least, to listen.

"Can we sit down or do you have somewhere else you'd like to go? We can go for a ride, if you'd like, or we could go for a walk. It's really too nice a night to be inside." He waits for an answer, but I still say nothing. "Jill, are you going to talk to me?" He gives me only a few seconds to say something and then takes me in his arms and kisses me.

I don't react and I know I'm behaving strangely, but I can't help it. Since he hadn't called all last week, I'd thought the fantasy world I'd been in was over, but now he's here again in my home. Finally, I find my voice. "Oh, I'm sorry. I guess I'm so surprised that you're here that I don't know what to say. Would you like to sit on the porch for awhile and then maybe go for a walk, or vice versa?"

"That sounds like a plan,: he chuckles. "I'm glad you've finally decided to emerge from that trance you were in so I can enjoy holding you in my arms and maybe getting a real Jill Hale kiss. Since I've been sitting in the car while driving down here, why don't we walk first and then sit on the porch?" When we get to the foyer, he puts his hand on my shoulder, turns me around to face him, and whispers, "Only first, let's try that kiss again, shall we?"

That most likely wasn't the best idea because when he finishes that kiss, I really do need to sit down because my knees are weak and I find myself leaning against him to try to get my balance. My arms find their way around his neck, but now his arms are pulling me so close that I can feel his heart beating against my chest. I let my arms drop quickly and push away.

"I th--think we--we'd bet--better wa-walk now," I stammer as I try to look anywhere but at him.

He tilts my chin and looks straight into my eyes, smiles, and then kisses me on the forehead. "You're probably right, Sweetie," he chuckles as he grabs my hand and heads for the door. "You do something to me, Jill, that I don't remember ever feeling before, even when I was engaged. I guess God knew that it wouldn't work out long before I did."

He never lets go of my hand as we walk for almost an hour, although he does bring it up to his lips a few times to kiss. He explains why he hadn't called. "I didn't want to do anything to disturb the family reunion. You really didn't have that much time to spend with Jessica, with all of you working every day, so I felt you needed your evenings together. I did have quite a busy week myself with appointments so I spent a few evenings working on reports.

I also played golf Wednesday afternoon for some exercise. So, tell me about your week."

"I guess the most thrilling part of the week was seeing the excitement in Jessica's eyes when we came home from work the day C.J. had called and finally told her about the building he'd found for the pre-school. He'd wanted to wait until she got there and surprise her, but he'd said just enough to peak her curiosity and she begged for a little information which he reluctantly gave her. We had some good conversations at the dinner table, Jodi and Richard joined us a couple of evenings, and the two of us got together with a bunch of our friends one night to say goodbye. We also went one afternoon to play our amateur type of golf. We were terrible, but we had a great time."

"So you enjoy golf. I'm glad to hear that because it's one of my favorite pastimes, and I like to go to some of the PGA tournaments, too. Would you like to accompany me if I can arrange to get some tickets for one that isn't too far from here?"

"You're kidding, aren't you? Those tournaments are usually for four days. How do you expect to manage that? I'll have you know right now, T.J., that I don't share a bed with any man. I'm telling you now so there will be no misunderstanding if we continue to see each other."

"I'm glad to hear that, too, Jill," he chuckles, "but we'd go just for the weekend and I would get a two-bedroom suite or two separate rooms, depending on availability and your preference. I wouldn't try to take advantage of you, Jill, I promise."

"Todd promised Jessica, too, and we both know how that ended. I guess his promise was just for a two-bedroom suite, though, so I shouldn't compare the two."

"C.J. and I were both raised to believe in abstinence until marriage so you really don't need to worry about your little sister with C.J. either. In fact, we just discussed that recently and we're both still on the same page. Of course, neither of us expected to be this old without being married, though, so we do like to play around a little."

His chuckle sounds a little too dangerous, and I feel him looking at me most likely to see how that last statement might have affected me. I'm certainly not going to give him the satisfaction of knowing it shocked me a little, but I suppose my face is giving me away with a stupid blush. I wish I could learn to keep my emotions under control.

We get back to the house and sit down on the glider. He is still holding my hand but switches to his other hand so he can put his arm around my shoulders. "I guess I should thank you for the assurance, T.J. Not having dated much, it has always been a fear of mine, since I've read a lot about date rape, drugs, and promiscuity among the youth today. As we get older, the reports make it sound as if most guys and gals just take sex as a natural part of a date. Sometimes it's on the very first date, I've heard, and sometimes it's been a pick-up. I just can't imagine doing that."

"Getting to know someone well is the basis for a good marriage, and I intend to take plenty of time to learn about the girl I ask to marry me. I made one mistake, and I certainly don't intend to make another if I can possibly help it."

"Are you saying that you've actually been married?"

"No, Jill, I haven't been married and I haven't been in bed with a girl, either. At my age, I guess it sounds a little strange, but I thought I'd found the one I wanted for my wife when I was a junior in pre-med. We'd dated for over two years and I gave her a diamond shortly after I started Med School. We'd planned to marry the following June, but in April, while we were on a date, she begged me to take her to a motel room because she couldn't wait until June. I refused to do that, but I told her I'd agree to get married sooner although I'd prefer to wait until June because my studies were quite hard that first year.

Well, she got enraged, took off the ring and threw it at me as she informed me she was carrying another man's child. She just disappeared then and I couldn't find her. I came to the conclusion that she'd lied to her parents, who lived in another town, because they blamed me for the pregnancy and wouldn't give me any information about where she had gone. I finally had to give up so I could concentrate on becoming a doctor. That's my sad story, Jill, but I'm hoping it won't turn you against me. I'd really like to get to know you a whole lot better."

"Thanks, T.J. for sharing that with me. There is no way it could turn me against you, but rather it makes me admire you more. You and C.J. are two exceptional guys, and I'm sort of glad now that Jessica had to be rescued from Todd. She got to meet C.J. and, consequently, I got to meet you." I can't stop my giggle until T.J. finally covers my lips with his, successfully sending those tingles all over my body. Is this what he means by playing around?

I grow a little apprehensive and try to wiggle free, but he continues to hold me tight as his lips leave mine and he softly whispers, "Don't be afraid, Jill. Those little tingles I think you're experiencing are a sign that we have some good chemistry, and it gives me hope that we just might have a future together. What do you think?"

"I think it's very scary and I'm not sure I'm ready for all these reactions. The kiss in the foyer was rather weakening in the knees, but I don't know how I would stand up at all after this one. Don't you think it's about time for you to head home?"

He lets out a laugh that I think Mom and Dad could've heard way back in the den, if they're still up, and I don't really know how to react. As he turns the light on in his watch, he stands up quickly and then helps me up. "You are so sweet, Jill, and I'm sure you're right again. I didn't realize it had gotten so late and I've got a little drive yet ahead of me. I've had a wonderful evening, Sweetie, and I look forward to seeing you again. May I have just one more little kiss before I leave?"

Of course, he doesn't wait for an answer as he pulls me against him and kisses my cheek and then lightly on the lips. He opens the door for me, runs his fingers through my hair as I go by, and then takes the steps two at a time on his way to his car. I can only stand and stare when he flashes the car lights as he backs out and drives away.

I say a short prayer as I lock the door and climb the stairs to bed. "Please keep him safe, Dear Jesus, as he drives on the busy highway tonight."

CHAPTER THREE

*W*hen I wake up Tuesday morning, I decide that there are two things I have to do as soon as possible. One, I need to talk to Jessica, and two, I'm going to sign up for some golf lessons. I'm not going to be embarrassed if T.J. asks me to play golf with him; and I want to make sure I know all the rules for scoring the booboos I'll probably make because I'll be so nervous. Jessica and I both played on the girls' golf team in High School, and I even played during my first two years in college, but that was 6 to 8 years ago. Some practice and some reviewing definitely need to be done.

Mom and Dad are interested to know how the surprise visit had gone last night and I actually tell them about the kiss that sent tingles up my spine. They look at each other and grin, which doesn't help me a bit. I start to walk out of the room to get ready for work, but they call me back and explain, the best they can, that the tingles are only one signal that the other person meant something more than friendship to me.

Oh, Whoopee. I knew that without those tingles telling me. I think my intelligence is a bit more sophisticated than having tingles tell me I like T.J. better than any other friend I ever had. I must admit, though, that the more I think about those feelings, the more I like them, and I hope he'll come back and cause them again. Oh, I sound so naive.

Right after work I go to the golf course and sign up for lessons on Tuesdays and Thursdays and I get to start my first lesson immediately. With just a few tips from the pro, my swing improves greatly and the ball is going straight down the fairway, but my putting will need a lot more practice. It was a good lesson and I'm looking forward to Thursday.

Jessica called tonight and we talked for almost an hour about all the reactions we're having to these handsome brothers. I felt so much better when we'd hung up although it's a little embarrassing to have my younger sister know more about the dating game than I do. Well, she did date Todd for almost two years so she is a great help, and she assured me that Todd and C.J. are nothing alike. She is quite sure now that she never really loved Todd.

Jessica has been staying with Emily, the one who works in the Resort and had also grown up living next door to the guys. During their talks, she told Jessica about the losses T.J.

and C.J. had faced with their first loves. Jessica was so glad T.J. had confided in me.

When Sunday came and T.J. hadn't called, Dad asked if I would like to play 9 holes of golf with him because his usual partner was out of town. I agreed and he also asked Mom, but she elected to just ride along in the golf cart with him. I took a cart by myself since I wasn't sure if I'd be very accurate in a real game and I might be all over the fairway. Actually, I think I did pretty well after just two lessons, and Dad only beat me by 9 strokes or 1 stroke per hole. He said he was impressed.

I'm really surprised when the phone rings fairly late the next Sunday evening. Dad motions that it's for me and whispers, "You may want to take it in your room," and I notice he has a big grin on his face. I hurry to my room although I have no idea why T.J. would call so late if he wants to see me tonight. Of course, he'd surprised me that Monday night after Jessica had left, so maybe he's doing it again. "Hey, this is Jill."

"Hey, Yourself, Sweetie, has your week gone well?"

"Yes, I've had a very interesting week. How about you?"

"Aren't you going to elaborate at all on your interesting week before I tell you why I'm calling? You sound like you're in a good mood so I'm rather curious about what you've been doing. Come on, Miss Hale, tell me."

"It's really nothing. It's actually been almost two weeks since I've heard from you so I've talked to Jessica a couple of times and that was fun. I took a couple of golf lessons and

Dad and I played 9 holes last Sunday. He only beat me by 9 strokes so I'm happy that my skills haven't been completely lost. Otherwise, I've just been working and seeing some of my old friends."

"I'm sorry I haven't called you before now. The life of a doctor, I guess. You did tell me you liked golf, but not that you could play that well with your dad. What else are you holding out on me? Are these old friends going to be some competition for me?"

"I'm not telling. You'll have to find out as time goes by." I really try to sound just a little sarcastic but I don't think I'm very convincing.

"I can see you don't always play fair, Little Miss Hale, so I guess I'll have to hire me a detective to investigate your past and your present."

"You wouldn't spend good money on something like that, would you? Please don't bother because there's not very much to learn. Now, why did you call?"

"I don't know whether I should ask you now since you're being so mysterious, but I need to know your answer no later than Tuesday so I guess I'll have to bend my rules just a little and give you a break. There was a local golf tournament last weekend that Dad and I got involved in and somehow we were able to win the father and son match.

Now there's going to be a banquet on July 28th, when the various awards are given out, and I would be most appreciative if you'd attend with me. Mom will be there with Dad so you'll know someone besides me. I'll need to drive down and get you Friday night, though, since we have our Saturday morning office hours, and then take you back Sunday afternoon or evening. It's fine with Mom if you stay with them unless you'd rather stay with me," he chuckles.

"Now who's playing with fire?" I laugh. "It sounds like a fun weekend, T.J., but I do have a couple of questions: 1. Is this a casual or a formal affair, and 2. Do you have two bedrooms and are your beds twin, double, queen, or king?" I try to sound as serious as I can, but his hesitation causes me to start giggling.

"You little devil, Jill. Just for that, I should make you stay at my place and sleep with me in my extra long twin size bed. How would you like that?" he chuckled.

"Actually, I don't believe that you sleep in a twin size bed, but there is always the floor if you have an extra pillow. I'll just pray for a good night's sleep at your parents, but before we get completely carried away here, what about the banquet?"

"Oh, I forgot to tell you, didn't I? Everyone is going in their latest birthday suit so you won't have to worry about packing much in your suitcase."

"O.K. we've carried this far enough, T.J.," I giggle. "What am I really supposed to bring to wear to this banquet?"

Unable to control his laughing for a good 10 seconds or more, he then remarks, "I'm sorry, Jill, but this has been the funniest conversation I think I've had since I was a kid. You seem to bring out all the silliness in me and it feels so good. I guess I've been serious for too long. But to answer your question about the banquet, it is sort of casual, not shorts or swimsuits, of course, but a sundress or a skirt and blouse would be fine or even a nice summer pantsuit would suffice. Now, are both of your questions answered to your satisfaction?" His laughter is starting again, and I can't help but join in.

I've probably checked my closet ten times trying to decide what I want to wear to this banquet that is slowly coming up next Saturday night. I have several modest style dresses that I wear to the bank, but I can't get my thoughts off of one I saw recently in a store window. Finally I couldn't resist going in and trying it on, and of course, buying it. It's a pale yellow cotton knit styled with a somewhat daring vee neckline on a nicely fitted sleeveless bodice. The skirt flares down to the knee where the material ruffles a little from the handkerchief hemming. It has a narrow colorful sash that can be worn or not, although it doesn't have a defined waist and can be dressed up or down with the jewelry and shoes selected. I hope it's not too dressy, but that's the one I want T.J. to see me in. I'll take a pair of my Bermuda shorts and a pair of crop pants with a couple of tops, plus another dress to wear to church if we should go Sunday morning. That should do it. Now, all I need is for this final week to quickly slip by so Friday night will be here. I can hardly wait.

T.J. and I had talked a couple of times since his invitation to the banquet, but he hadn't made another trip down to see me. Now, with my two golf lessons and another lengthy conversation with Jessica, the week does seem to fly by and I'm excitedly waiting for T.J. to come. He hadn't said exactly what time he would be here, but when 8 o'clock comes and goes, I begin to worry. Could he have been involved in an accident, had he gotten tied up with a critical patient he just couldn't leave, or had he changed his mind about coming?" *Why haven't I thought to ask for his cell phone number?* I chide myself as I pace the floor until almost 9 o'clock when the phone begins to ring.

"T.J. is that you?" I'm crying by now, but I can't help it. "I've been so afraid that you were in an accident or had decided you didn't want me to go with you to the banquet after all."

"Yes, Jill, it's me. I'm so sorry, but Dad and I both got called in to help with victims of a three-car pile up, and I didn't have time to do anything but care for the patients. Every thing is calm now and I know it's terribly late, but can I still come and get you?"

"Are you sure you aren't too tired to drive down here? I could drive up there in the morning while you're at the office if that would help."

"That's awfully sweet of you, Jill, but I need to have you with me and in my arms for a little while tonight to help get the past several hours back in their proper places. I'm already to our city limits, so I could be there in 30 minutes or less. Is that all right, Jill? Please say yes."

"I'll be waiting. How about some coffee before we start back?"

"That sounds great. I'll see you soon."

CHAPTER FOUR

*A*s he'd predicted, T.J. turned into the driveway at 9:30 and hurried toward the door where I'm waiting. He picks me up in his arms and twirls around and around in our small foyer. When he finally sets me on my feet again, he whispers, "I'm so happy to see you, Jill. It's been too terribly long since we were together." Of course, he proceeds to kiss me like he really meant he had missed me, and those tingles are now messing with my brain.

"I have the coffee ready, but I wasn't sure whether you'd had time to eat so I fixed a little something for you. I'm glad I did because your stomach is talking to you big time," I giggle. "Come on into the kitchen and we'll try to pacify that crying tummy of yours."

"I'd considered stopping and getting a sandwich, but then I decided I was in too big of a hurry to see you so I thought we could stop on the way back. I should've known you'd anticipate my hunger."

"I just hope it's enough. I made two turkey, cheese, and lettuce sandwiches with a few olives on the side, some chips, and a big piece of chocolate cake that Mom and I baked this afternoon. We also have cottage cheese if you'd like some of that."

"It all sounds wonderful, and I do love cottage cheese if it's not too much trouble. Are you going to join me? I'll share," he grins as he takes his first bite of sandwich.

"I'll join you with a piece of cake and a cup of coffee, when you get to your dessert, but right now I'll just sit and watch you eat and thank God that you're safe. I really started to worry when you hadn't come by 7 o'clock, but then I was pacing the floor from 8:00 on until you called at 9:00. I was thinking I need to have your cell phone number, but you probably wouldn't have been able to stop to answer today if I had been able to call."

"It would've been wonderful to hear your voice and realize you were so worried about me, but you're right, I wouldn't have been able to talk. There were 7 adults, 5 teens, and 2 children in the three cars, and each one had an injury of some kind. A lot of prayers were sent by the crew of doctors, and He answered by letting us save all of them. Four are critical but stable, and we expect all of them to recover fully.

I'm ready to eat this yummy looking cake now, so are you going to join me? I can't thank you enough, Jill, for fixing this for me. You went way beyond the call of duty, and I'll try to make it up to you, maybe a little at a time." He then gives me that fabulous plus very sexy smile.

After the dishes are in the dishwasher, we decide we'd better be on our way. "May I say hello to your parents before we leave or are they not here?"

"I'm sorry but they aren't here. They were invited over to some friends to play some bridge and have dessert. They were hoping to see you before they left, but it wasn't to be this time."

"I guess I have some making up to do there, too. Shall we go then?" He lets out a big yawn as we head for the door.

I hesitate to say anything, but I can see that he is very tired and I don't want to take any chances of our being the next victims of an accident. I spoke very quietly when I said, "T.J., I'm wondering if you'd consider letting me drive so you can relax after the ordeal you worked through this evening? I saw the yawn and I wouldn't want you falling asleep at the wheel."

"No, Jill, I'll be okay," as another big yawn escapes. "On the other hand," he grins, "I don't want us to end up in the hospital tonight either. Do you think you can drive this car of mine? I guess it's not much different from any other once you put it in Drive and get it moving except it does react quickly when you turn the wheel and moves fast when you step on the gas pedal."

"I think I can manage. You might instruct me while we're still in town and then I'll be fine when we're on the highway." He opens the door for me and then scoots around to the passenger seat. I hold out my hand for the key, but his eyes are already closed. "T.J., I need the keys," I say as I pat his arm.

"Wha--what?" he jerks awake.

"I need the key to the car," I repeat.

"You can't have the key to my car," he smirks, "because I'm driving. See?" He reaches out for the steering wheel and then snaps awake. "Sorry, I guess I really am too tired to drive." He digs into his pocket and hands me the key.

Before I have backed out of the driveway, he's asleep again. The car handles well and it's a thrill getting to drive a sparkling new sports car. There weren't too many cars on the road, actually, and we're approaching Chapel Hill within minutes, it seems. I hadn't really watched the speedometer and now I wonder how fast I was really driving. When we reach the city limits, I pat his arm again to see if he'll tell me where I'm supposed to go. I think I remember how to get to his parents', but I'm not totally sure. It's a community that's out a ways and I was never there before the night we'd had dinner with his parents. "T.J., please wake up now. I need you to give me some directions."

He finally opens his eyes. "You mean we're here already and I slept all the way with a girl driving my car? I must really be slipping because no girl has ever driven a car of mine before. I guess that means I'll have to marry you," he laughs, "but why don't you pull over and I'll take it from here?"

"Are you sure you're awake? You're talking rather crazy, you know."

"I'm awake and ready to party, thanks to you, Sweetie. There's a little restaurant up here where you can turn in, and I'll show you how awake I am."

The restaurant is already closed so the parking lot is empty. As we are switching seats by walking around the back of the car, he stops me for a little kiss just as a car full of teenagers drive by. The cheering and hollering is embarrassing, but T.J. just gives them a wave and continues with the kiss until one yells, "Hey, Doc, I didn't know you had it in you. More power to you." That remark makes him quickly look at the car that had stopped and was turning around.

"Get in the car, quick," he says as he heads for the driver's side which is nearer the street. About the time he opens his door, the car has pulled up beside him and a young male voice says, "Dr. Peterson, this is Johnny Bradford. You took care of my leg last year when I hurt it playing football. You seemed to be all business then, very efficient but you also seemed a little sad. My parents told me about your earlier loss so I'm happy to see that you do have a social life. Sure hope we didn't scare you with our yelling. We're sort of a crazy bunch of rowdy teenagers, I guess, enjoying our summer vacation. You aren't having car problems, are you?"

"No, Johnny, we were just changing driver duties. You guys be careful because I had to help patch up about five of your age group earlier this evening."

"We heard about the wreck. Was anybody killed?"

"I'm happy to say that everyone has survived although there are some still in critical condition. So, I say again, please be careful, and watch the curfew hour. Thanks, Johnny, for remembering my work on you, and I'll try to smile more around my patients. Is your leg still doing OK?"

"It's great, thanks to you. Goodnight, Sir."

"Goodnight, Guys." He'd been standing on the inside of his partially open door and now he climbs on in. "Whew, that was quite an experience. I never dreamed that a good teenage football player would remember what a doctor looked like, let alone his name. Next time, I'd better let you continue driving until we're at our destination. I did enjoy that little kiss, though," he chuckles as he's adjusting the seat and mirrors.

"It's so nice to see that there are teenagers who are respectful of their elders, even if they do it in a somewhat unusual way," I remark and suddenly feel like praying. "Thank you, God, that our experience tonight was with good, decent boys who just wanted to say hello to a doctor they were grateful to. We ask that you watch over them and see that they arrive home safely. Please watch over us during the last leg of our trip, especially now that we have changed drivers."

T.J. throws his head back against the headrest and just sits there and laughs. "Jill, you are such a fresh breath of air, and I'm so glad that I've met you." He puts the car in gear and pulls out onto the road. We are soon turning into the driveway at his parents'. I notice that it's totally dark, and then I hear T.J. quietly question, "I wonder why they didn't leave a light on? They knew you were supposed to stay with them tonight. Let me check."

He's back shortly with a confused look on his face. "I thought they may have left the door unlocked, but no such luck. I don't know what to say, Jill, but it looks as if you're going to stay at my place tonight whether you want to or not. I promise I won't hurt you, but I know this isn't what you agreed to, either."

"You never did tell me whether you have one or two bedrooms or the sizes of your beds. I guess I'll see for myself now, won't I?"

"You aren't terribly upset with me?"

"If I thought you'd done this deliberately, I'd be extremely angry, but under these circumstances, we'll just have to play the hand we've been dealt. Isn't that the way that old saying goes?"

Not being able to control his chuckling, he backs rather slowly out of his parents' driveway and heads for his condo. "Jill, you are a super sport, and I must say that I admire you tremendously. By the way, would you like to know the answer to your question, or do you want to have the pleasure of checking it out yourself?"

"I'll check it out myself, thank you. I've always liked looking at people's homes to see the different arrangements, furniture, decor, and how much dust I can find. It'll be fun to see what your tastes are in furniture and colors. Will they be antiques like the beautiful pieces your folks have, or are you more a modern freak? Yes, I think this is going to be a delightful adventure."

"Oh, boy! Jill, will you give me the benefit of the fact that I'm a busy doctor and I don't have much time to keep my home spic and span? I sure hope this was the week my cleaning lady came; otherwise I'm probably going to flunk your white glove treatment."

Before long I watch as he pulls into a private parking garage under a building I can recognize as one I've admired many times. "How long have you lived here, T.J.? When I was in college, I loved to ride my bike around this area and always thought it would be a great place to live."

"Really? I've only lived here since I started practice with my dad three years ago, but I'm buying the building now so I'm my own landlord. When it went on the market about 18 months ago, Dad recommended that I check into the price, have an expert check out the condition of the building, and then consider buying it. He knew it was a very desirable neighborhood, and I couldn't go wrong by owning it. It has really worked out for me." We are now inside the building and he whispers, "Here's the elevator."

"Oh, the owner doesn't get to live on first floor?" I whisper back.

We're inside the elevator before he answers, "The owner doesn't want to live on first floor. That would make it too easy for the complainers to find him. The owner lives on the top floor and has made a rooftop garden to enjoy when he has a leisure moment."

"Do I get to continue my adventure up there, too?"

"It would be my pleasure to take you up there tonight and enjoy the moon and stars, if you aren't too tired. Did you happen to notice that big moon as we were driving along? It almost looks like a full moon but I didn't think it was quite time for that. Anyway, this one is absolutely gorgeous, not to mention romantic." Of course, I notice the devilish grin.

"I got to see it all the way from home to here, while you were getting your beauty rest. It was so big and bright that I couldn't help but think of the Magi following the star to Bethlehem. Wouldn't that have been a wonderful experience?"

"I guess it would have, but I'm not sure I would've enjoyed the living arrangements they had to put up with back then. I guess I'm pretty spoiled when it comes to all the neat modern conveniences we have today."

I feel the elevator stop and then T.J. says, "We're at the end of the line, Jill. Come into my parlor said the spider to the fly." He gently puts his free hand to the small of my back and we walk together toward an entrance door which could welcome a queen.

My heart is pounding and in a way I want to turn and run, but since there's no place to go and he's promised to behave, I need to relax and enjoy his company. I do have some mace in my purse, but it's so old that there's probably no strength left in it. I'll just have to trust that as a doctor he values his integrity and my friendship.

Chapter Five

*H*e sets my suitcase down on the marble tile of the large entry area and turns to look at me with that dazzling smile and dimple. "Well, Sweetie, what would you like to see first now that we're here? There's a powder room right over there if you need it. The bedrooms are on down the hallway to your right, you can see the living room ahead of you, the dining room is rather obvious, and the kitchen is to the right of the eating area."

"Since you said bedrooms, I assume that there are two."

"Actually, there are three, but I've taken the one nearest the master bedroom for my office. Let's take your suitcase and hanging bag first and check the guest room. You can hang your clothes in the closet before they get anymore wrinkled from my carrying them over my arm. It's getting pretty late, so if we're going to the roof, we should go rather soon because you're most likely getting tired. I've had my nap so I'm good for several hours, but I don't want to keep you up."

"You're the one who has to work tomorrow so you decide what we should do."

"How about taking a quick tour of the bedrooms and my office now, then we'll go up on the roof for a little while. When we come down from there, we'll decide if you want to see the rest of the rooms tonight or tomorrow."

The first stop is the guest bedroom and it is lovely. The antique furniture is there, a charming dresser with mirror, a chest of drawers, and a rocker with a table and lamp. One wall is papered, where the queen-size four poster bed and night stand are located, and the others are painted a soft creamy yellow. Natural linen drapes are at the double windows in a shallow alcove holding the rocker and lamp. The chest of drawers is across from the foot of the bed, next to the door to the bath, and the dresser is on the entrance wall facing the side of the bed and the windows. It is inviting to say the least.

His office contains a couch in sable leather against the wall next to the door to the bath that is shared with the guest bedroom. Two upholstered chairs, one at each end of the couch, make a nice seating area which faces a built-in oak entertainment center. His desk of weathered oak is separated from the seating area and is surrounded on three sides by oak bookshelves, one section being the back side of the entertainment center. I can see that the shelves are literally overflowing with his books of all kinds, including a lot of medical manuals, of course, but also mysteries, non-fiction historical books, and even a few rare biographies. The fourth wall has a rectangle table with a lamp, a chair on each side, but the single large painting above the table is outstanding. The upper walls of the room are painted a creamy deep tan while the lower section is paneled in unstained oak and topped with a chair rail of the same wood.

The master bedroom is probably twice as big as the other two and really something to behold. At one end there is a king-size bed with an ornate headboard that I could have drooled over. Large night stands are on each side with the most outstanding manly brass lamps. A stack of 3 or 4 books is on one of the tables while a clock and a radio appear to be on the other. A seating area, at the other end of the room, which must be behind both the inside and outside hallways as well as part of the elevator, has a very comfortable looking recliner on each side of a fireplace, a large square coffee table with an array of candles and a stack of medical papers. I'll definitely have to check out the picture above the fireplace later, but it really looks impressive. There are also fairly large built-in shelves in here with a few more books, which look like some sports manuals and photograph albums, but I see that the majority of these shelves hold framed pictures.

What is really impressive in this room, though, is the bathroom. It is huge, with two showers, a hot tub, two walk-in closets with built-in drawers, shoe racks, and shelves as well as the hanging rods for zillions of clothes. I notice T.J.'s is far from full, but the other one, I'm glad, is completely empty.

"This is a fabulous condo, T.J. It's homey, elegant, and beautiful as well as very practical. You, or your interior decorator, did an outstanding job."

"Thank you very much, Miss Hale. Are you ready to explore the rooftop now? It should be at its best this time of night."

"Just show me the way, Dr. Peterson. I'm really very anxious to see this night time phenomenon of yours."

He grabs a rather large bag in one hand as he starts for the door, holding my hand in the other. The enclosed stairway has about 15 steps up to a most unusual space which has been turned into a fantasy garden. A light in each corner gives just enough illumination to see that there are small evergreen bushes, tall grasses, flowers, a large fountain that almost sounds like a river cascading down the mountainside, a swing for two with a canopy top, plus a few other individual chairs. Over in one corner is a mesh enclosed sunroom which would provide shelter when the sun is too hot or the mosquitoes are too bad. He'd dropped the bag when we first got up here, but now he opens it and pulls out two blankets and two pillows and starts to put them down on the soft artificial grass.

"What are you doing?" I ask unbelievingly.

"Jill, you can't look at the stars and moon correctly if you're not lying on your back. Don't you remember going out in the yard, when you were little, lying on the ground and being mesmerized by the stars? Em, C.J. and I used to spend hours lying on our backs in the back yard trying to find the big dipper and all the other constellations. It was even more exciting when we'd see a shooting star streaking through the sky. Come over here and lie down. I've made it pretty comfortable with a pillow for your head." He sits down on one of the blankets and pats the other for me to come join him.

"I don't know if I should. It looks rather suspicious to me."

"Jill," he laughs, "You have a separate blanket and I won't even touch you if it'll make you feel less nervous. I'll even move your blanket over more so I can't even reach you." He gets up and proceeds to pull my blanket about five feet away from his. "How's that?"

I still stand there motionless, feeling absolutely ridiculous for not being able to lie down and look at the stars. I want to, so what is my hang-up?

All of a sudden I'm in his arms and then on the blanket that he'd said was mine. I'm ready to fight, but when I look around, he's five feet away on his own blanket. I just start crying.

"Jill, what is wrong? Have you looked at the stars and that beautiful moon at all?"

"No, and I don't know what's wrong. I guess I'm shaking because this is so new to me, and I'd love some warm arms around me, like my dad's. I'm really scared, T.J."

"Do you want me to come over there with my warm arms and see if that will help? I'm not your dad, but I'll be happy to hold you like he would."

"I guess so if you promise I won't regret it."

"I promise, Jill, with all my heart, that I won't hurt you."

He drags his blanket next to mine and pulls another one from the bag. He puts the new one over me and pulls me into his arms. He is so warm that I apparently snuggle up to him without even realizing it, and in minutes, I'm asleep.

The next morning, I find myself under the covers in the guest room, my sandals are off, but I'm otherwise still dressed. I smell coffee brewing and it makes me realize I'm really quite hungry. I slip my sandals on, go to the bathroom to freshen up a little, and then head for the kitchen that he'd pointed out last night. A gourmet cook would be in his glory with a kitchen like this to work in.

T.J. has his back to me as he stands at the stove but without turning around he says, "Good morning, Jill."

"Good morning, T.J.," I whisper as I try to take in all the extraordinary features of this room. "It must be so exciting to come in here every morning and fix a nice gourmet breakfast for yourself as you watch all the goings on outside. The windows are fantastic in the whole condo, but I think the ones in here outdo all the others."

"I'm glad you like it. I did quite a bit of remodeling after I bought the building, and I've been really satisfied with the results. Did you sleep well? I'm so sorry you didn't get to enjoy the night time sky before falling asleep, but it was late and I knew you were tired."

"I'm sorry, too, but the bed is extremely comfortable. I don't know why you didn't wake me, though, so you didn't have to carry me down all those steps. I feel ashamed of the way I acted, but everything seemed to loom like ignominy to me up there on the roof. Can you forgive me?"

"There's nothing to forgive, and as far as carrying you down the stairs, I felt like I was carrying a little baby. I didn't want to get myself in any big trouble by taking any of your clothes off, so I just slipped your sandals off and tucked you under the covers. I have the coffee made and an omelet almost finished if you would like to try my unprofessional culinary expertise."

"I'd love to, but is there anything I can do to help?"

"If you'd like to pour the orange juice and coffee, I'll bring our plates over in just a couple of minutes. I put the silver and napkins on the table earlier. I usually eat here at the counter, buy I wanted to give you the royal treatment your first morning in my home."

I want to throw my arms around his neck and get a good morning kiss, but I keep my mind on the task at hand. "It's a unique plan having a space on the counter that can be either an eating area that will accommodate two or a sit-down work space with even a sink nearby." He puts our plates on the table, and I take my first bite of the omelet. "T.J., this is delicious, so fluffy and good that it almost melts in my mouth. The coffee's very good, too. You're quite the chef and I'll have to get your recipe for this omelet.

I'd like to change the subject for a minute, though, and find out what the plan is for today. I know you have to go to the office, but do you want me to stay here this morning or will you drop me at your parents?" Oh, there's that confused frown and then a grin again, and I've gotten to the point now that when I see that particular look, I'm almost certain that something is going to happen that isn't what I'm expecting. "Now what has happened to change the schedule?"

He slowly reaches over and takes my hand in his and then starts massaging the palm with his thumb. He raises my hand to his lips for a kiss that starts my heart pounding like a big bass drum as he looks into my eyes. "It's like this, Sweetie. My grandparents have been on a Caribbean cruise the last two weeks and they'd planned to fly to Vegas for a few days before coming home. Apparently, Grandpa decided he was tired and wanted to come home now, but their plane connections weren't as direct as he thought when he made the change in reservations.

They'll land at the airport in Charlotte instead of Raleigh-Durham, so they asked Mom to drive down there and pick them up. Dad called to say he could be at the office until 10 o'clock if I could come in from then until noon. He isn't too keen about Mom driving down there by herself. You see, we don't make any scheduled appointments on Saturdays -- just emergency calls or walk-ins, but one of us has to be there. He remarked that I'd still have time to drive down and get you this afternoon, but I haven't had time to ask why he thought you weren't already here or why they weren't expecting you last night.

Anyway, I'll work from 10 until noon and Mom and Dad will be back for tonight, but not much before--which means, Sweetie, that you're stuck with me all afternoon, all evening, and hopefully, again all night. Maybe I can get you to see the moon and stars this time."

"Maybe so, but will you please give me my hand back before you have me wanting something I know nothing about and shouldn't even be thinking about?"

As he put my hand back on the table, he was laughing. "I'm so glad I can affect you that way, Jill. You have just made my day."

Of course, I'm trembling a little as I continue trying to eat this delicious breakfast, because I'm wondering what I've gotten myself into by accepting this invitation to spend a weekend with this captivating guy. Has Jessica experienced the same difficulties with C.J.? Oh, how I need to talk to my sister.

CHAPTER SIX

*W*e work together to get the kitchen back to spotless and then go to make the beds. I offer to do that while he's at the office, but he insists on helping. I want to climb onto his big comfortable-looking king-size bed just to see how it would feel, since I've never been on one before, but I hold myself in check. I'm thinking, a little guiltily, that I might sneak in here while he's gone and get my curiosity satisfied, but apparently he spots the grin on my face.

"What's that grin for, Jill? Is there something awry with my bed or me?" He shoots a hand quickly to his zipper, which gets my giggles started, and that brings him around the bed to grab my shoulders and gently shake me. "What are you up to, you little imp?" He's taken hold of my chin and tilts my face up so he can look right into my eyes, which only makes me giggle harder. His lips are suddenly over mine and I wilt into his arms which are wrapped around me like a cocoon. He deepens the kiss and all I can think of is that the bed is too convenient beside us.

What does he have in mind, I wonder, and then I panic. I push away, and he slowly and reluctantly lets me go. "You-you'd bet-better go t-to the off-office," I stammer as I turn and run from the room. I don't know exactly what to do or where to go, but I slip into the guest room and lock the door.

I can hear him coming down the hallway and then he stops at the door. "Jill, I'm sorry if you got the wrong idea in there. You had the most devilish grin on your face and I just wanted to know what you were thinking. Will you come talk to me before I leave? In fact, I was wondering if you'd like to go shopping for a while or do you prefer to stay here while I'm at the office? I'll wait in the living room, but I do have to leave shortly."

Well, just how foolish can a person feel? He is the most in-control man I have ever heard of. Okay, I don't know much about men, but I've read plenty of stories about how all they want to do is get a girl into bed. How is a girl supposed to know if she can trust a man or not? Right now, though, I guess I need to go out and send him to the office knowing I'm not going to run off while he's gone.

I slowly open the door and practically creep into the living room. "I guess I acted a little foolish, didn't I? I'm sorry, T.J., but I just don't know what to think or how to react to some of the things that are happening. I've never been in a guy's house before, let alone his bedroom, so I panicked when you were kissing me so--so passionately. Forgive me?"

"There's nothing to forgive, Jill. I thought you might be having some problem with the kiss being in the bedroom. I wasn't completely at ease, either. I've never had a girl in my bedroom before, and there's only been one person in the bed you're sleeping in, and that was C.J. when he came back for a weekend. We'd been out for something to eat and then we went up to the roof and lost track of time. He didn't want to wake up the folks so late so decided to spend the night here. But," he chuckles, "that doesn't answer what that grin on your face was about. Are you going to tell me?"

"Do I have to? You may not trust me to stay alone here while you're gone." His look is complete confusion and I can't hold back another giggle. "Oh, well, you can't do anything to me except make me stay outside and roast in this heat, so I'll tell you. I'd never really seen a king-size bed, except on TV commercials, and yours is so unique that my very inquisitive mind wondered what it would feel like to be lying on it. My grin, I guess, was when I was conjuring up a plan to maybe try it out while you were at the office."

His dazzling smile, with that cute little dimple, lets me relax a little as I wait for his reply, but then he is on his feet and holding me in his arms again. He gives me a quick kiss on the cheek, and then with one swift sweep, he picks me up and is carrying me toward his bedroom. "T.J.," I cry out, "what are you going to do now?" I'm squirming in his arms but he holds me tightly until he is beside his bed and then just drops me on it.

"You only have to ask, Sweetie, and I'll try my best to accommodate. I have to leave now, but you stay on my bed as long as you like."

"Can I go up to the roof garden? I brought a book I've been reading and I thought it would be fun to sit in the swing and read."

"Whatever you like. The neighbors just below me are retired and they like to use it occasionally. They helped me quite a bit with the planting and landscaping, but they use it mostly on weekdays because they know I'm at the office. They also know I like to be up there on the weekends. I don't think they'll bother you, but I just wanted you to know that it's not mine exclusively. The other two tenants on this side of the building have never shown any interest in the garden. There is a roof area atop the other side of the building, too, but other than putting some chairs and tables out, I rarely have seen or heard them. I should've told you to bring your bathing suit so you could have gotten some more of your beautiful tan. I've got to run now so I'll see you around 12:30." He bends down and kisses me lightly, runs his finger down my cheek, and then he's gone.

What a bed! I feel like I'm floating on a cloud. Not that the guest room mattress isn't comfortable, but this is so spacious. It must be fun trying to locate the other person in a bed like this. I'm laughing as I get up and head for 'my' room. At the last minute, when I was packing, I'd put in a pair of short shorts and a halter which I'd thought I could wear if I was alone during the day while everyone was at work. Well, I'm alone and the roof garden is a great place to get a tan. T.J. had said he wished I'd brought my swim suit so I quickly change, grab my book and am going to head up the stairs when I realize I don't have a key to his place or the roof, if one is needed. I certainly don't want to leave the condo door unlocked. "So, now what do I do?" I'm mumbling to myself as I try to decide my next step. I'm just about ready to sit in the living room and read when I see four keys on a key ring lying on the table in the foyer. The first one I try in the lock works and I'm on my way up the stairs to my sunny getaway.

"This is so much fun," I smile as I get comfortable on the thickly padded cushion of the swing with the canopy shading my eyes but letting the sun hit my arms and legs. I read for almost an hour and then I put the cushion down on the artificial turf so I can lie on my stomach and get some sun on my back. I apparently fall asleep.

"Who is this beautiful, although barely clad individual asleep in my garden?" I hear a chuckling voice whispering in my ear. I jump so fast I almost hit him in the face with my head as my eyes try to focus on my surroundings.

"Wh-where am I?" I stammer as I look at the cushion I'm sitting up on, and then at T.J. who is smiling as he lies on his side holding his head in his cupped hand. He is just staring at me, or do they call that ogling? "Are you supposed to be back already? I guess I must have fallen asleep."

"You're beautiful when you're sleeping, Jill, but where did you get that outfit? You weren't wearing that when I left, or I may not have gone, and you also forgot to inform me you'd brought such tantalizing attire with you." He reaches over with his free hand, puts it around my waist, and before I know it, my back is against him on the turf. "I could so easily get used to you being beside me," he says in a very sexy voice as he turns me just a little so his lips can reach mine and very slowly but deliberately urges me to open my mouth. After a wonderful kiss, his hand begins massaging my back for a few minutes, but now he's brought it to my face and his thumb is gently stroking my cheek as his fingers bring my head even closer. "You're my dream girl," he murmurs as the hand that had been holding his head slips under my neck and his face hovers over mine. His body is definitely becoming tight against me and his lips again take control of the situation. I can't stop the whimper that escapes from me, and he immediately backs away. "I'm so sorry, Jill," he says as he gets to his feet and then holds out his hand to help me up. "Shall we go down now and decide what we want to do about lunch?"

"T.J., please don't be upset with me. I love your kisses and your soft touches, but as I told you this morning, I've never been in this type of situation before and I'm not sure how to handle a lot of it. I think I heard you whisper something about my being barely clad, too.

Actually, I didn't mean for you to see me this way, but I didn't think I had less on than if I'd been wearing a swim suit. I'm so sorry if I've disappointed you."

"Oh, Jill, I'm not disappointed in you. I'm disappointed in myself for getting carried away with your appeal and scaring you with my aggressiveness. I'm pretty sure I would've come to my senses and stopped, but that doesn't excuse my actions. I'm just afraid you'll feel you can't trust me anymore."

"There is a lock on the bedroom door, isn't there?" I give him a big grin as I feel we need a little humor to get past this rather awkward moment.

"I should've known you'd do or say something to get over this stupid thing I did. You are really someone special, Jill Marie Hale." He pulls me into his arms and kisses me lightly on the lips and then picks up the cushion and puts it back on the swing. Holding out his hand to me, he is smiling as he says, "Let's get out of the sun before you get too toasty. It's the wrong time of day to be exposing your delicate skin to that hot sun."

When we reach the kitchen, he says, "I guess lunch is in order. Do you want to go out and get something, or shall we try to find something here?"

"I imagine we'll be eating rather heavy tonight, so I suggest that we go a little light for lunch. Do you have some lettuce for a salad or a can of soup?"

"I think I may have both but are you sure that will be enough for you? I know I have lunch meat because I just bought it yesterday. Could I interest you in a sandwich?"

"I'd really be satisfied with a small salad, T.J., but I'll be happy to fix you a bowl of soup and a sandwich, if you'd like that."

"You may fix your salad, Jill, but you're not going to fix my lunch. The lettuce will be in the crisper over there in the fridge. I don't know what else you'll find to go with it, but whatever you find, you may eat," he chuckles.

"I don't know whether I like the sound of that or not. I'll check rather closely to see just what kind of food you eat around here." When I open the crisper, I'm amazed to see a wide variety of fresh vegetables and fruit. There's a zucchini with just a portion used, a new carton of grape tomatoes, a bunch of green onions, and a package of torn lettuce with red cabbage and carrots added. "T.J., there's a lot of salad fixings here. Are you sure you don't want me to fix you one along with mine?"

"Well, if you don't mind, I'll forget about the soup and just have a sandwich and a salad. Did you find everything you like?"

"Everything looks great. Do you have someone who shops for you or did you buy all this thinking you might get me to come over? You would've been eating a lot of salad if you'd had all of this available and then I hadn't come." Whoa, I'm thinking, let's wait just a blasted minute. Could this have been a real clever set-up to get me to stay here?

I guess the truth will come out when we meet his folks at the banquet tonight. Or is there going to be a banquet and are his parents actually going to be at this golf awards ceremony? Well, I'm not going to worry about it right now. I'm here and so far I'm having a good time, but I will keep my defenses up. I just hope I don't end up having to take the bus home.

"Hey, Jill, I think those salads are big enough for The Hulk." I hear him laughing as I glance down at the huge amount of lettuce I've tossed in the bowl and feel like I should be turning green. "I've been watching you and I get the impression that your mind has been on something other than salads. Do you want my help to put some of that lettuce back in the package?" When he reaches me, he slowly turns me around to face him and gently tilts my chin so he can see my face. I was looking down at the floor and trying to resist because I didn't want him to see tears forming in my eyes, but one rolls over the edge and runs on down my cheek. He wipes it away with his thumb.

"What's wrong, Sweetie? Are you reliving my stupidity earlier and wondering if you really are safe here with me? You know you can stay at my folks' tonight if you'd feel safer by doing that. I'm anxious for you to enjoy the moon and stars, but I don't want you to be afraid staying here."

I push away but then look directly into his eyes. "Will you be honest with me, T.J.? Some things are happening here that suddenly have me wondering if I'm the naive fool in a clever plot like the one Todd tried to pull on Jessica. Do you really think I'm that naive just because I come from a small town? If so, maybe I should warn Jessica. What I see is, your folks were conveniently in bed or gone last night, and you haven't yet mentioned the fact that your dad might have apologized for that mistake. Instead, it just happens that they are now going to pick up your grandparents and hopefully, but not definitely, will be back in time to attend the banquet which I'm beginning to doubt if there will even be one. And, of course, added to all of the above is the incident upstairs earlier. Can you see how I might be just a little suspicious, T.J., or do you really believe you have all your bases covered? I need some good reasonable and honest answers or I'm out of here and on my way home."

CHAPTER SEVEN

*P*utting his arm around my waist, he guides me into the living room and motions for me to sit on the couch. He sits down beside me and reaches for my hand, but I pull it into my lap and clasp it to the other. He does the same with his and tries to give me a dimpled smile, but it is a rather sad one.

"Jill, I hardly know where to begin because your description of what you've seen has chilled me to the bone. I can so plainly see what you've observed and it makes me so extremely angry with myself. I'll start by assuring you that there was no plot to get you under my roof or into my bed. I'd thought that you might like to see my home and had planned to ask you to have lunch with me here today and to see the moon and stars tonight before I took you back to Mom and Dad's. The accident yesterday and the following several hours of treating the injured was definitely unplanned.

I talked to Dad just briefly before I started to Sanford last night, but I guess nothing was exchanged as to where I was going, about you or the weekend. We just remarked that we were both bushed and would be glad to get to bed as soon as possible. Apparently, he assumed that I was not going to drive down after you, so they went to bed. When he called this morning, his mind was on Grandpa's call and the office schedule and, of course, he still didn't realize that you were here nor did he give me time to tell him.

When I got to the office, I found out his reasoning that I would still have time to get you this afternoon, but with the happenings since I got back, I haven't had a chance to tell you that he was very upset about the mix-up, they do plan on being at the banquet which is really going to be held. They would be very happy to have you stay with them tonight, but that is up to you. And, by the way," he added with one of his dazzling smiles, "he's very, very glad that you were the driver last night. What can I do, Jill, to make it up to you?"

"Well, I guess, we'd better eat our lunch, after which we could possibly go for a short walk, and then, unless I need a little nap, I'll start getting ready for the banquet. I'll save my final judgment of your actions until after I've seen your parents tonight. Is that fair enough?"

"I'm most grateful, Jill, and if you're not satisfied with our explanations and humble apologies, I'll drive you home right after the banquet." He stands and extends his hand to help me up, but while I'd rather grab him and hold on tight, I hesitantly reach out my hand.

Our lunch is eaten pretty much in silence with an occasional comment about our calls with C.J. and Jessica. They both seem to be thriving on the plans for the pre-school and also spending a lot of time together. Emily is acting as their chaperone, so she says, since Jessica is staying with her most of the time. She'll make other arrangements when school actually opens in August.

After I change into my Bermuda shorts and t-shirt, we relax a little on the walk. It's really a beautiful, although quite warm, afternoon so we decide to stop and get some nice cold ice cream and a drink. T.J. gets two scoops while I only order one, but he still finishes before I do. "How did you eat twice as much as I did and still beat me?" I ask with a smile.

"A much bigger mouth and less manners," he laughs and I let out a big yawn at the same time. "Oh, I see that we'd better get you back for a nap before you have to get dressed for the big evening. I'd hate to have you fall off your chair and make the organizers think they'd planned a terribly boring evening for all of us."

"I really wouldn't mind lying down for an hour or so. Being in the sun always does that to me. What time do we have to leave for this shindig?"

"It's supposed to start at 7 o'clock, but you don't sound too enthusiastic about going, Miss Hale. Would you rather stay here at the condo and make me explain why my date deserted me for the evening?"

"That I would like to see, Dr. Peterson, but I will not stay at the condo and miss out on a good meal and getting to clap like an enamored school girl when you and your dad get your trophy. Plus, you must remember, I have to confirm your interesting story with your parents." With his sunglasses on, I can't make out exactly how he's taking all this ribbing, but I do want to get my message across that I'm not going to accept any cockeyed plans he might come up with. He can't see my eyes either because of my sunglasses, so hopefully my smile, my beaming face and racing heart, just from being near him, haven't been giving me away.

～

The Club House is glowing with lights all through the building, and it's really quite impressive as we approach. Inside, each table for four is covered with a white tablecloth and the centerpiece is a golf trophy with two small mounds of flowers lying on a lovely piece of rumpled green silk. Name cards are at each place and we soon find ours on the far side of the podium, and we realize that the mounds of flowers are wrist corsages for the ladies. They're made with miniature ivory roses which will match anyone's outfit. "Do you want to put it on now, Jill, or wait for Mom and Dad?"

"Let's wait for everyone to get here so the decorations will look the same as they all arrive. Your mom and dad should be coming soon and then she and I can put ours on at the same time." I give him that rather doubting look, but he grins as he watches the door.

My hands are resting in my lap but he reaches under the table and finds one. "I'm so lucky to have you with me tonight, Jill, even if you are upset with me. As I told you earlier, you are so lovely in that dress. The color does magic to your complexion and brings out the highlights in your hair. It's definitely a color you should wear often."

"Thanks, T.J., you look pretty sharp tonight, too, but flattery will get you nowhere if your parents don't arrive." As hard as I try, I can't keep the smile off my face.

"You won't have to wait long, Miss Hale, because they are coming in the door." He waves to get their attention and to guide them to the table.

"I'm glad you got here first so we didn't have to hunt for the right table. I can't ever remember them doing this before so it must be a new group doing the planning this year. And Jill, my dear," his dad sighs as he leans down and kisses my cheek, "I must say you look absolutely stunning, and I believe I owe you one huge apology for last night.

When I spoke briefly with T.J. after we'd finished patching up the accident victims, I just assumed he was too tired to drive down to Sanford to get you. I was exhausted and told Jeannette that T.J. was, too, so I'd plan to go to the office this morning and let him pick you up. Of course, I didn't realize then we'd get a call from the grandparents and have to make a trip ourselves. I was sound asleep by 9:30, but it was truly unconscionable of me, and I hope you'll be able to forgive me."

"I'm at fault here, too, Jill, and I feel just terrible about the whole thing. I think we'll have to give the key to the house back to T.J. so you can come in and make yourself feel at home. You know where the room is and please remember it's always open to you."

His mother looked so sad that I just had to do or say something. "It wasn't such a big deal. I at least didn't have to sleep outside on the ground and in the heat. Let's forget it and enjoy the evening." I give them all a big smile and then say, "Did you notice the wrist corsages that are here for us, Mrs. Peterson? Shall we put them on now since it looks like most everyone is here and are putting theirs on?"

Immediately the two men pick them up and proceed to put them on our wrists, and then, to my surprise, they bring our hands up to their lips and give us a memorable kiss, at least to me. Although I've seen my dad kiss my mom's hand many times, this is definitely a new experience for me. "Thank you," I whispered and couldn't keep from giving him one of my very sincere smiles.

"You are so welcome, Jill," he says as he pats my hand and lays it on the table. That dazzling smile is spreading across his face and I then realize just how much I had missed while I was acting like an unforgiving snob this afternoon.

The rest of the evening was wonderful. After the delicious buffet dinner, they had some entertainment with music, a comedian sharing mostly golfing jokes, and a short speech by the Golf Pro about the tournament that had been held. At the end of the speech, he began announcing the winners in the different categories, having them stand for a big round of applause as he called their names. He then informed them, all at once, that they'd been looking at their trophy all evening because it was the centerpiece on their table. The banquet ends with all of us standing and singing God Bless America.

"Jill, would you like to spend the night at our house?" his mother asks as we're walking together to the door. The guys are a little ahead of us trying to decide who gets to keep the trophy. I wonder who will win that debate? Maybe they'll put it in the office.

"I appreciate your offer, Mrs. Peterson, but I've already messed up the guest room bed at T.J.'s and my other things are all there, too. He wants me to see the moon and stars from the roof garden, and I hate to disappoint him since I fell asleep last night when he wanted to show me the garden after we got back. I guess the drive had tired me but T.J. was wide awake after his little nap on the way back," I giggled. "I hope you feel that it's OK."

"Did I hear something about the guest room bed being messed up?" T.J. had turned around with a big grin and a chuckle. "I think I found my bed a little rumpled, too, when I came back from the office." His mother got a very strange look on her face, but T.J. just pats her cheek and laughingly continues, "Whoa, Mom, don't get all upset now because it's all very innocent. We decided to help each other make our beds this morning, and Jill got the cutest grin on her face, while we were in my room, but she wouldn't tell me why. Later, I coaxed it out of her that she had never seen a king-size bed before, except in a TV ad, and she was thinking about sneaking in, while I was gone, just to see how it would feel.

Well, I picked her up, carried her to my room, and dropped her on my bed as I was leaving. I'd told her to stay there as long as she liked, but she was up in the roof garden, when I came home, adding to that beautiful tan. She looked mighty good then, but not as beautiful as she does tonight." He just had to smile teasingly and say, "I love making you blush, Jill."

To say the least, I am blushing when he finally shuts his mouth, but then he bends down and kisses my forehead as his fingers are caressing my cheek. Is there no modesty in his bones? Putting his hands on my shoulders, he turns me to face him and whispers, but I'm sure his mother can still hear, "Have you decided where you'll spend the night? You do know I want you to see the moon and stars with me, and my earlier promise is sincere."

I notice his mother smiling as she takes Brian's arm and then mouths silently to me, "It'll be fine." I nod that I understand.

"I believe you, T.J., or I wouldn't have decided to go back to the condo. By the way, are we going to church in the morning?"

"We certainly are." He turns and calls to his parents as they are walking slowly to their car, "We'll see you in church in the morning."

"That's wonderful. We'll see you there then. Goodnight," his mother calls back.

Taking my hand, T.J. starts running toward his car which he had parked in a very secluded spot that had only two parking spaces and a wide golf path was between the two.

"Not so likely to get dents out here," he'd chuckled when we'd parked. Now I notice that there are bushes protecting the driver's side.

"Yes, we must protect this expensive sports car," I grin and mumble as he opens the door and assists me in. The door closes but I continue to mumble. "Men and their cars, I'll never quite understand, but after all those years of schooling, internship and residency, why shouldn't T.J. have the car of his dreams?"

Getting in on the driver's side, he turns and looks at me with a rather disturbing look on his face. "Did I hear what I thought I heard, Jill? Do you really think I'm being a little too protective of my car?"

"No, T.J., I don't think that, but when I was in college it did disgust me a little when I would see those young freshmen come to school in their brand new cars, which was their high school graduation gift from their extravagant parents, and then try to be so extremely demonstrative of their worth. I'm sorry you didn't hear the rest of my thoughts about you and your car."

"Are you going to tell me exactly what you were thinking?"

"I remarked in my mumblings that after all those years of schooling, internship, and residency, why shouldn't you have the car of your dreams."

"Thanks, Jill. All during my medical training and up until last year, I drove a Caddy that was 20 years old when I traded it in on this car. That's why I can tease C.J. about the old Caddy he drives, because I know it's something he has driven for at least 11 years and it may be a few more before he's in a position to buy what he'd really like. In return, he teases me now about my sports car, but he's actually very happy that I can finally see a brighter future. I pray every night that things continue to be as satisfactory and profitable for him as they seem to be right now, especially since he has met your sweet sister who has given him a chance to love again."

"That's so sweet of you to say, T.J., because from our conversations, Jessica thinks C.J. is about the most wonderful person she has ever met. Of course, I think my sister would be a perfect catch for anyone." I giggle and he reaches over and pats my cheek.

"That may be so, but from what I hear, Jessica thinks she has a pretty exceptional big sister, too. And so do I."

CHAPTER EIGHT

*A*rriving back at the condo, we quickly go to change so we can get up on the roof to watch the moon and the stars. I put my Bermuda shorts on again and a t-shirt that has UNC across the front. I'd bought it when we attended Jessica's graduation over two months ago. The summer is really flying and college students will be invading the area in another two or three weeks. In one way, I'd like to be one of them, but in another, I'm so glad that part of my life is over.

"Are you ready, Jill?" His voice suddenly brings me back from my thoughts of a summer almost over. I check my hair and my make-up and head for the door.

"Yes, Sir, I'm ready for this great adventure to the moon and stars." I take a quick glance at him in shorts and a well-fitting t-shirt and almost swoon into his arms. "Aaah, could we possibly take something cold to drink with us, though, or is it not allowed on this journey?" I give him a big smile as he holds up a thermos and two glasses with ice in a wicker basket that has sections to keep items separated. "My hero."

"Always aim to please." He holds the door with his free hand and we're on our way.

"Did you leave the blankets up here?" I ask as we reach the roof and then gasp as it looks so romantic with tiny lights flickering all around the perimeter of the garden tonight. My heart is doing flip flops because I'm totally in awe as I try to take in every little thing. I then glance up at the sky which is actually full of twinkling stars, and I see the beautiful big moon that seems so close I think I could reach up and touch it. "Oh, T.J., it's absolutely unbelievable."

He takes my hand and leads me to the blankets that he'd spread out while I'd been gawking. "It will be even more intriguing if you'll lie down so you don't have to strain your pretty little neck to see God's beauty." Picking me up in his arms, he kisses my cheek and then stoops down to put me on the blanket with my head on the pillow.

I can't keep my eyes off the sky and wonder why my sisters and I had never done this while we were growing up. I wonder how many other things we missed by not having a brother to do outdoor things with. I'm looking forward to the discovery of so many things with T.J. if he continues wanting to see me. I turn my head to look at him lying at least four feet away and wishing I could be in his arms. I'm surprised to find that he's lying on his side watching me.

"Are you comfortable, Jill? I have that other blanket I can put under you if you'd like a little more padding."

"This is very nice, T.J., except I feel a little lonesome with you so far away. While we're watching the night sky and trying to find the constellations I've read about, couldn't we be just a little closer without causing too much trouble? Maybe we could even hold hands."

"I'll be happy to oblige, Sweetie, if that's what you'd like. I didn't want to frighten you again after promising I would behave myself." He pulls his blanket over next to mine and we lie there quietly, holding hands, for almost an hour. He'd started pointing out the Big and Little Dippers, The Milky Way, and the North Star when suddenly a shooting star goes streaking across the sky. "You're getting to see quite a show tonight, Jill. There's another favorite of mine, which is called Orion, but it appears mostly during the winter. Maybe we can arrange for you to see that one, too."

For some reason, I turn toward him just as he turns toward me and we are instantly aware of our closeness. His arm comes over me, drawing me even closer, and his lips are on mine playing havoc with all the built-up tension in my body. I realize that we're still holding hands, but my other arm suddenly wants to go around his neck. It isn't long before I'm opening my mouth in response to his coaxing and even inching closer to his warm, manly scented body that I've been admiring all evening. With both of us in shorts now, our bare legs are part of the togetherness from head to toe.

"I wish you were still in your shorts and halter," he whispers as his hand slips under my t-shirt and slowly and gently massages my back. "You're so soft and you smell so good from the banquet," he murmurs as he kisses my cheek and then moves his lips down to my neck. He's still on his side as he removes his hand from my shirt so he can roll me over on my back, and his fingers gently caress my arm as he slowly moves them down toward my elbow. Oops, somehow his hand is now along my side which is sending all kinds of tingly sensations down through my stomach. I quickly remove his hand as I shake my head, but his hand just returns to the bottom of my t-shirt, pulling it up and kissing my midriff. Just where is he going to stop, I wonder?

I squirm and try to move away but both of his arms are holding me now as his lips are back on mine, and I'm actually shaking with anticipation. "I promise I'm not going to hurt you, Jill, but you might enjoy this a little more if you'd relax just a little," he chuckles as he continues to tenderly move his mouth over my lips, my ear lobes, my neck, my arm and again to my midriff where he gets me giggling with his antics of blowing raspberries. I can certainly understand now why a baby giggles when someone does that on their little tummies.

I am so overwhelmed with the feelings I'm having that I find my fingers starting to run through that thick sandy blond hair of his. I discover, by doing that, my apprehension subsides a little, but then I realize his lips are moving up from my midriff. "T.J., you need to stop." I put my arms across my body to stop him, but I'd certainly found that I could enjoy his kisses, especially all the tingles that seem to go with them. I guess my folks were right. Those tingles can mean you feel something more for that person than just a casual friendship.

His chuckle surprises me, but then his lips return to mine and his kiss is so soft and sweet. "Thank you, Sweetie. That was wonderful and you are everything a woman should be. I'm glad your parents gave you good advice. Are you about ready to go and get a good night's sleep? I think it's getting close to 1:30 and we've got church in the morning."

"Yes, I guess we'd better get to bed. It's beautiful up here, but this floor, or grass, or whatever you call it, might've become a little uncomfortable before the night was over. Do the lights stay on all the time, or do you have a magic switch to control them?"

I only get a smile, but we're both on our feet now folding the blankets which he puts into a big storage chest along with the pillows. He takes my hand as we head for the stairs and I see the switch where he turns off the twinkling lights.

We get to the door of the condo, however, and he looks sheepishly at me. "You may get to sleep on the roof yet tonight, Jill, because I forgot to bring my keys. The set I left for you this morning is usually out here in a special hiding place. It has one for the condo, one for the roof, when we lock it, an extra for my car, and also the master key for certain areas. Do you remember where you might've left them?"

I think for a moment and then shake my head. "I don't remember bringing them down since I was rather upset at that time, if you recall. They're probably still up there with my book. In fact, I did put both of them in the drawer of that table when I took the cushion off the swing."

"You're a doll. Stay here and I'll be right back." He kisses me quickly on the cheek and then takes two steps at a time up to the roof to retrieve the keys and my book. We're finally inside the condo and the air-conditioning feels so good although the breeze had been wonderful up on the roof.

"I can't believe how tired I've suddenly gotten, but I'm also very thirsty. I guess we didn't quite get to that thermos, Dr. Peterson. Would there be something I could have to drink before I go to bed?"

"What would you like, Sweetie? There's water, of course, but I also have sodas, iced tea is made, there's milk, or maybe you'd like some ice cream."

"I think I'll just have a glass of water, and if I can take it to my room, I'll drink it while I'm getting ready for bed." He quickly fills a glass and I head down the hall to the guest room. "Goodnight, T.J."

"Do I get to watch?" he chuckles as he follows me to the bedroom door.

"I think you've done enough of your watching and touching tonight, T.J., so you may now head on down the hall to your own room with that big king-size bed."

"How about joining me, then, in my big king-size bed? You can find out how it'd feel with two in it instead of just one." He's now leaning against the jamb of the doorway watching me with that dazzling smile. I'm standing in the middle of the room with my heart pounding so hard, I don't know if it's because of fear or just the exciting thought of being asked to sleep with him in that big comfortable bed. We just stare at each other for a couple of minutes, me with a scowl and him with that grin.

"T.J., you promised that I wouldn't be sorry if I decided to stay here again tonight. I have already experienced something that I definitely wasn't expecting, and that's more than enough for tonight. Please take that sexy body of yours on down the hall after you tell me goodnight."

Oops, wrong thing to say. With one quick long stride, he has me in his arms, tilting my chin up with his hand, and his lips are heading for mine once again. "No, T.J., please don't do this, it's late and we need our rest," I sort of stammer as I push him away.

"I'm sorry," he chuckles. "I can't seem to keep my eyes or my lips off of you, so can I help you take your shirt off? Did you bring pajamas, or do you wear a gown?" He grins as he flutters his eyelashes and looks around the room.

I reach for my folded gown but he thinks he still gets to help and proceeds to take it out of my hand. I give him a very disgusted look, quickly grab a part of my gown, and jerk the rest which he releases. My arm goes out pointing the way to the door. I'm afraid to talk for fear I'll start crying.

He grins as his fingers caress my cheek, and he ambles toward the door. "You're not going to wear all those clothes to bed, are you? I could help you take them off before I go to my big comfortable king-size bed," he chuckles.

"Get out of here now, T.J., and I mean it. I'll never be able to believe you again." As hard as I try, I can't hold back the tears, and of course, he has me in his arms again. He sits on the bed beside me, apologizing over and over for being an absolute fool. He even gets his handkerchief out of his pocket to dry my tears. He kisses my forehead and cheek again and again, but he never comes close to my lips. When I'm finally under control, he tenderly says goodnight and slowly leaves the room. I go and lock the door, slip out of my clothes and crawl into bed. I am exhausted, and even though I'm terribly confused and upset about all that has happened, I quickly fall asleep.

CHAPTER NINE

*J*have no idea what time it is, but I'm suddenly awakened by a swooshing, fluttering noise around the room. I listen for just a minute before something swoops down right over my head. Well, I'm out of that bed and into the hallway, fast. Pulling the door shut behind me, I'm running into that master bedroom full speed. "T.J.," I call as I jump onto the bed, "there's something flying around in my room swooping down like a bat. Do you have bats in your belfry?" I try to laugh but I realize that he's still sleeping right in the middle of the bed so I quickly sit down beside him and shake his arm.

There's a moan, a groan, and then an arm goes around me as he sits up and looks at me as if I were out of my mind. Yawning and grinning, he stupidly asks, "What did you say Sweetie? Do you want to sleep with me after all?" I slap his face and he's suddenly awake enough to grasp the fact, I guess, that something isn't right if I'm in his room. "Hey, Jill, you're trembling. What's wrong?"

After repeating my plight, he snuggles me against his warm chest. "Did you shut the door so it'll stay in there?"

"Yes, I did, but what am I supposed to do now?"

He throws the sheet back, lifts me into the bed, and covers me as he sits on the edge of the bed rubbing his eyes. "I'll see if I can do something about what's bothering you. We had a bat in there when C.J. stayed here, so maybe it doesn't like visitors," he chuckles.

"How can you be so nonchalant about a bat flying around your house at night? You make me wonder if it's another scheme of yours to get me into this bed. What are you, a witch that can call bats into action whenever you wish?"

He doesn't answer me as he's already down the hall, and I hear the door to my room open and then close. I sit up and wrap my arms around my bended knees and try to listen to the muffled sounds coming through the door. "Whoa, you're quite an active one tonight, aren't you? Hey, just calm down. I'll open the window so you can get out. Just let me get over to it. How'd you get in here anyway? I'm going to find out, one way or another. O.K. I'm not too fond of you, either. You're really a menace. There, the window is open---now fly away. Oh, come on, Bat, I'm a little too big to be your kind of food. Now, get out of here and hunt somewhere else."

I think I hear a thud, a kerplop, and then "Sorry, but that's what you get for trying to attack someone bigger than you." I'm giggling as I hear the window go shut and his footsteps are coming back this way. He goes into the bathroom and the water turns on in the shower. After a few minutes, he comes back to the bed with at least the bottoms of p.j.'s on, a bare chest, and his hair still a little damp, but the clean smell of soap and shampoo is certainly intoxicating. I scoot over to the opposite side of the bed from where he'd gotten in, but he follows me and puts his arm over me. "I got rid of the intruder for you, Jill, and I'm so sorry you had to have another unpleasant experience while under my roof." His lips are kissing the back of my neck and his fingers are combing through my hair until they slowly caress my cheek. You are so beautiful."

"W-well, may-maybe I-I'd b-better go ba-back to the oth-other room na-now."

"You're not going anywhere near that room until I check it out in the morning. Just relax and go to sleep. I'll scoot over to the other side and try to forget you're in here with me. Can you trust me enough to get some sleep, Sweetie, or would you prefer that I sleep on a couch? I don't even know how much of the night is left to get any sleep."

"I-I'll try to ge-get some sle-sleep, T.J. I-I don't wa-want you to thi-think you have to sle-sleep on the co-couch. Goo-goodnight, again."

"Goodnight, Sweetie," he chuckles. "You are such a good sport," he whispers as he works his way to the other side of the bed, and I find it hard not to follow that warmth and the manly smell of spice. Why did he have to put that on after his shower, anyway, and I find myself debating whether I would really want a king-size bed if I had T.J. in there with me, but I soon drift back into dreamland.

When I wake up in the morning, I glance at the clock on the table beside me. It's 7 o'clock and the sun is shining into the room making it bright and so warm as it lands on my back. I roll over to see if my bed partner is still asleep, but find him lying way over there on his side watching me. "Didn't you get any sleep, T.J." His eyes look bright and clear, but why is he staring at me so intently. "Did I keep you awake by snoring or something? Surely I didn't take part of your space." I smile as I sit up and pull the sheet up to my neck.

"You're a wonderful bed partner, Sweetheart. As far as I know, you didn't move an inch after I left you alone, and I slept well, too. I just woke up about ten minutes ago and have been admiring my sleeping beauty. I was a little concerned whether you'd be able to sleep, but you seemed to be resting well. Are you ready to get up, or could we snuggle for awhile?" he grins. "You want to know just how comfortable a king-size bed can be, don't you?" He's inching his way toward me, but I'm out of the bed and heading down the hall. Of course, he's told me he doesn't want me to go into my room so I head for the kitchen.

I only get to the entry area before he catches up with me, scoops me into his arms and heads back to his bedroom. "T.J., I don't think this is a good idea. We need to get some breakfast and get ready for church."

"Church isn't until 11 o'clock, Jill, and I don't intend to keep you in bed all morning. I just want to cuddle for a little while so we can find out how my bed reacts to two people on it." I'm suddenly on my back in the middle of his bed again, like yesterday morning, but this time he's beside me with his arm over me and his face pressed against my cheek. His face has short stubble, since he hasn't shaved, and the idea that he is OK with that is rather exciting to me. I'm glad to know that he doesn't think he always has to be so clean shaven.

His lips are soon there, urging mine to open as his hands cup my face. He raises his head to look at me and smile. "You don't know how much I've missed the closeness of a woman the last three years," he murmurs as he turns on his side and his hand slides down my arm and brings my hand to his lips. He is kissing one finger at a time and also doing something with his tongue that is hair raising.

I jerk my hand away and try to hide it behind me. "I thought you and C.J. were both adamant about waiting until marriage to have relations, so what is this about missing the closeness of a woman for only the last three years? What did you do before that?"

"I told you one night down at your house that we like to play around a little. Do you remember that conversation? It's only been the last three years that I haven't dated at all." He's looking into my eyes now with his twinkling like the stars we were watching up in the sky last night. "I'm having the time of my life playing around with you, Jill," he chuckles, "but I may have to keep myself a little more under control with you or I might find that I'm getting in over my head. You're certainly more of a challenge for me to behave than any woman I've ever been with."

He's bringing his lips toward mine again when I give him a shove with my hands as hard as I can and then kick him in the shin which almost breaks my toe. While he's trying to figure out what has just happened, I'm out of the bed and hopping into the guest room whether he wants me there or not. I lock the door, fall on the bed, and cry. How could I have imagined he was or could ever be serious about me?

"Jill, I don't want you in that room, remember? Please let me help you get your things and you can take your shower and get dressed in my bathroom. There are the two showers so you'll have all the privacy you need."

I wonder if he knows what privacy even means as I ponder what I should do next. I hate to miss church and have his parents thinking the worst, but I'd also like to catch the early bus home. I'm not about to be just another plaything in his life, and he'd better get that through his thick skull right quick. The privacy he's referring to is probably me being in the shower with him standing outside watching. Well, the answer to that is a big N-O.

"I'll be fine in here, T.J. I'm going to take my shower and get dressed for church, so I'll see you later in the kitchen, I guess."

"Jill, I'm sorry if I did or said something wrong again. Won't you please come and talk to me so we can get it straightened out?"

"No, T.J., you go back over what you've said and done since I came and maybe you can discover why I'm upset. I'm taking my shower now." He may have said more but I make sure the door opening to his office from this bathroom is still locked, turn on the water and try to wash all of his kisses and touches down the drain because that is where I'm thinking this relationship is going.

I take my time getting dressed because I dread having to face him again. He'll most likely act so innocent and try to make me the misunderstanding fool. Well, I might be a novice at this dating game, but I do have morals that I try to live by, and he has done every thing in his power to lead me astray this weekend. I'll admit I was vulnerable to his charms after I'd heard the sad story of his struggle with Adele, and also Jessica telling me about him having only one date with each girl he'd dated until three years ago when he'd started his practice and stopped dating completely. I must say he didn't lose his touch.

I get my dress from the closet that I'd brought to wear to church, and it lifts my spirits a little as I like it a lot. It's white cotton knit with medium-sized flowers scattered here and there. It's styled with a boat neckline and inset cap sleeves, a fitted bodice and a short skirt falling just above my knee. I'm wearing the same white high-heeled sandals that I wore last night at the banquet, and the white dangling earrings will again complete my outfit. My hair is behaving well as it falls to my shoulders with just a bit of a wave at the ends. I hurriedly pack my suitcase because I'm asking to be taken home or to the bus station as soon as church is over unless we're to have lunch with his parents.

I look in the mirror again, check the room to make sure I haven't forgotten anything, and then reluctantly open the door and carry my suitcase to the foyer. His footsteps startle me as he's coming from his bedroom. "You look lovely, as usual, Jill Marie. Shall we have some breakfast?" There's no smile, no grin, no dimple. He walks beside me as we head for the kitchen, but he looks so handsome in khaki slacks and a navy polo. "Is there something special you'd like this morning?" he asks as we reach the table area.

"No, thank you, T.J. I'll have a slice of toast with jelly, if you have some handy, along with that wonderful smelling coffee. I'm not a big breakfast eater." I start toward the counters to help myself, but he takes my arm and leads me to a chair at the table.

"As long as you're my guest, I'll fix your breakfast," he says softly and immediately turns away to go toward the toaster, but I notice a quick swipe of his hand across his eyes. Has he realized what I was referring to?

He brings me my toast and coffee, but only a cup of coffee for himself. "Aren't you going to eat something?" I ask, actually surprised that this incident would keep him from eating on his set schedule. "Surely the banquet food has digested by this time, and you don't want your stomach talking to you during the church service?" I try to give him a smile, but I'm afraid it was a half-hearted one.

"I'll try to eat something before we leave, but I don't think I could keep anything down right now. Jill, what do I say? I can't even start to forgive myself for what I've put you through. As much as I respect you, I certainly haven't given much thought to your feelings as I've gone about satisfying my male ego. I was hoping you were enjoying my touches and kisses, but I was completely out of line. I have surmised that the last straw for you was my referral to missing the closeness of a woman the last three years and having to watch myself around you to keep from getting in over my head. What can I say except that I have acted like a complete fool and I don't deserve anyone as sweet as you anywhere near me? If you like, I'll take you home as soon as you're ready and then explain to my parents what a disgrace I am to our family."

"We promised to see them in church, T.J., and I don't like breaking promises. I'd like to go to church, but then you can take me home unless they want us to have lunch with them. I don't want to cause any friction between you and your parents, and I'm pretty sure I can bluff my way through church and lunch. I'm just so sorry I didn't, or couldn't, stop all your advances a lot sooner. Apparently my feelings for you have already gotten a little out of control. I guess I was totally mesmerized by your charms, which certainly doesn't help our situation one little bit." (Yep, I knew that one way or another I'd try to take the blame for all of this, but I'm not about to let that happen, Dr. Peterson.) "Of course, you're the older and more experienced so you shouldn't have led me, the innocent, on. So, it really was your fault."

Now, why is it that I can't keep from giggling? "I don't know why that struck me so funny, T.J., but I'm feeling better about the whole situation. I'm still quite upset that you can consider me just another plaything in your life, but I have to appreciate the fact that you didn't try to act like so many men in those romance novels do. I've learned quite a big lesson, and I accept your apology, too, because I feel you're very sincere.

Now, do you think you can get through the church service with me by your side? Maybe you should drop me at the bus station. You can tell your parents I just remembered that I'd promised a friend to do something for her, or that we had a misunderstanding and I'd made it very clear that I wouldn't let you drive me home."

He reaches for my hand and holds it in both of his as he says, "You're really a gem, Jill, but I don't deserve any of your sweet, forgiving nature. Let me assure you, though, that you're not a plaything to me. You are someone I care about so much that I can't act like a platonic friend when you're around. You also mentioned that you have learned a big lesson, but let me tell you something. I have learned more in these last 36 hours than I have in the last 13 years about how to show respect for a lady when I find one, and I've definitely found one in you. Let's try your plan and go to church, have some lunch with or without the folks, and then I'll take you home unless you'd like to spend the hot afternoon at the movies before venturing out on that smoldering highway."

"I'll think about that, but right now you'd better get something in your stomach so we can be on our way to church. I'll have another cup of coffee while you're eating."

"Thanks again, Sweetie, You're the greatest, as Ralph Kramden used to say on The Honeymooners." He kisses the top of my head on his way to the cupboard for the box of cereal.

So, what are my feelings right now? I'm in total disbelief that this weekend could really be happening, but what a handsome guy to be spending it with even if it is a fairy tale.

CHAPTER TEN

When we get to the church, a little later than we should have, the pew where his parents are sitting is full, so we slip into one a few rows back on the other side. They must have sensed that their big, handsome son had arrived as they turned around and smiled.

I'm so glad when the first hymn is one I'm very familiar with so I'm singing along enthusiastically, but I am really surprised to hear the beautiful baritone singing next to me. I glance up at him, he smiles and puts his arm across my shoulders as the song continues. "You have a wonderful singing voice," I whisper after we sit down again.

"Thanks, Jill, and I must say yours isn't bad either. Do you sing in your church choir or another singing group?" he whispers back.

I shake my head and try to settle back to listen to the service. The announcements are made and then a prayer, another hymn, the Children's time, the Bible reading, the Choir Anthem, and then the sermon about God fulfilling our every need. I have my hands cupped in my lap when he reaches over, lays one hand over mine and then works them apart. He takes one and holds it on the seat between us all during the sermon. After the last hymn is sung, we meet his parents and his mom asks if we'd like to join them and another couple for lunch.

"I think we'll decline that invitation, Mom, because Jill is rather anxious to get back home. We'll grab a quick lunch and then see how things go."

His mother is all over that remark in an instant. "Are you trying to tell us something that we might not like to hear, T.J.?" Her face is so full of concern I feel I have to come to the rescue.

"What he's trying to say, Mrs. Peterson, is that I do have some things to get done at home before going back to work tomorrow, but he has also asked if I would like to go to a movie this afternoon while it's so hot. I haven't given him my answer yet."

"Oh, all right," she smiles. "A cool movie theater would probably feel pretty good on a hot day like this. "Okay, we'll talk to you later, T.J., or tomorrow. It was fun getting to see you, Jill, at the banquet and here, and we hope you'll come back soon." They move on with the crowd toward the front doors but T.J. motions toward a side door, puts his hand in the small of my back and we are outside in no time.

"How can you do that, Jill? I get myself in a situation I don't know how to get out of, and you're always there to come to my rescue. I wish I knew how to repay you."

"Well, for starters, how about some lunch?" He puts his arm around me and we head for the car and quickly pull out of the parking lot. I'm really surprised when he pulls into the same restaurant where C.J. had taken my family after graduation. It's fairly busy, but we're seated in about five minutes on the outside patio with the beautiful shade trees protecting us from the sun. There are huge fans in each corner circulating the air which makes it quite comfortable. "Well, you brothers must have the same taste in restaurants, too. C.J. brought us here after graduation, but it was cool enough that we ate inside that day. It's really lovely out here."

"I'm glad you like it, Jill. I'd do almost anything to make you happy after the way I spoiled your weekend with my bad behavior. Do you see anything on the menu that looks good to you?"

"Yes, too many things in fact," I giggle. I then feel the blush coming because I can't stop the giggle and it's embarrassing.

"What's the giggle about? Don't tell me you want to order the whole menu." He has to grin but then continues, "If that's what you want, however, just start ordering."

"No, not the whole menu, but I would like more than just a sandwich and drink, if that's all right. You'll have to promise not to buy me popcorn at the movie, though." I give him a mischievous grin and his eyes are now sparkling again which sends my heart into thumping overtime mode.

"You're a precious gem and a little devil all in one beautiful body, Jill, and I'm not sure what to do with you."

Our server is suddenly at our table to take our orders, so I give her my order of a half-sandwich of chicken salad, an order of onion rings, a large iced tea, plus a piece of chocolate cream pie for dessert. Not only does the server smile at me, but T.J. is trying so hard not to laugh. I just look at him and say, "All right, Smartie, just try to outdo me."

"Oh, I can do that, Sweetie," he chuckles. "I'll have the large steak sandwich, one of the large French fries, a medium chocolate malt, and one of those delicious chocolate eclairs." He then looks at me and continues to chuckle. "Do you want to change anything on your order now before she leaves?"

"Yes, please. Change my onion rings to one large order of fries, and my iced tea to a large chocolate malt."

The server just smiles and murmurs, "I don't know what the challenge is between the two of you, but I think there's going to be a lot of food that's not eaten here."

We look at each other and start laughing. "I can eat what I ordered, but I'm not so sure about this young lady." After the server leaves, he continues, "I'm probably at least twice as big as you are, Jill, and you did order a lot of food for that little body of yours."

"You just wait and see, Dr. Peterson. I can put away a lot of food when I'm hungry, and I only had a piece of toast for breakfast, if you remember. Of course, that is my usual breakfast," I quietly confess.

"I guess that's right, so we'll just wait and see what you can do with their extra large portions." His grin is exasperating and I'm beginning to wish I hadn't made that remark so soon about the popcorn at the movie. I'm sort of committed now to spending the afternoon with him in a movie where it'll be cold. I'll want an arm around me, and what will that lead to in a dark movie theater. Well, his kisses aren't really something I would want to miss or discourage, but he may not even want to hold my hand again, except in church, after the way things went last night and this morning. Oops, I must be frowning or something. He has a concerned look on his face.

"Is something wrong, Jill? Were you thinking about something that disturbed you? I really wish I could wipe last night and this morning away and start over, but what is done is done. Will you ever be able to forgive me?"

"I think I'll be able to forget it, T.J., if you'll stop bringing it up. As you say, what is done is done and we'll have to go from there. It really wasn't that bad, I guess, but it was all so new to me that I probably over reacted. Let's try to eat our lunch and enjoy the rest of the day if you really want to go to a movie."

"There's my special angel again. I'll have to say a special thank you to God in my prayers tonight. I just hope there's a good movie on so we can relax and enjoy it."

Our food comes, I bow my head to say a short prayer and notice that he is doing the same. I eat slowly so I can consume more, but as T.J. had said, they are very large portions. I'm determined to have my chocolate cream pie, so I leave about half of the fries and also a large part of the malt to see if I can finish them after I enjoy my pie. Why didn't I order the small malt? Of course, T.J. is downing all of his food with the appetite of a hungry bear.

"You're not quitting, are you?" he chuckles.

"No, I'm waiting for my pie, and then I'll finish my malt."

"What about your fries?"

"We'll see. Maybe I'll sneak them into the movie in my purse."

"There's a rule against that, I think."

"I'll leave them in the car, then, and eat all of them in front of you on the way home when you're hungry again and wanting me to share."

"Cold French fries? I'd really have to be starving to beg for cold fries."

⁓

There are six movies playing and we finally pick one neither of us had seen. It's one rated PG so it shouldn't be too scary or too sexy, I hope, although it's surprising what they put in a PG rated movie these days. About the middle of the show, I'm suddenly covering my face during an explosion which is throwing things all over the place, and T.J. does put his arm around me. I snuggle up a little closer, but oh how I'd love to get rid of the armrest between us. "Up on the roof was a little more comfortable, don't you think?" he whispers in my ear as he leans down and kisses the top of my head. I can't resist looking up to smile at him but find his lips waiting to claim mine. They linger until a whistle behind us brings him back to reality.

It's almost 4 o'clock when we leave the movie but the sun is still pretty high in the sky and very hot. "Do you want to drive home with the sun in your face or would you be willing to wait until it cools down a little?"

"What's the alternative, may I ask?"

"Well, we could drive out to the lake and see if we can find a shady spot, we can go to a restaurant and get a cool drink to sip on for a couple of hours, or we can go back to the condo and relax in the air-conditioning. We can fix a salad or whatever you'd like before we go to take you home. I promise I won't even touch you."

"Not even for a kiss like in the movie?"

"Not unless you want me to," he says, but you should see the grin on his face.

"I don't think this dress is very appropriate for the lake, and I'm not much in the mood for a long, drawn-out drink after that lunch we had. I'd really like to change into a more comfortable outfit for going home, so if you'll promise to behave, I'll go back to the condo with you. I think we have to pick up my suitcase, anyway. We were in such a big hurry to get to church on time we didn't put it in the car."

"Did you put that beautiful dress you wore last night in that little suitcase of yours or is it still hanging in the closet?"

"I guess it's still in the closet," I sheepishly admit. "I was so upset this morning that I only concentrated on the things that were in the room to put in the suitcase. I guess the condo is a necessary stop."

Chapter Eleven

*W*ell, I'm back in my own realm now, working at the bank during the day and alone with a book at night. My thoughts, of course, keep returning to the weekend and all the new things I experienced. At 26, I suppose most girls have done all that and more, but I'm just so glad it was a guy like T.J. that I was spending the weekend with and not some over- powering romantic who wouldn't take 'NO' for an answer.

It's Wednesday already and I haven't heard from T.J. When he brought me home Sunday night, he declined my invitation to come in. He said he had some papers he needed to go over so he'd better get back home. He left after a rather short kiss and an "I'll be in touch," whatever that means. Maybe it means that the relationship is over, maybe that he'll call me if he needs a convenient companion for another banquet or dinner, or maybe when he feels a little lonely and has no one else to turn to.

We'd actually had fun when we returned to the condo. He'd put on some good CDs and we'd danced around the kitchen and even into the big entry hall. He's a good dancer and it was terrific being held by him. There were a few songs we both knew all the words to, so we'd sung along together. We'd finally fixed a large chef salad which we shared. Of course, he ate three-fourth of it to my one-fourth, but it was good and it was fun. He seemed to be enjoying himself, but only once did he kiss me, and it wasn't a long, romantic kind to cause trouble.

I talked to Jessica earlier tonight. She has her 50 students enrolled now and is so excited for the beginning of classes. She and C.J. are getting along fine. He has been such a great help to her, as well as Emily and this Jackson fellow who so unexpectedly showed up on the scene. I guess, since he's the owner of the building where her pre-school is, it's perfectly normal that he'd be around to keep a check on his investment, although she says he's been wonderful coming by with different things she really needed.

❦

Now it's been almost three weeks and I still haven't heard from T.J. I'm keeping up with my golf lessons and I've met four others who are also trying to refresh their skills. The two girls, Penny and Ellie, who are both older than I am, seem to be real nice, and we're going to have lunch together Saturday and then play 9 holes. Actually, Ellie is married and is trying to get good enough so she can confidently play golf with her husband. The two guys are either very shy or a little snobbish, but they have little to say to us girls.

Saturday is really fun and I actually shoot a great game, for me anyway. Ellie beat me by one stroke, but Penny had a bad day. On Sunday, Mom and I were invited to play with Dad and his partner, but I doubt if we'll be asked again. Mom hadn't played for a few years and I'm worried about her keeping up, so I guess I didn't do very well either. I'm really looking forward to my lessons on Tuesday and Thursday when maybe I can figure out what I'm doing wrong.

❧

Time passes, there's still no word from T.J., and it's already September 1st. Our whole family has made plans to go to the beach next weekend to surprise Jessica and get to see the pre-school as well as C.J.'s Beachside Resort, and the ocean. I'm so excited about the trip that when the phone rings early Sunday afternoon, I don't have any expectations of it being T.J. anymore. I've finally resigned myself to the fact that he's no longer a part of my life, and I've actually done quite well the last two weeks.

"Jill," my dad softly calls, "this phone call is for you. Would you like to take it in your room? It may be personal."

As I'm running up the stairs, I think it's most likely Jessica calling with some news about C.J.'s brother. (of course, that's T.J.) She was going to check and see what she could find out although I have no idea why I'd care anymore. "Hey, I didn't expect you to call me back today," I answer rather excitedly.

"I'm sure you didn't," a deep male voice that I recognize immediately comes over the line, "but I'm also pretty sure that excited greeting wasn't meant for me, either."

"Oh, hello T.J. You're right, I was expecting it to be Jessica although we just talked Thursday night so it would've been rather soon to hear from her again. What, may I ask, are you calling about?" My heart is pounding like a jack hammer, but I won't let him know that I've been pining for him the last five weeks.

"Please, Jill, don't turn your back on me until I can talk to you face to face. I need to explain several things, and I'm wondering if I can come down this evening for just a little while. I'd like to take you to dinner so we can talk privately, if you'll agree to see me."

"I'm sorry, but I have something already planned for tonight, T.J. We're all getting ready to go and see Jessica next weekend so I'm afraid I don't have time for you."

"I know you're going to the beach and that is why I need to talk to you tonight. It can't wait until you get back. Please give me at least 30 minutes. I'll be there anytime you say. I'm begging you, Jill, please don't turn me away because my whole future is at stake here."

What in the world can that mean, I wonder, and what would I have to do with his future? I thought he'd made it pretty clear that he had no room for me in his life, but he's definitely aroused my curiosity. "I have no idea why you need to talk to me about your future, T.J., but I suppose I can spare 30 minutes to hear your story. Would 6 o'clock be convenient for you?"

"I'll be there, Jill, and I want to thank you so much for giving me a chance to talk to you. It means more than you can possibly realize right now."

"Yeah, I'm sure. I'll see you at 6:00 then. Goodbye, T.J." I slowly get up to go tell my parents that he's coming.

When I tell them he's coming to talk to me about something that seems to be bothering him, they decide not to add to the difficult situation by being around. I explain that he's taking me out to dinner, but they decide to go over to see Jodi and Richard for a little while and then get something to eat before they come home. Jodi's pregnancy is doing well, but she has quit working so Mom doesn't get to see her every day at the bank like she used to.

After showering, I decide to wear my short denim skirt with a taupe batiste blouse styled with short puffed sleeves, a mandarin collar and Y neckline. My tan flats will give me a very casual look.

Our grandfather clock is just beginning to strike 6 o'clock when T.J. pulls into the driveway. How he does that, I'll never know. I think he must wait at the corner until just the right second to come the rest of the way so he can arrive at the exact time. I wait for the doorbell to ring and then slowly walk to answer it. It's terribly hard to do because I'd love to run and jump into his arms.

"Hi, T.J., you're right on time, as usual. Do you want to come in or should we be on our way?"

"I would say hello to your folks, if they're here, unless they want to stay as far away from me as you're trying to make it appear you are." His dimpled smile tells me he's seeing right through my hard shell, which is really irritating, and I can't seem to keep myself from an old habit of sticking my tongue out when I'm upset.

"They're at Jodi and Richard's so you're stuck with just me, Smarty Pants. Did you make reservations again, or would you like to have something to drink here before we go?"

"Let's go on to the restaurant, Jill. When I get started with my humble apology and explanation of what has been going on in my life since you last saw me, then I won't have to stop until I've made my point."

"That sounds intriguing. What restaurant are we going to?"

"Unless you have a suggestion, I thought I saw a Perkin's on my way here, and they are usually a little quieter than some of the others, so we could try that one."

"Sounds good to me. Let me grab a sweater real quick because that restaurant is a little chilly at times."

"I could lend you an arm, if you'd like," he says but then chuckles because I couldn't help but look a bit surprised at that remark. "Sorry, I guess you're not in the mood to hear my wishes or desires."

"It does sound a little far fetched after five weeks without a single word from you. Shall we go?"

It isn't far to the restaurant so little conversation is needed. He does ask about my golf lessons, and I tell him about the four others in my class and about playing the 9 holes with the girls last Saturday. I also laughingly tell him about Mom and me playing with Dad and his partner on Sunday.

"I've found it to be distracting to my game, too, when I'm concerned about the one playing with me. It's usually when I team up with someone at the club who needs a partner and I'm not familiar with him or his game."

We're lucky to get a booth which is separated a little more from the others and fairly quiet. After placing our orders, he reaches out his hand and motions for one of mine which is in my lap. "Please let me hold your hand, Jill. I'll feel closer to you that way and hope I can convince you of the sincerity in my words." He waits as our drinks are placed on the table and then smiles as I reluctantly put my hand in his.

"I see that I've got my work cut out for me tonight. You, of course, remember the rather difficult circumstances I created for us during the weekend of the banquet. When I brought you home, I didn't know what my next step was going to be. I was afraid that I was getting myself too involved too fast, and I'd made a vow that I wouldn't let it happen again, after Adele. The girls I dated during Med School, internship and residency were either nurses or blind dates whom the other guys set me up with, and after one date with each, I'd had enough of their trying to push themselves into my life with promiscuous actions and promises. So, when I started practicing with Dad, I decided to stop dating and concentrate on my practice, and although I was lonesome a lot of the time, I thought I was doing quite well.

And then you came along. The moment I saw you with Jessica and C.J., the night you came to the folks for dinner, I was wondering what in the world was happening in my chest, and I haven't been able to stop its pounding since. I don't remember ever feeling this way before, even with Adele. In fact, every time I see you, my heart is telling me one thing but my mind is telling me something else.

So, when I finally realized my hopelessness, after making a complete fool of myself that weekend with you, I decided to talk to Dad at length about all my feelings and also my apprehension about the future. He told me a few things that made a lot of sense, including the fact that I'm not 21 or 22 years old anymore, love is love, and our feelings are still the best indicator of what we want out of life. He reminded me that I don't have time to take two or three years deciding what my next step is going to be, if I want to have a family, and then he gave me a suggestion."

Our meal comes and we try to eat, but I know he's anxious to continue. We've both taken only a few bites when I push my plate away, put my fork down and tell him to go on.

"Dad said there was a conference for doctors being held in Chicago later that week and also an AMA meeting the following week he thought I'd enjoy. I knew he'd made all the reservations to go himself, but now he wanted me to go instead. I tried to argue, but he insisted that I go and even take a few extra days to relax and try to get my thoughts about the future straightened out. I came home on the 19th and wanted to call you, but I was so afraid it had been so long that you'd refuse to talk to me. I finally called C.J. and he first encouraged me, but then just plain told me to get off my big fat behind, show him and the folks and myself that I have good Peterson blood in my veins, and call you. If you refused to talk to me, that would be the time to panic. So, here I am."

"And you feel that this is enough to cause you to be so disturbed that it could affect your whole future?"

"No, Jill, there's more. While I was at the doctor's conference, a mention was made that there are openings for doctors with special training in pediatric care and medicine, and I'm qualified for that. One is in California and the other is in Florida, but it was stressed that the deadline for sending in a resume is the 10th of this month.

I honestly don't want to leave Chapel Hill or my practice with Dad, but if I can't get some solution to my feelings for you, it is my intention to pursue this option. If you refuse to see me because of my previous actions, and I have no future with you, I will just have to leave. To be so close to you and yet without you just couldn't be tolerated.

You see, Jill, I have realized that I'm definitely in over my head with you, but right now I'm unable to proceed like any normal guy, to give you a ring and ask you to marry me. I'm just not ready to do that after knowing you for only three months." He's grimacing and he's running his fingers through his hair as if in anguish.

"I guess I can see your dilemma, T.J., but I don't know exactly what you think I can do to help. This is my home, and Jessica is my sister, and I can't control what is happening between her and C.J., so what is it you want to happen? If you'd just like to get to know me better without a commitment, I'd be willing to do that if we can plan to do things that won't create problems. Is there another plan that you have in mind other than shipping me off to Antarctica or Africa? I wouldn't particularly like to live in either of those places."

Oooh, I think I see that dazzling smile appearing. He reaches for my hand again to get it to his mouth and kiss it, which, of course, sends those tingles acting up again. I think that's enough in the now crowded restaurant so I pull my hand back and look at my food. It is completely cold and unappetizing. "Do you think we could order some dessert, T.J. or will that not be enough for you. Do you want to order another meal?"

Of course, he can't keep from laughing. "What am I going to do with you, Jill? You are the most interesting and intriguing, the most exasperating and provoking, and the most darling and sweetest human being I have ever met. Are you sure you could give me time to learn to know you until I can get my head on straight?"

"I see no problem in being friends, and I can even pay my part of the tab if that is what friends do. That is, unless you decide you want to go to a golf tournament that is way out of my price range."

"I don't think I suggested that this would be a totally platonic relationship, Ms Hale, but we'll talk about that later. What kind of dessert did you have in mind?" He motions to the server who comes immediately and looks concerned when she sees the uneaten food.

"Was there something wrong with your food?" she asks.

"No, not at all. We just got involved discussing something and forgot to eat. We'd like to order some dessert, however, if we haven't overstayed our welcome."

"Oh, of course not. What may I get for you?"

We both order a piece of their Chocolate French Silk pie and a cup of coffee which she brings almost immediately. It tastes terrific, but I enjoy the smile on his face so much more than I do the pie. I'm just glad to have our friendship back, or whatever he wants to call it.

CHAPTER TWELVE

"*D*id you really have another engagement tonight, Jill, or were you just being a little hostile toward me when you told me that on the phone?"

He gives me that smile I wish I could wipe off his face that tells me he already thinks he knows the answer to that question. I don't even respond as he starts the engine and pulls out of the restaurant parking lot. I really don't want the evening to end, but it isn't long before I begin to wonder where he's taking me when he's going the opposite direction than to my home. "You're not going to kidnap me are you, T.J.? Do you have directions to my house turned around tonight in this little town?"

"No, I'm just fine, Sweetie, and we'll be to our destination in just a couple more minutes if I have my address correct.

Yes, there it is," and he turns into the parking lot across from the movie theater. "Is it all right with you if we go to a movie so I'll get to have at least one of my arms around you?"

"Do friends do that?" I ask as I give him my mischievous grin.

"I don't know about friends, but I'd like to do that with the girl I adore unless she'd rather go to a motel room where we could really get more comfortable."

That remark and then his chuckle, as he glances over at me, make me realize that my face is probably as red as a beet. "You're not getting off to a very good start, Doctor, if you're going to pull those type of tricks after your so sincere apology and asking if we can be friends while we get to know each other better."

"I think I know you pretty well after the one weekend we shared, although you are so unpredictable and spontaneous that I wonder if I'll ever know you like I'd love to. Let's go to the movie." He's around to open my door so quickly that I only have time to grab my purse. As I get out, his lips are kissing my hair and then my cheek which sends a flutter of emotion through my body. Maybe this isn't a very good idea. How can I be only a friend when my feelings are telling me something so different?

As he takes my arm crossing the street, he remarks, "I'll behave myself, Jill, truly I will, although I'll admit it's going to be hard. Remember what I told you in the guest room that night when I wouldn't go to my room like I should have? Well, keeping my hands and lips off of you is still going to be a problem."

"I guess we'll have to be careful about where we spend time with each other then," which, of course, brings a hearty chuckle from him as he stops on the sidewalk and kisses me on the lips.

"I'm not sure it'll make a whole lot of difference where we are if I get an urge to kiss you, Ms. Hale, but let's see what's playing at the movie." We stop to look at the marquee to study the only two choices at this theater. Our timing is good because the one we decide to see has just ended and the commercials and coming attractions are now being shown as we find our seats. He steers me toward the last row in one of the side sections, and when I resist, he whispers, "I don't want someone to whistle again, like the last time, if I decide to kiss you when you get scared or a little romantic." He takes my hand and pulls me into the very dark corner of the last row.

The movie is good and he gets so engrossed with it that the only attention I get is his arm around my shoulders until a romantic scene comes on. "I've got a prettier girl in my arms than he has," he whispers as he leans over to kiss my cheek. His arm tightens a little around me and he pulls me as close as he can with that chair arm between us. His attention is then back on the movie. I'll have to remember the kind of show that holds his attention if I want this to remain just a friendship or a time to get to know each other, as he describes it.

It's 10:15 when we leave the movie and he's talking all the way home about the outstanding job of photography that was done in making the picture. "Are you interested in the scenery and photographic detail of a movie more than the story line?" I ask.

"Photography and art are my hobbies, and I've spent a lot of weekends or vacations at a lake, a campground or even along the highways getting ideas for paintings. I'm sorry I didn't show you some of my paintings when you were there. I have three or four hanging in the condo and at the clinic, and there are several more stored in the closet of my office."

"I remember seeing an outstanding picture of a lake over the fireplace mantle in the master bedroom Saturday morning. Does that one happen to be one of yours? I so admired the detailing where the artist wanted to emphasize a certain item or area."

"You're very observant, Jill. Yes, that is one of my best attempts at painting a lake scene. It happens to be a wonderful Minnesota lake where our family vacationed almost every year when C.J. and I were growing up. I'd love to go back and see how much it has changed from a boy's perspective over the years."

"Maybe you can some day. Do you like to fish, too?"

"You bet. That was the main reason we went, but I had my drawing pad and pencil with me, too. Well, I guess I got you home safe and sound, so I'd better be getting myself on back to Chapel Hill. Thanks again, Jill, for a wonderful evening and for giving me the option to stay with Dad in the practice that I love."

Walking me to the door, his arm is again around my shoulders, and then he turns me in his arms so I'm facing him. "You are so precious, Jill, and I promise I'll try my best to treat you as an angel should be treated. Don't hesitate to slap my face, or at least tell me, if I ever get out of line again. Goodnight, Sweetie." He tilts my chin up and lowers his lips to mine for the softest, most gentle kiss I've experienced. "I'll call you because football season is going to be starting soon, and I hope we can get to a few of the games," he says as he softly caresses my cheek with his fingers and gives me a smile that will last for several days. Then he's gone except for the blinking of lights as he backs out the drive. I wave and, like always, I pray that God will keep him safe on his way home.

I've got to call Jessica. I have to know if she and C.J. had anything to do with this miracle tonight or was it, as he told me, that he was afraid I wouldn't talk to him after he'd waited so long to call. He said C.J. had told him there was only one way to find out. Oh, Jessica, I hope you're up late tonight because your sister needs to talk to you.

Everything worked out well. Jessica had been with C.J. and had only been home a few minutes when I called. Everything T.J. had told me seemed to be the truth, as far as she knew, and all my doubts were lifted. I can be his friend, or even girlfriend, for as long as he wants to satisfy his need to know that I'm not another Adele.

I know my dreams are going to be about the possibilities of true happiness with the man I have truly fallen in love with, and I know that my arms and lips are also going to find it hard to leave him alone.

I turn in my Bible to the 13th chapter of Corinthians because I want to read the 'love chapter' and memorize what it says. "Love is patient, Love is kind, it does not envy, it does not boast, it is not proud, it is not rude, it is not self-seeking, it is not easily angered and does not keep a record of wrongs. Love does not delight in evil, but rejoices in the truth. It always protects, always trusts, always hopes, and always perseveres. Love never fails."

"Dear Jesus, This is a lot to remember, but I'll try my best to show the love in my heart toward you, my family, and my new friend, T.J., as well as all others you put in my path. With your help, I will succeed. Amen."

CHAPTER THIRTEEN

After church on Sunday, Dad has his usual golf game and Mom and I putter around in the kitchen baking some cookies and then putting the roast in the oven for supper. I then decide to curl up in one of the recliners and try to finish reading the book I've been trying to complete for the last two weeks. When T.J. wasn't calling, I read so many books that I was out of the mood when I started this one so it has taken me ages to even get close to the end, but if I'm lucky, I'll get it finished today.

I'm actually on the last chapter when the phone rings. Mom has gone to visit one of the ladies from church, so I guess I'll have to answer. It'll probably be just another of those telemarketers or kids dialing the wrong number, which seems to happen quite often on the weekends, so I answer "Hale residence," hoping it's a wrong number and they'll hang up.

"I'm surprised to hear you answer the phone, Jill. I'd gotten the feeling that your dad screens all the calls coming into your home. I'm glad I don't have to wait to hear your sweet voice this time."

"T.J., I certainly wasn't expecting you to call today since I just saw you last night. I assume you got home safe and sound. Dad is playing golf and Mom is visiting a lady who had surgery last week. She took her some cookies we'd just baked. As far as the phone is concerned, Dad is usually the closest to the phone in the evenings and he has a few clients who call after office hours, so we let him answer most of the time. Is there a special reason for your call?"

"Am I interrupting something? You don't sound too happy to hear from me. I just thought I'd call to see if you're still my girl. You haven't changed your mind, have you?"

"Answer to your first question: Yes, you're interrupting my reading of a book that hasn't been the most interesting so I'm trying real hard to get it finished today. The answer to your other question: I'm a girl and I hope I'm still your friend, so I assume that makes me your girlfriend, and I haven't changed my mind. You didn't really waste a phone call to just ask me that, did you?"

"It's very important to me, after our talk last night, but I do have something else to ask you. I just received the UNC football schedule, and there is a game two weeks from yesterday, and I was wondering if you'd like to go with me.

There's only one problem: It's an afternoon game, so I'd have to come get you Friday night like I did for the banquet. I also wanted to ask if you'd be willing to drive up if I were to hit a snag like before. I don't expect you to do that unless something unusual happens again, and that is really rare."

"I'd love to go to the game, T.J., but would I be staying at your parents for sure this time? I could drive up, if need be, and I know how to get to your parents' house now, so that isn't a problem."

"I've talked to Dad and Mom and it's fine with them that you stay there. In fact, she said we could plan to eat with them Friday night, if the timing is right, and then I'll plan to take you out for dinner Saturday after the game. They have tickets for the game so they'll be going, too. We'll go to church again Sunday morning, if you'd like, after which I'll take you home."

"That sounds like fun and I'll be looking forward to it. What else have you been doing today? Did you play some golf?"

"I went to church this morning and then Dad and I played 9 holes. The course was so crowded that it wasn't much fun so we quit after the nine and came home. I suppose I'd better let you get back to your reading now. Is it a romantic novel to put you in the mood to dream about me while you're sleeping tonight?" he chuckles.

"Don't you wish? Actually, it's a historical novel that was recommended by one of the girls who works at the bank, but I found it a little boring to start with. The plot changed quite a bit today, though, and the last six chapters have been quite interesting. For some reason, I thought I was starting the last chapter when the phone rang, but I see now that I have three chapters to go and I'm really anxious to see what happens to her family when they get back to their plantation after the Civil War."

"I have some great books on the Civil War if you like to read about that period of our country's history. I really enjoyed learning about the lives of our young struggling men and women after I wasn't forced to remember all the dates and places in school."

"I may have to check them out sometime because I've always enjoyed reading about our country's first important leaders and all the trials they faced trying to get everything running as well as they knew how. I have read some of the romances, too, that took place in those days, and I'm very happy that I live in today's world and not back then."

"Yeah, me too. You wouldn't have been there for me to irritate if I'd live back then while you'd lived in this modern world. That would've been a calamity," he laughed. "I'd better sign off for now, Sweetie. If I don't talk to you again before you go to the beach, do have a great time and tell my brother I took his advice and it worked pretty well."

"Of course, I'll be sure to do that. Goodbye, My Friend."

"Not goodbye, just farewell until we meet again, Jill, and here's a kiss for you." A loud smooch comes over the line, he chuckles as he whispers, "I've never done that before in my life," and then I hear the click of the phone.

I'm laughing but also thinking it's going to be a long two weeks. I go back to my reading and am just finishing the book when Mom comes in the door. The aroma from the roast is beginning to tempt my empty stomach and it's time to add the potatoes and carrots. As I set the table, I tell her about T.J.'s call and invitation to attend the football game. "His parents also have tickets so they'll be at the game, too. I really like his folks and they make me feel so welcome in their home. It was so easy to talk to both of them at the banquet, and T.J. also seems close to his family. He was ready to tell them that he had behaved badly, when I had to stay at his place that weekend, and his mother was quick to question one of his humorous remarks before he continued with the full explanation of why his bed was rather rumpled when he came back from the office."

"I can understand her concern after hearing your report on the wild weekend, but I'm so glad you've found someone with high morals and a belief in God that will keep you safe when you're with him and keep him on the right path most of the time, anyway," she laughs. "The other times will be up to you to let him know he's out of line."

"Changing the subject a bit, can you believe it's not even five full days now before we leave for the beach? I'm so excited to see my sister and her school. She sounds so excited that everything is falling into place for her, and we'll get to meet Emily and this Jackson as well as seeing C.J. again. Oh, here comes Dad, and I can imagine he's hungry. Is there anything else I can do to help?"

"I think everything hot will be ready by the time he takes a shower. You can help me fix a fruit salad, if you'd like, and I think some cookies will be enough for dessert."

∽

I'm trying to push the week along, and my two golf lessons and a Wednesday night call from Jessica certainly help except I could hardly keep from telling her that we would see her in two days. Thursday night, when I get home from my golf lesson, I go to my room to finish packing. Mom calls me to eat before I finish, so I go back as soon as we get the kitchen cleaned up. About 9 o'clock I hear the phone ring, but I'm really surprised when Dad calls to say it's for me. Who would be calling me this late?

"This is Jill," I answer.

"I would know that voice anywhere, Sweetie. Are you all packed and ready to go tomorrow? I just wish I were going with you."

"T.J., you're so sweet to call just to tell me goodbye. I'm almost packed and am so excited I probably won't sleep a wink tonight. What are you planning to do this weekend?"

"Well, I just learned on Tuesday that there's a ProAm golf tournament this weekend and I was able to get tickets, so I'm looking for someone to go with me. I guess I'll have to get out a little black book and see who I can come up with unless you'll change your plans and go with me. I'll take you to the beach the weekend after the football game if you'll do that for me."

"Very tempting, T.J., but I can't miss this weekend with my family. The anticipation has been growing for weeks and nothing can make me change my plans, not even you."

"I was afraid of that. Will your family always come first with you, Jill, even after you're committed to someone in marriage?"

"I'm not sure how to answer that, T.J., and I'm not sure it's fair for you to ask at this time. After all, you're the one who's afraid to commit, remember, so how can you expect me to jump through hoops to satisfy only what you want to do? I'm sorry, My Friend, but you sound just a little selfish tonight."

"Thanks for clarifying how you feel, Jill. I won't keep you any longer, but I hope you have an enjoyable, even though lonesome, time with your family the next four days."

I hear the phone click and soon there is only the dial tone buzzing in my ear. "How dare you, Dr. T.J. Peterson. I don't remember you showing me this side of your personality before, but I won't soon forget it." I was about to throw the phone across the room, but I decide to take my shoe off and throw it against the wall instead. I'm not going to waste an expensive phone on an egotistical blankety blank like him. I throw myself across the bed and sob. I had been so happy just a few minutes ago and now I see my future in ruins. Of course, I'm wondering if he might send that resume to California and Florida yet. But, so what if he does? I can't be responsible if he's going to be so controlling that he messes up his own life, too.

There's a knock on the door and Mom is asking, "Are you all right, Jill? I thought I heard something fall. May I come in?"

"Sure, Mom, come on in." I quickly sit up on the bed and try to wipe the tears out of my eyes, but it wasn't fast enough to fool my mom.

"Your dad said it was T.J. on the phone." She sees my shoe over against the wall and then looks back at me. "Did the conversation cause you to react by throwing your shoe or did a critter of some sort get in your room?"

"I almost threw my phone, but I decided it was too expensive an item to waste on an absolute jerk. Oh, Mom, I've probably lost him, but he asked the impossible, and when I called him selfish, he hung up on me."

"Do you want to elaborate on that so I can understand what the impossible was that he asked?"

I reiterated most of our conversation and she looked somewhat shocked herself by the time I'd finished. "What do you think of the fine young doctor now?" I ask.

"Well, I am a little surprised that he would expect you to change your plans at the last minute, but sometimes men don't think quite clearly when they want something so very badly. T.J. found something to fill his empty weekend, but then he realized it wouldn't be an exciting time, like he wanted, without you. He even came up with an alternative that he thought you might accept. I remember a similar occasion with your dad, not long after he'd given me the engagement ring. One Sunday we were both supposed to go with my parents to let my grandparents finally meet him, know about the engagement, and to see my ring. I was so excited and could hardly wait.

On Saturday, your dad called and made some excuse that he couldn't go and asked me to change my plans. I refused and it was two full weeks before he finally called and apologized. He said he'd gotten cold feet about meeting anymore of my family. So, don't be too upset, Jill, he'll probably realize how it hurt you and will want to make up before the football game next weekend." She gives me a hug and leaves me alone with my thoughts.

I get ready for bed and have a good long talk with Jesus before I try to fall asleep. I repeat the few characteristics of love that I have memorized so far and now feel determined to overlook the hurt that T.J. caused by his remarks. After all, I have a great weekend ahead and I'm not going to let anything or anyone spoil it for me.

CHAPTER FOURTEEN

O ur suitcases are in the car and we plan to leave so we can arrive at the beach about the time the afternoon preschool is being dismissed. It's a beautiful September day, a few fluffy clouds in the Carolina blue sky, and everything is so lush and green. It reminds me of our family vacations except Richard has taken the place of Jessica so it can't be all girl talk today.

We easily find the Beachside Resort and have time to meet Emily before C.J. walks with us over to the school. Cars are pulling up in front of the attractive building, and the front door is just opening when we're about 40 feet away. We stop to watch as Jessica hugs each child as they come out one by one. She shakes hands with the parents as they claim their child, and she even gets a hug from a few of the mothers which we think is amazing after just two or three weeks. When the last one has gone, she glances toward the resort to apparently see if C.J. is coming, but then she sees us and lets out a scream. We run toward her and almost knock her down when all of us try to hug her at the same time.

"Come on in and see my school. In fact, you can all help me tidy up the room," she laughs. She then looks at C.J. and gives him a cockeyed grin. "You knew my family was coming today, didn't you, and you helped them surprise me." When she sees the smile on his face, she adds, "For that, you get to sweep the floor."

"Ah, gee, Miss Jessica, I thought I'd get to do something different today. You assign the sweeping job to me almost every day." He tries to pout but can only chuckle.

The room is so organized that it takes little time to put things away so after seeing her office and the rest of the area, we head over to the resort to get something to drink and then find our rooms. I'm going to stay with Jessica in her room while we're here, and I'm looking forward to sharing the latest about T.J. with her. I'm debating, though, about giving his message to C.J. following the upsetting conversation we had last night. Insinuating that C.J.'s advice had worked pretty well might not be so true now.

There's room for the seven of us in Dad's van, so he lets C.J. drive and he shows us around the area. We stop at one of the seafood restaurants for dinner and then C.J. invites us into his apartment so we can visit. Although it's not quite as large as T.J.'s condo, it's a beautiful place, and I realize both brothers have wonderful tastes in decorating.

Most of Saturday is spent on the beach and doing a little shopping. A wonderful meal is served at the resort that evening. Emily joins us and C.J. has also invited Jackson so we can all meet him. He seems so thrilled to meet Jessica's family. I don't know if Dad appreciated him referring to Jessica as his newly adopted daughter, but he did seem to enjoy visiting with him and even invited him to come see us.

After we attend church Sunday morning, we spend most of the afternoon on C.J.'s sailboat, and that is so cool. When we thought we were heading back to the marina, we end up right in front of the Beachside and almost immediately two servers from the restaurant are on a small raft bringing a large cooler out to us. We anchor out a little ways and get to eat on the boat. It's fantastic, and after a rather short sunset cruise, it's almost dark when we finally dock at the marina and walk back to the resort. We're all so excited but ready to call it a day.

Jessica and I finally get a chance to talk. I tell her about my conversation with T.J. Thursday night, and she is really surprised to hear that he would expect me to change my plans at the last minute. "I understand your confusion and I'll talk to C.J. about it, but, if you care for him at all, I suggest that you not call it quits until you've given him a chance to explain his actions and hopefully apologize."

"What else can I do since I'm totally under his spell, so to speak? But that doesn't mean I'm going to put up with him expecting me to jump whenever he gives a command."

Jessica was laughing, "No, Jill, he'll never get by doing that. I remember when you would even butt heads with Mom and Dad when they were insisting that you do something you didn't want to do. Of course, you stayed in your room without supper those nights, and couldn't use the telephone either."

"I guess I am pretty stubborn, but I'm memorizing the characteristics of love given in I Corinthians 13, and I'm determined to be more patient and all those other nice things that the Bible says love does."

❦

Monday morning, after telling everyone goodbye, we watch as the morning students arrive and get to see the big smiles on their faces as they're greeted by their teacher. Jessica turns and waves to us, but then the door is closed. It's time for us to head home.

We are back in time to have a fast-food lunch and then Dad drops Mom and me at the bank, Jodi and Richard at their house, and then he heads to his office. We are all back in our familiar surroundings although my thoughts seem to be constantly on next weekend when I'm supposed to go to the football game with T.J. Will he come to get me as planned, call and cancel the date, or maybe not contact me at all? It has my nerves so taut that I feel as if I could scream.

Why did I have to meet him? It certainly wasn't my lucky day, or was it? Maybe God thought I needed a challenge like T.J. so I would learn I Corinthians 13.

I'm certainly not ready for the phone call that comes Wednesday night around 7:30. When Dad says it's for me, I'm hoping it's Jessica calling to tell me how C.J. reacted to his brother's actions. I answer, "Hey, Jill here."

"Hello, Jill." I hear T.J.'s voice which has no emotion whatsoever, and as hard as I try, my temper is rising rather rapidly as I listen to his instructions. "I plan to leave the office at 4 o'clock or shortly thereafter on Friday afternoon, so I should be there by five. Please be ready to go because we're eating with the folks, if you recall."

"It's really not necessary, T.J., that you fulfill your invitation to take me to the game if you'd rather not. It's perfectly fine with me if I stay home."

"The folks are expecting us, and they're looking forward to seeing you. Let's not disappoint them, OK?"

"Oh, I'd never want to disappoint your folks. I'm definitely looking forward to seeing them again."

"Fine, I'll see you Friday then." The phone clicked off before I had a chance to say another word, which, I guess, was a good thing.

"Ooooh!!!!! Who do you think you are, Dr. Peterson? Do you treat your patients like this, too, if they disagree with you or question your orders? Well, I won't disappoint your parents, but you're going to receive a piece of my mind, and you can take it or leave it. I don't need and will not take your high and mighty actions." I was sitting on the edge of my bed repeating my promise to be patient, but also trying to figure out just what I'd done to deserve this treatment. About twenty minutes had passed when Dad calls up the stairs to inform me that I have another call.

"Jill, here," I say despondently.

"Whoa, what's wrong with you tonight? Did the big weekend get you down, or has something else happened? Oh, no, Jill, has T.J. called and caused you more heartache?"

"You guessed it, Jess. He was absolutely overbearing as he gave me orders about Friday evening, and if it wasn't for his folks expecting us for dinner, I would refuse to go anywhere with him."

"I'm sorry to hear that because when C.J. was just talking to him he brought the situation up himself, said he was ashamed of the way he'd talked to you, and had to figure out someway to make it up to you. What exactly did he say?"

I repeat our conversation almost word for word and then ask, "Does that sound like someone who is sorry?"

"I wonder if this was the conversation he was referring to when he talked to C.J.? It sounds like someone who is so embarrassed that he's at a loss on how to do an apology. He resorted to trying to be in control by any means he could grasp onto. Jill, he is used to having the answers to his patients' problems, but it appears he lacks the know-how to have the answers to problems of his own heart. C.J. tells me he's one of the kindest guys anyone could ever know, but I guess it'll take a lot of patience and understanding on your part if you want to pursue a relationship with him."

"Yeah, that's the problem. I'm afraid I'm in love with the guy but he only wants me when he needs a date like to the banquet, the game, or a movie. I'm not sure I'm ready to be a convenient tag-along, so to speak. We'll see what happens this weekend, and I'll try to give him the benefit of the doubt, but I can't promise any miracle. If he continues on this course of action, he'll soon be without the girl he thinks he can control."

"Just be your sweet and humorous self, Sis, and I'm sure your weekend will be one of the greatest, and of course, we want a win for UNC."

❦

T.J. pulls into the driveway ten minutes before 5 o'clock and slowly walks onto the porch to ring the bell. I have my suitcase in the foyer, say goodbye to Mom and then go to the door. "Hey, T.J.," and I really do try to give him a convincing smile. "I have my things right here so we can be on our way."

"Do I get to say Hello to one or both of your parents this time, Jill, or did you ask that they be gone to save any embarrassment?"

"Mom is here, but I thought you wanted to start back to Chapel Hill as soon as possible. Come on in, I think she's in the kitchen."

Mom is at the sink with her back toward us as T.J. slips into the room and says, "Hi, Mrs. Hale, I didn't want to leave without at least saying hello. I'm sorry I missed you the last time I picked Jill up."

A shocked look was on her face as she turns around and quickly puts her hand over her heart. "T.J. you startled me. I wasn't expecting you to take time to say hello to me. Jill thought you wanted to get right back on the road." She wipes her hands and extends them both which he takes in his and kisses.

"There's always time for me to greet Jill's parents and assure them that I'll do my best to see that she has a good time this weekend. Will you please tell Mr. Hale that I'm sorry I missed him? Is he all right?"

"Yes, T.J., he's fine and he'll be sorry he missed you, too."

"We won't linger, then, because Mom and Dad are expecting us for dinner and we'll be driving in some of the heavy evening traffic. It was so good to see you."

Well, he was as nice to my mom as I plan to be to his folks. Of course, just what happens on the way to Chapel Hill is anybody's guess.

He takes my arm with one hand and carries my suitcase with the other on the way to the car. One part of me wants to jerk away while the other part wants to grab him for a big passionate kiss. I'm so tense he surely notices, but he opens the door for me and then puts the luggage in the trunk on his way around to the driver's side.

When he's seated, his belt fastened, and he's starting the engine, he looks over at me and smiles. "Jill, are you going to let me apologize for my atrocious actions the last few days, or is it your plan to make me suffer mercilessly? I can't blame you for giving me the option to cancel our date for the game after my insane request that you change your plans just because I wanted you to. My only excuse is that I desperately wanted you to be with me and I started giving you orders instead of thinking sensibly. All I could think of was that it would be another whole week before I'd see you. My mom and dad were so furious when I told them what I'd done, I was afraid they were going to disown me."

We're on the highway as he continues, "I didn't tell them about my call Wednesday night or I may have been without my parents for sure. I was actually afraid to talk to you because I was so sure you were going to tell me to go jump in the lake or worse. That's why I hung up so quickly.

I didn't go to the golf tournament either, Jill. My dad refused to go with me, so I gave the tickets to one of my patients who is a good player and talks golf all the time. He'd never been to a PGA tournament, so he and his wife were thrilled to get away and spend a weekend together and stay in the hotel room I'd reserved. The best was that they got to go without their kids who went to stay with their grandparents."

"I'm really sorry it was the same weekend I had the other plans because I would've loved to follow the tournament with you."

"I'm so glad to hear that, Jill, and I'll find another tournament to go to, if you'd like and the time is right for both of us. We'll get down to the beach together, too. I haven't met this Jackson fellow yet, but right now I'm feeling fortunate just to have you speaking to me after I was such a fool."

I can't help but smile as he seems to be squirming a little trying to make up for the mistakes he'd made. But, I'm not quite through with him yet with the long weekend just beginning. "Don't get too comfortable in that cocky skin of yours, Dr. Peterson, because my revenge is far from over. I may have given you the opinion that I'm just putty in your hands by coming up here for the game tomorrow, but you're going to find out I am more like solid unbending steel by the time you take me home Sunday."

"Okay, Sweetie," he says, but then he has to give me that dazzling smile that makes my heart go thumping like crazy and he knows it. "I'm ready to accept anything you want to hand out because I realize that I deserve your anger and retaliation."

"Then stop your smiling and at least act a little remorseful." I stubbornly hold on to the scowl on my face, but with his smile getting bigger and those eyes sparkling like big pools of diamonds, my defenses are quickly receding.

He reaches over and tries to caress my cheek with his fingers, but I slap them away.

"Don't think you can avoid my revenge by pulling that little stunt, Dr. Peterson. I'm onto your come hither antics and I'm not going to fall for them. You just keep your hands on the wheel and your eyes on the road."

"Yes, Ma'am," he chuckles, "but what do I do now that we're not going to be in the car or on the road anymore?" I glance up to see him turning into his parents' driveway.

"Maybe I'll have to tie your hands behind your back," I smirk and try to be as angry and serious as possible.

"You may need some help to do that," he smiles as he exits the car, quickly reaches my door, and before I know what's happening, I'm in his arms. His lips are suddenly on mine to make me forget, I suppose, all about making him pay for his stupid mistakes.

Well, I do a pretty good job of struggling for a minute, at least, before my arms go around his neck and I melt into his embrace. What else is a girl supposed to do when she loves the guy and has a chance to get a fabulous kiss?

"You don't play fair, T.J.," I say as I give him a slap on the arm and then a big push which he wasn't expecting. It causes him to stagger a little before he gets his balance and looks at me rather surprisingly.

"You're stronger than you appear, Little Lady. I guess I'd better be well prepared to defend myself from a hefty punch or a karate blow if I'm a bad boy again. Have you taken some lessons in martial arts?"

"I'm not telling you. You'll just have to discover the answer to that when you find yourself on the floor one of these days." Now I wish I did have some defense training, but it was never one of my motivations in life. Of course, I'll not tell him that.

"I've heard it said that all is fair in love and war, so I'll be sure to be on my guard, but I'm warning you, you'd better keep your eyes open, too." He's laughing as he takes my hand and starts toward the house.

"Mom, we're here," he calls. "We'll take Jill's things up to the room and then we'll be down."

"All right, Dear. Everything's almost ready."

CHAPTER FIFTEEN

I immediately notice the aroma from the beautiful bouquet of pink and white roses when I step into the room. I almost run over to admire them and put my nose close to inhale the wonderful smell of each one until I feel T.J.'s arms around my waist. "No, T.J., this is neither the time nor place for you to try out your affections on me," as I push his hands away from my waist and then turn to face him.

I look into those eyes that are dancing with something, but I can't believe it's what I'd like it to be--namely, love. "Did you buy those roses for me, T.J.?" He nods so I then continue, "They are so pretty, and I appreciate your thoughtfulness. I love roses and I'll be able to enjoy them the entire weekend." My arms reach up to encircle his neck,

I stand on tiptoe, and my lips move lightly across his cheek as they get closer and closer to his mouth.

Am I being too forward, I wonder, as I decide to ask, "Are they just another part of your apology, or could it possibly be that you have a few little feelings for me?" I really try to sound as sexy as I've seen in some movie love scenes, but I'm certainly not an actress.

"What did you say about this not being the time or place, Jill," he murmurs softly as he turns just enough for his lips to find mine for a short pleasant kiss. He takes my hands from his neck and asks, "Do you have some things to hang up in the closet?"

I slowly turn away from him realizing this romantic moment is gone. I get to my suitcase and then stop. "Why don't you go on downstairs and I'll be down as soon as I get my things put away."

"That's probably a good idea although I don't want to leave you. Will you promise you won't run away?" he chuckles.

"I shouldn't promise you anything, but I did agree to have dinner with you and your folks so I'll be down shortly." He pats the top of my head and leaves.

"I'm not a little child, Dr. Peterson, that you're trying to get in a good mood so you can give it an unwanted shot," I murmur although I know he won't hear me as I hang up my pant suit that I'll wear with a cami on Sunday. I brought a pair of jeans to wear to the game. I'll layer a sleeveless V-neck blue knit top under a white chambray shirt that has

UNC on the pocket and I'll carry a blue sweater in case it turns cool. Another outfit is there, too, just in case I need something a little nicer than my game clothes if we decide to go somewhere else. I'm set now so I quickly wash my hands and check myself in the full length mirror, and then I run down the unique curving staircase and on into the kitchen.

"Hello, Mrs. Peterson. May I help with anything?"

"Oh, Jill, it's so good to see you again." She turns from the sink, wipes her hands and quickly comes to give me a big hug. "Can you ever forgive that son of ours for the awful way he talked to you before you went to the beach?" She definitely was looking to see my reaction, and I see she's extremely upset about the situation.

I smile and nod. "I was rather angry when I thought he was going to try to be one of those controlling guys, but I also realized that I have some pretty deep feelings for that son of yours. Because of the exceptional way he'd treated me previously, I felt there had to be some reason for his behavior and I should give him a chance to explain. I didn't know if he'd come to get me today, call and cancel, or just not show up, but we had a good talk on the way up here, and I think I understand him a little better than I did. He also understands that I won't tolerate that kind of treatment. He's usually been very gentle, fun loving, and even protective so when the green-eyed monster came alive, it was hard to accept, but he agrees to work on that."

"Brian and I were so furious when he came by and told us what he'd done, but we could see that he was carrying enough blame for all of us, so we tried to understand. I'm just so glad he apologized, but don't hesitate to make him pay," she grins.

"Where is he, anyway?"

"He went out to the garage for something. He still has some carpentry tools out there that he loves to work with when he comes over. I think he's trying to build a secret something, but he keeps whatever it is all covered up and his dad tells me I should leave it alone. I guess they found each other; I hear them coming in now. Would you like to set one of these dishes on the table? We'll be ready to eat as soon as they wash their hands."

"Everything looks and smells delicious. By the way, did you have anything to do with those beautiful roses in my room?"

"No, but they are gorgeous, aren't they? He brought them over on his lunch break, and I just happened to be home from the store. I also need to go in for a few hours in the morning, and I was wondering if you'd like to go with me. We'll be home by the time the guys close up the clinic at noon. You're welcome to stay here, of course, if you'd rather."

"Oh, I'd love to go to the store with you, Mrs. Peterson. I understand it's quite an unusual antique store, and I love to browse around furniture, antique or otherwise."

"Good, I think you might enjoy seeing our collection. Well, here they are ready to put some food in their stomachs.

Please sit down, you two, while Jill and I bring the other dishes to the table."

Dinner is a delicious chicken and rice casserole, lightly buttered asparagus spears and a fresh lettuce salad. The conversation continues very upbeat as I realize Dr. Peterson has a charming personality that I imagine delights his little patients as well as the mature ones. As I listen to him, however, I think I could be hearing T.J. since he has that same soothing tone to his voice. I'm sure his patients are just as pleased with his care as those of his dad, and my earlier thoughts about him come back to haunt me. Mrs. Peterson had just finished telling them that I'd agreed to go to the store with her in the morning when a young girl suddenly appears to clear the table and then brings in the dessert. It's a delicious apple cobbler that hadn't been out of the oven long and then topped with whipped cream. I learn that Sara is a college student who works at the store two or three days a week after her classes, and when needed, she also comes to the house to clear the table and clean up the kitchen. I look forward to seeing Sara again at the store tomorrow.

Bringing my thoughts back to the present, I hear Dr. Peterson asking his wife if she's had any luck finding someone with financial knowledge to help her with the store's bookkeeping.

"No, I haven't and I'm getting a little desperate. I have invoices piling up that need to be entered, and I have some statements that need to be checked. I've been able to get most of the checks written but a few still have to be mailed."

"Maybe I could help you with some of that tomorrow morning, Mrs. Peterson, if you'd like. I work with figures every day at the bank. I fill in as a window teller, when needed, but most of the time I'm in the finance office."

"Oh, Jill, that would be wonderful. I'll show you what I've done, and hopefully you won't scream at my attempt at bookkeeping. You see, our bookkeeper was with us for over forty years and I never had to worry when I took over after my parents retired. She was diagnosed with cancer recently, however, and apparently it's serious. She decided, on the spur of the moment, that she wanted to do a little traveling before the cancer starts taking its toll. She gave me two weeks notice and then was gone, but I miss her terribly."

"I'm so sorry, but I'll do my best to catch you up while I'm here."

"Mom, that was a wonderful meal, as usual. I'm thinking about asking Jill to walk to the exercise room with me and maybe work on those muscles that she about knocked me down with earlier. On second thought, maybe I should just take her for a leisurely walk."

"I want to go to the exercise room. I need a little more strength in my arms so I can land you on the ground next time," I giggle.

"You two run along. We'll see you before you go home, T.J." Dr. Peterson is chuckling as he steps between us, puts his arms around both T.J. and my shoulders as he walks us to the door. "Try not to have a knock down, drag out fight tonight," he laughs.

When I finally get back to my room, I'm exhausted. I had really exercised and I'm wondering now just how sore I'm going to be in the morning. I'd lifted weights, walked five miles on the tread mill, rode the stationary bike, and did a few of the arm and leg lifts. I tried to keep up with T.J., but I'd finally had to quit. He didn't do very many more, though, when he saw that I was quitting.

As we'd walked back to the house, T.J. had reached for my hand which made me so happy. It was so romantic as he'd massaged the palm of my hand, and gently squeezed it as he took it to his lips, but then he'd stopped before we reached the door and turned to face me. "Jill, I want to get my kiss goodnight before we go in, if you don't mind, and also ask you a rather important question. It is to me anyway," he grins. "I think I'll get my kiss first, though, just in case you don't like my question and follow through with your threat of landing me on the ground. After all that muscle building exercise, I might be in trouble."

His kiss was fabulous, as usual, but I was really curious about the question he was going to ask. He'd seemed very serious as he put his hands on my shoulders and looked me directly in the eyes.

"You've been wonderful, Jill, through all my inappropriate actions toward you, plus my trying to order you to change your plans last weekend. My question concerns why you've put up with me. Are you doing it for Jessica, thinking it'll help her relationship with C.J. if we aren't at each other's throats, or could it possibly be that you really care for me, at least a little bit? I need to know where I stand with you, Jill, before I can make a decision about my future. So, would you be able, at this point, to give me a glimpse into your true feelings?"

"I believe I asked you somewhat the same question when I was admiring the roses in my room, but I didn't get much of an answer. Why do you think I should open up my heart to you when you're not willing to give me an idea of how you feel?"

"I can understand your reasoning, Jill, and my only explanation is that I've had one experience of living in hell, so to speak, and I promised myself that I'd be positively sure the next time before I gave my heart away."

"You've told me that before, so I'll answer your question as well as I can without possibly getting myself hurt. The night I met you and you became my so called escort, my heart tried to tell me something; and it still does whenever you're around. It has nothing to do with Jessica and C.J. because it seems that their relationship is good, but if I didn't have feelings for you, T.J., I would certainly not have been here tonight. I *will* make a promise, though. If I make a commitment to anyone, now or anytime in the future, it will be a solid lifetime commitment that no one could come between unless it were the other involved person asking for a release. Does that answer your question fully enough?"

"For the time being," he grinned and took me in his arms for another quick kiss.

His folks were waiting when we entered the den. We had a cold drink with them, visited for about 30 minutes and then T.J. said his goodbyes. He looked at me, winked, pulled me into his arms for a quick goodnight kiss and then quickly left. I then excused myself and came to my room because I'm now expecting my dreams to be sweet ones tonight. I remember a Bible verse, which I learned quite a few years ago from Psalms 119: 9-10 in which David not only asked a question but also answered it. 'How can a young person live a pure life? By living each day according to your word, seeking You with all my heart; so don't let me stray from your commands.' "This is my prayer tonight, Dear Jesus," I whisper as I get into bed.

Chapter Sixteen

*CW*hen I awake Saturday morning, I'm so glad I brought another set of clothes to go to the store with Mrs. Peterson. The light khaki slacks with a navy turtleneck top will be fine for the store, and I have my navy cardigan, which I wore yesterday, for all the wrap I'll need. The last few days have turned a little cooler than usual for late September, but a light jacket or sweater is sufficient. I'm so excited to get to see the store and to even help out by doing some financial work.

"Good Morning," I call out as I see Mrs. Peterson sitting at the table having a cup of coffee but gazing toward the window facing the back yard.

"I guess it's a good morning, Jill," she says rather sadly as she points to the window. I hadn't taken time to look outside as I was getting dressed, but now I see that it's raining, although rather lightly. "It's not going to be a very good day for our first home football game, I'm afraid."

"It's still early, and my grandmother used to say if it rains before seven, it'll be over by eleven. If that holds true, it'll have time to dry up and be nice by 2 o'clock."

"Oh, Jill, you're such a joy. What would you like for breakfast? We usually grab something light on Saturday mornings and then have a nice lunch, but I'll be happy to fix you whatever you'd like."

"I'm not a big breakfast eater, so I'll just have a piece of toast with jelly if that isn't too much trouble. I'll fix it if you'll tell me where the bread is."

"Don't be silly. I'll fix you some toast and jelly."

It isn't long until we're on our way, and we get to the store about 8:45. The building stands by itself and appears to have some years on it. Just what you need if you're going to have an antique store, right? It appears that the siding has recently been painted and all the windows are double-paned Anderson or Pella Windows. The sign, Cameron Antiques, is an antique, too, but it's definitely in keeping with the type of store you're entering. It's just so unique that it sort of draws you inside.

When Mrs. Peterson opens the door and flips on the lights, I'm totally in awe. A few beautiful pictures are displayed on the walls, the crystal and china are all spotless as they're arranged on tables, buffets, and shelves like you'd have them if in use in your home. All the furniture has been dusted as if they were expecting a white glove inspection at any time.

"It's absolutely gorgeous, Mrs. Peterson. I have been in several antique stores, but I have never seen one like this."

"Thank you, Jill. My grandparents were very particular about how the items were to be arranged and cared for and also what to buy to display and refuse any items they thought would not move. Of course, that is how my parents and I learned the business. I couldn't have it any other way. Why don't you look around while I get things ready to open? I have Sara and Jane coming in today around 11:00, and then I'll come back after the game to help them close at 6:00. I'll show you the bookkeeping set-up in a few minutes."

I'd only gotten about a fourth of the way through the store when she's back to join me. I ask, "Did you decorate the apartments, or condos, for the boys or did they pick the items they wanted?"

"They both seem to have a love for antiques, I suppose from being around them so much here, at home, and at the grandparents'. They'd picked the items they wanted from here, but both of them found items in other places, too. Are you ready to see the mess I have our books in?"

"Lead me to them. I'm sure they're not as bad as you think they are if you aren't too familiar with financial work."

The bookkeeping was a simple procedure which didn't take me long to understand, although I was surprised to see that it was still all done by hand. "Have you ever thought of putting your accounting on a computer, Mrs. Peterson?

It would make it so much easier and faster to keep it up to date."

Laughing, she replies, "I mentioned it once to our bookkeeper, and she let me know very decisively that if I ever brought one of those computers into this store, that would be the day she walked out. Well, she did such a good job for us that I didn't push it, plus the fact that I wasn't sure I could learn what would have to be done to even enter a sale. So, consequently, it's the same system my grandfather, no, it was actually my great grandfather set up when they opened for business way back in 1910. This desk is one of the first items he purchased and although he had quite a few offers from folks who wanted to buy it, he would never part with it. He said it was his good luck piece."

A chime starts to ring, meaning someone has come in, so Mrs. Peterson leaves to take care of the customer and I get started on the bookkeeping. A few minutes later, she's back with two men standing near the desk. "Jill, this has been one of our best customers over the years and his grandson who is visiting from Boston. They happened to see a new face back here and wanted to meet you. Mr. Galen and Andrew, I want you to meet our older son's friend, Jill Hale, who is here to go to the football game with him this afternoon. I'm very lucky, however, because she offered to help with my bookkeeping this morning."

I stand and extend my hand to Mr. Galen. "It's very nice to meet you. This is the first time I've been in the store and I'm truly impressed. Do you come here often?" I then continue to address Mr. Galen because I'm a little ill at ease when I see that Andrew, a nice looking young man with brown hair, between 25 and 30, I'd guess, is just standing there staring at me. All of a sudden he reaches out and grabs my hand, pulls me toward him and immediately puts me in a bear hug that brings our bodies quite close together. "I beg your pardon, but release me, please."

"I'm so glad Grandfather wanted me to see this store because otherwise I would've never had the chance to meet the one I want to be my future wife. You're beautiful, Jill Hale, and I'm going to marry you. Grandfather, will you make the arrangements for me?"

"What in the world are you talking about, Andrew? You can't walk up to someone and say you want to marry them and think it's going to happen just like that."

"Why not? You've always given me whatever I've asked for, and I'm telling you now that I want this girl for my wife, so please make it happen."

"Material things are one thing, but a human being is not an article that you can buy and possess. We'd better go. Let go of her right now and let's get back to the house."

"No," he shouts as he pulls me tighter into his arms. "I'm taking her with me!"

I notice that Mrs. Peterson had slipped away and my only thought is that I'd gotten my muscles tightened up last night for a reason. My knee quickly makes an impact with his private area which causes a loud scream, a release of me, and he's bending over toward the floor. My hands are now free, of course, and I'm ready to give him a blow to the head when I hear:

"Wait! What's going on here?"

I glance up and see two policemen and Mrs. Peterson coming toward us.

Mr. Galen steps up and gives an accurate account of his grandson's inappropriate actions and my very well placed defensive move. He's actually chuckling, which surprises me, because Andrew is still bent over and moaning.

"Where did you say he was visiting from?" the one officer asks.

"He's been living in Boston for about six months, but he travels a lot in his work so he doesn't keep a permanent address."

I notice the officers looking at each other and then one says, "We're going to take him down to the station. There's something we'd like to check out. Come along, Andrew, let's take a little ride."

"I don't think I can walk," he moans. "Why aren't you arresting her for assaulting me? I didn't do anything to her."

"You did enough to get yourself in the condition you're complaining about, so let's go talk to the Captain." He turns to me and says, "I'm sorry you had to protect yourself on our patrol, Ms. Hale, but it's amazing that you had the strength to do what you did. You aren't very big to have that much power in your legs." They then take Andrew by the arms and are on their way.

I just smile. It's satisfying to know that I have the strength and the confidence to at least try to protect myself. I go back to my bookkeeping, but Mrs. Peterson is soon there to give me a big hug, apologize for letting something like that happen, and then laugh a little as she sees that I am fairly calm as I enter invoices into the ledger.

By 11:15 I have the book work done and only need to put stamps on the statements to be mailed. Sara arrives and remembers me from last night, and Jane is just now coming in the door along with a nice looking guy who looks like he could be a pro football player. He is introduced as Jane's husband, Wyatt Fulton, and he is going to stay with the girls this afternoon. I realize that Mrs. Peterson didn't waste much time making arrangements for the safety of the girls this afternoon, because there had also been several customers in the store while I'd been busy with the books. She'd spent quality time with each of them which had resulted in a few sales, too.

We leave about 11:45, drive by the Post Office and get home a few minutes before the doctors arrive. While we're having a cold drink, the story is told by Mrs. Peterson about how brave I'd been, and I think T.J.'s face could have been set in a plaster cast. There's no emotion and no color as he appears to be transfixed by a great trauma. He's staring at his mother and then he looks at me as if just realizing I'm sitting next to him. He reaches over, lifts me up in his arms and sits me on his lap. "Are you sure you're OK, Jill? Did he hurt you at all? Oh, I'd like to get my hands on that jerk."

"No, T.J., he didn't hurt me. I hurt him. I'm glad you took me to the exercise room last night, though, because it gave me the confidence I needed to do what I did." With a big smile on my face, I run my fingers down his cheek as I remark, "All I can say, Big Guy, is that you'd better watch the way you treat me from now on or I may have to use my talents on you." Of course, I can't keep a straight face and everyone has a good laugh.

Chapter Seventeen

$\mathcal{W}$e all change into our game clothes and decide that we'll get something to eat at the stadium. My grandmother's old saying about the rain has proven true today since the sun is shining and everything's dry except for a puddle here and there. I'm surprised that we don't all go in one car, but then I remember Mrs. Peterson saying she'd go back to the store and help the girls close. Maybe Dr. Peterson is going with her.

We don't have any trouble finding them because we find parking spaces right next to each other. I wonder if they have them reserved since they seem very supportive college sports fans, but I elect not to ask. It is still quite a walk to get to the field. We take time to buy our sandwiches and fries before going to our seats, but then T.J. and I go back for the drinks. We are seated on one of the 40 yard lines and about 10 to 14 rows up. We should be able to see all the action just fine although I wonder if T.J. will see any of the game if he continues to have his eyes fixed on me.

"The game is going to be played out there on the field, T.J.," I smile and also try to convince him that I'm perfectly all right. It's being announced that the National Anthem will be sung today by a member of the University Choir, and we all stand. I hope that will change the protectiveness that T.J. is displaying so he can enjoy the game.

"Did you remember to bring your sunglasses?" he asks as we sit back down to wait for the coin toss.

"Yes, they're in my purse and I guess it would be wise to put them on. That sun is really getting warm. Do you have yours?"

He pats his shirt pocket. "Always come prepared," he grins.

UNC won the toss and elected to receive. The offense was doing real well and got the ball down to the opponent's 20 yard line, but then there was an interception. Luckily the other team went 3 and out so we got the ball back. This time we take it in for a touchdown. We manage to be ahead 10-7 at the end of the first half, but it has been a hard fought game.

With the large drink I'd had, I excuse myself to go to the restroom, but T.J.'s up and following me out. Although it's nice to be protected, it's also a little embarrassing to have an escort to the restroom. When I emerge, however, I find myself looking directly into the eyes of Andrew. Why did they let him go this morning?

"I've been watching you," he says, "and I was hoping you'd come out during half time. Let's get out of here before you're missed." He grabs my arm and starts pulling me toward the exit as I glance quickly to see where T.J. might be. I see him just leaving the hot dog stand, but he's looking toward the restroom I'd gone into. I raise my arm that's not being squeezed tightly by Andrew and try to wave but I don't think T.J. sees me. I begin to panic. Can I get into a position to hurt this crazy guy again and somehow get away?

As we near the exit I see an officer not too far away. I yell, "Please help me," but Andrew pulls me even faster toward the door. I try my best to resist, but he actually gets me outside and I'm afraid the officer didn't hear my call for help with all the other noise.

"You be quiet now or I'll have to tape your mouth shut. My car isn't too far away so I'm going to have you as my wife. I won't let what happened this morning happen to me again, so don't get any ideas." He's looking at me and not watching where he's going, as he continues pulling me toward the parking lot, and awkwardly runs right smack into T.J. who is standing with his arms folded across his chest and a horrible scowl on his face.

"And just where do you think you're going with my girl, you spoiled little twerp?" T.J. asks as he lands an uppercut to his chin. As Andrew starts to fall, T.J. catches him and sets him down on the ground. I follow his gaze toward the doors and see the officer and T.J.'s dad coming toward us. I can't keep the tears from rolling down my cheeks.

The officer takes control of Andrew and T.J. takes me in his arms. "I'm so sorry I left to get myself a hot dog. I was so sure I'd get back before you came out."

"I-I didn't th-think yu-you saw me and I-I was so-so scared." I had my arms tight around his waist and didn't ever want to let go.

"Actually, Mom had sent Dad for some tortilla chips, and he was the one who saw Andrew grab you. He ran to me and sent me on my way. With you resisting as much as you could, I was able to come out another door and get ahead of you, especially when he sort of stopped to say something to you just after you got outside."

"He told me to be quiet or he'd tape my mouth shut." I can giggle now that it's over.

A squad car pulls up and two officers come over to where we are. Dr. Peterson had told the officer at the game what the situation was so he conveyed the instructions to the other two who then helped Andrew to his feet and headed to the squad car. Turning then to Dr. Peterson and T.J., he said, "Thanks for all your help, Gentlemen, and I'm so sorry I didn't see or hear you in distress, Young Lady. I'd better get back to my post and keep my eyes fastened on the crowd. I hope I don't have anymore trouble this afternoon."

"Well, shall we go back and see what's left of the game?" Dr. Peterson smiles and starts back toward the entrance.

"Do you feel like watching the rest of the game, Jill?" T.J. still has his arm around me and looks so concerned.

"Of course I do. I just wish I could've kicked Andrew again, but does a guy like that ever learn anything?"

"I don't know, but maybe our team has learned how to hold onto the ball this second half. Let's go see." We quickly catch up to his dad.

Mrs. Peterson looks at her husband's empty hands and smiles, "It certainly took you long enough to buy me nothing." She studies our faces and sobers immediately. "What happened out there, Brian?"

"Andrew showed up again," he whispers. "He grabbed Jill when she came out of the restroom, and if you hadn't sent me for tortillas, I wouldn't have seen her trying to motion to T.J. and that scum would've kidnapped her. He did get her outside, but T.J. was waiting for them not too far away. The police have him now."

"Oh, Dear. I never gave a thought that anyone with Mr. Galen would be a weirdo like that. They must not have held him very long this morning."

The game is finally over. We'd won by 6 points although it had been a struggle. I hope they can get a lot of practice and improve before the next game.

"I'm going to the store with your mom, T.J., so are you going ahead with your plans to take Jill out to dinner?"

"Yes, I want her to have a nice evening and try to forget all she's been through so far today. It seems like a nightmare to me so I can imagine how she feels. I'll bring her back to the house later. You will be up this time, won't you?" he chuckles.

"I'll make it a point to be up, but remember your curfew," his dad laughingly retorts.

We reach the car and T.J. opens the door for me. When I'm seated inside and feel as if I'm finally safe, I realize that I'm trembling and can't seem to stop. T.J. gets in his side, glances over at me and immediately knows that everything is finally catching up to me. He puts his hand on my arm. "Jill, you aren't in any condition to go to a restaurant right now, and it's still a little early to eat anyway. Would you like to go to the condo and relax for a little bit? I can give you something to relax you and I'll just be there until you can put this crazy day behind you. Does that sound like a plan you could tolerate?"

"I-I guess, if you'll hold me. I wish my dad were here now to hold me. He was so good when we needed comforting. If not your arms, I'll need a dozen blankets be-because I-I'm so cold." I have my sweater on, but he gets his jacket from the back seat and puts it around me and then starts the car.

"I'll try my best to comfort you like your dad would, Jill, but I'll turn the heater on now to see if that'll help warm you up. Let me know if you'd like my arm around you. I'd be happy to accommodate you."

I know he's going to suffer from all that heat that comes pouring out and I'm not sure that's the kind of warmth I need. "You can turn the heat down, T.J., so you don't get too hot. I'll be fine with your jacket around me."

"Don't worry about me, Sweetie, just try to relax and enjoy the warmth." Of course, with all the traffic leaving the game, it's about 35 minutes before we reach the condo and I'm beginning to feel a little better since I'm certainly warm enough.. However, we get into the condo and I pull his jacket a little tighter around me because of the air-conditioning.

"I'm sorry, Jill. I forgot that it would be rather cool in here. Do you want to go to the guest bedroom and crawl under the covers? I'll close the register in there so it won't be as cool as the other rooms."

Without saying anything, I head for the bedroom. Thinking he is right behind me, I ask, "Da-do you sti-still have ba-bats in he-here?" as I pull the quilt and sheet back, kick my shoes off, and crawl in. I then see that he's coming in carrying two blankets and covers me with them.

"I'll be right back with something to help you relax," and he turns to leave the room. "To answer your question, though, there are no longer any bats in this room or the condo. I had an inspection done and they found that the vent to the exhaust fan in this bathroom had no cover and there were several small bats using it as their home. I don't know where their parents were. Maybe one was the one I konked on the head that night and threw him out the window."

"T.J., I do-don't really wa-want to take any-anything. I-I think I'll feel all ri-right as soon as I-I can get my mind on som-something else be-besides Andrew. Do you suppose you could pu-put some music on and just hold me?"

I can't keep from smiling as he has a frown on his face as he asks, "Are you talking about me holding you in that bed or in my arms while we're dancing like we did before?"

"May-be bo-both? It de-depends on how fa-fast I-I can for-forget the re-rest of this da-day." He's out the door like a flash and I'm wondering if he'll be back soon or will he stay away until he thinks I've come back to my senses. I shortly hear music and he appears at the door.

"Are you trying to exchange one type of trembling with another, Jill?" he grins as he's slipping off his shoes and sliding under the covers beside me. His one arm goes under my neck and the other across my stomach as he lies on his side with his lips on my hair. "Our clothes aren't going to look too good to go to a restaurant, you know, if we stay in this bed very long." His lips start slowly down the side of my face but are soon on my mouth. It's a different kind of trembling, to be sure, but it certainly feels good.

"I-I was pla-planning to cha-change back in-into the ou-outfit I wore th-this mor-morning, b-but ma-maybe we'll have to set-settle for a-a drive-thru or-or fix something here."

He throws the blankets back and sits up on the side of the bed. "I'll drive over to the folks and get your clothes while you lie here and relax listening to the music. Then we can look presentable when we go to eat." He slips his feet into his shoes and quickly scurries out the door.

"He certainly acts differently when it's me making a play for affection than when he's the one doing all the moves," I mumble as I pull the blankets up around my neck and enjoy listening to a CD of romantic old-time favorites. I apparently fall asleep.

When I open my eyes, I find that the room is rather dark and as I glance outside, I see it's definitely evening. The music is still playing as I lazily stretch and slowly roll over on my back, but I quickly realize that I'm not alone. *When did he get back and how long has he been in this bed with me?* I see that his eyes are closed as he's lying on his side facing me, but is he just playing a game of possum or is he really asleep? "T.J., are you awake?" I whisper as I turn on my side to face him. I get no answer. I reach over and run my fingers down his cheek and over to his mouth. He shakes his head and his hand comes up to brush away whatever he thinks is there. I smile as I watch him slowly open his eyes, look at me, and then reach over to pat my cheek.

"Are you real, Cutie Pie, or am I still dreaming?"

"I haven't pinched myself, but I think I'm in the flesh, but how long have you been sharing this bed with me?"

"Oh, Ms. Hale, we had the most marvelous time romping in this bed before you fell asleep on me. Don't you remember?"

"It's a long time since or before April 1st, Doctor, so don't try pulling an April Fool joke on me because I'm not that heavy a sleeper. It does look like it's getting about time to get something to eat, however. Isn't your stomach talking to you yet?"

"That's what I was hearing, wasn't it? With you around, I can't feel anything except my desire to. .ah. .I'd better not express that desire. Are you ready to freshen up and go get our stomachs filled up?"

"I believe I could eat, so if you'll scoot yourself out of here, I'll take a quick shower, change clothes, and be ready to go."

"We could take a quick shower together and save on my water bill," he chuckles as he scampers out the door.

Chapter Eighteen

I'm thrilled that he's taken me to another restaurant that I'm not familiar with, but from the looks of the outside, I feel like I should be wearing a more dressy outfit than my slacks and navy turtleneck. When we get inside, I quickly glance around and see that the others are dressed about the same, though, so I relax. The decor is absolutely beautiful and everything is so plush. I thought the maître 'd smiled a recognizing smile, but we are then shown to our booth without a word except, "Follow me, please." I'm also surprised when T.J. slides in beside me instead of across from me.

"What are you doing now, T.J.? Wouldn't it give you more space to eat if you were on the other side of the booth?"

"I'll move over there as soon as I get my wake-up kiss. You spend hours sleeping in that bed with me and I don't even get a little kiss, and I can't eat until I do." He smiles as his one arm goes across my shoulders and his other hand is turning my face toward him.

"T.J., you're not supposed to kiss in restaurants," I whisper but his lips are on mine and I can do nothing but return the kiss with a passion I can't seem to control.

"Um, that was real nice, Jill. Would you like to try another one?" he chuckles as he scoots out and slips in on the other side. He reaches over saying, "Give me your hand, Jill, so I can give you a second kiss to really spark my appetite." His dazzling smile almost gets to me, but I resist.

"No, I'm going to look at the menu, and you'd better do the same. The server will be here wanting our order before we're ready." I hide my face behind the large menu, but I can hear him chuckling.

When the server does arrive, T.J. whispers something in her ear, she smiles and says, "Yes, Dr. Peterson, I'll be happy to do that." I look at his face in time to see a slight grimace, and I ask the question with my expression.

"Dad supposedly owns an interest in this restaurant because he helped a nice young couple, who were his patients, get started in the business. They have paid every cent of the loan back, but they still insist that he is a partner because they feel he did much more than just loan them the money."

The server's back rather quickly with two glasses and a bottle of Merlot wine plus a plate of the yummiest looking stuffed mushrooms. She pours the wine and then disappears. "How did you know that I love these?" I ask.

"I was taking a big chance, but I've noticed that you seem willing to try most foods that I've suggested, so I was hoping you'd at least try a stuffed mushroom. They're one of my favorite appetizers. May I serve you one?"

"Of course." As we enjoy the wine and mushrooms, however, I'm surprised that the server hasn't been back to take our order, but when the last mushroom is gone, she's there to remove those plates and place beautiful looking salads before us. I give T.J. one special raised eyebrow to indicate there is something just a little odd here, but he gives me that dazzling smile which, of course, gives me the answer to what he had whispered in the server's ear. After we've made a good dent in the salads, we are both served a plate of superb prime rib, garlic mashed potatoes, and assorted vegetables which is then followed with cherry cobbler ala mode.

"Would you like an after dinner drink, Sweetie, or would you rather have a cup of coffee? Did I do all right with the menu, or were you in the mood for something entirely different?"

"Everything was wonderful and you're always a surprise waiting to happen. If you want to have something, I wouldn't mind a cup of coffee."

"That sounds good to me, too."

On the way to his folks, I remember that my other outfit is still at the condo. "T.J., I'm afraid I left my other clothes at your place again. Should we get them tonight or can we pick them up after church?"

"We'll get them after church tomorrow, if that's okay with you. That way, I'll get to sleep with them tonight while I dream of you in my arms. It'll seem more real because I'll be able to inhale the scent of your perfume on them and I'll be in heaven," he sighs.

"If you're going to have my clothes in bed with you, what can I have of yours to go to sleep with?" I ask as my face feels like it's burning hot with embarrassment.

Now he's really laughing. "What would you like Sweetie? I guess I could leave my shirt without any problem, but anything else might cause a little embarrassment either as I'm getting it off or as I try getting into my condo." His laughter won't quit and I'm trying my best to think of something to say that will shock him, but my mind is a blank.

"Maybe I could just take your socks. They might not have the best smell, but I'll certainly know it's something different from what is usually in my bed." My giggles blend with his chuckles, and tears are running down our cheeks before we finally calm down.

"I don't want the evening to end, but I'm afraid we've arrived at your home for the night. Do you really want something of mine to sleep with?" he chuckles again.

"If you're coming in, I'd better not take anything. I'll just use my imagination if I start to dream. Maybe I'll get to be with one of those handsome young actors."

"Are you trying to make me cry, Jill? I thought I'd had your heart pounding ever since you met me right here in this house and now you want to dream of somebody else? I'm devastated, totally devastated, but hey, I just thought of something you can have." He pulls a clean handkerchief from his pocket, wipes his face with it and then hands it to me. "Does it have enough of my aftershave on it to make you swoon?"

"Not too bad, really, but I want some of your shampoo fragrance, too." I refold the hankie, reach over and wipe it across his hair, and then I pretend to swoon as I bring it to my nose. It definitely picked up his scent, and I'll love sleeping with it tonight, but should I give him the satisfaction of knowing that. "It probably won't last long, but it'll give me a good start on my dream with that actor making a play for me."

"That's enough. Give me my handkerchief back. If you're not going to dream about me, then I don't want you having my scent in your bed."

"No, I'm not giving it back. You gave to me and I'm going to keep it and put it in my scrapbook right beside the picture of my favorite actor." Of course, I can't keep from giggling so I add, "until I get a picture of you that is. Let's go in now so you can tell your folks goodnight."

"He's around to open the door for me quickly, but he pins me against the car with his arms on either side of me. "You're driving me crazy, Jill, and I'm not sure this is what a friendship is supposed to be like. In fact, I don't think I can be just a friend to you, so will you still be willing to give me time to sort out my life if we become more than friends?"

"That depends on what the words 'more than friends' mean to you, but it's too late to delve into that tonight. We'll talk on the way to Sanford tomorrow. We'd better go in."

He doesn't stay very long after making sure I'll be riding with his folks to church tomorrow and he'll meet us there. He almost misses my cheek with his kiss on his way by and then just whispers, "Goodnight, Jill." I'm not sure whether that's from a friend, more than a friend, or possibly a bygone friend, but I guess that's a problem for another day.

I excuse myself and come to bed. I guess it's time to read the Love Chapter again, especially the patience phrase. I don't think I said anything tonight that should've turned him off, but I definitely need to know what he means by 'more than friends' before I can answer his other question. If he's going to expect more than I'm ready to give, and still with no commitment on his part, I guess this relationship or friendship will have to be over.

In my prayer I ask for guidance and almost immediately I remember part of a poem I learned in Sunday School quite a few years ago.

Does it hurt too much to smile? Does it hurt too much
   to listen?
Does it hurt too much to love? Will it hurt if teardrops
   glisten?
Just open up your heart of stone; Open up compassion's
   door;
Someone may need your unselfish gift; Someone who's
   loved and lost before.
Do your best to be a trusted friend, Until love is found
   to be a delight again.

Although some of it's not from the original poem, the
words come to me as if they have T.J. in mind and are
commanding me to help him. What else can I do if answers
to my prayers are coming so fast and so clear? I'm smiling
as I get ready for bed, pick up T.J.'s hankie and crawl under
the sheet. I spy my cell phone on the nightstand and know
exactly what I need to do.

"I'm just calling to say goodnight to my favorite friend."

"Jill, this is so sweet of you. I'm in the guest room picking
up your clothes to take to my bed and was wondering if
you're really going to sleep with my handkerchief. I was
afraid I upset you again with my rather awkward goodnight
in front of Mom and Dad, and I really wasn't expecting to
get much sleep tonight. I wanted to bring you home with
me and I just had to get out of there quickly before I did
something stupid again. This is such a great surprise."

"While I was saying my prayers earlier, I remembered a poem I'd learned in Sunday sSchool and it made me realize how much friendships can mean. I wanted to make sure we were on the same page before I went to sleep with your wonderful aroma next to me. We're a little crazy, I guess, but I love being crazy with you."

"You haven't the slightest idea how much this means to me, Jill, and now I can go to sleep cuddled up with your blouse and knit top and just dream away," he chuckles.

"Well, since I'm already in bed, I'd better let you go so you can get to church on time in the morning. I'll save a place for you."

"Goodnight, My Love."

CHAPTER NINETEEN

I awake Sunday morning with 'Goodnight, My Love' still ringing in my ears. T.J. had never before used the word 'love' meaningfully in any conversation I'd had with him, let alone having it be my name, so to speak. Did something really get to him last night in my phone call, or was it as he'd said, that he'd had to leave quickly to keep from doing something stupid? Whatever, it was a thrill to hear him say it to me.

I'm humming and singing as I shower and get dressed in my ivory pantsuit with the tangerine cami. My ankle high dressy boots with 2-1/2" heels match the brown purse I've been carrying and my earrings are rather antique looking with an amber stone in the center of a filigree setting. I decide to pull my hair up high in the back and hold it with a large barrette, but just a few tendrils fall down around my face.

Dr. Peterson whistles as I come into the kitchen, and I know my face is turning red which, of course, won't go well with my tangerine cami.

"Brian, you should be ashamed of yourself," Mrs. Peterson scolds. "You've gone and embarrassed Jill. You should apologize although I completely agree with the meaning of the whistle," she laughs. "You do look very lovely this morning, Jill, and there's a glow about you that is quite different from the one I saw right after T.J. left last night. I was sort of afraid that trouble was brewing again."

"Yes, there was an unspoken misunderstanding last night, mostly on my behalf this time, I'm afraid. When I got to my room, I asked for guidance in my prayers and got an answer that I carried through on immediately. I called him and found out that we're both on the same page--for now anyway." I smile and continue, "Thank you for your concern."

❧

When we get to church, I'm surprised to see T.J.'s car already there, and he's in the narthex waiting for us. "I had the most wonderful night's sleep and was awake bright and early this morning," he whispers in my ear. "I don't think I'll let you take your clothes home with you."

I just smile, shake my head, and whisper back, "I can't get along without them and the perfume will fade rather quickly."

His mother turns back to look at us with a pretty smile on her face, and asks, "What are you two whispering about that's putting those smiles on both your faces?"

"The same page that we're on," T.J. answers her and it's my turn to look surprised. I never dreamed that he would remember the remark from my call last night. He winks at me, takes a hold of my arm, and we follow his folks into the sanctuary.

It's an inspiring service again, and my prayer is full of thanks for His guidance and the feeling of contentment in this place of worship and also in T.J.'s presence. It seems that the sermon "Agree to Differ, but Unite to Serve" is directed toward us, and T.J. must feel it, too, because his arm comes around my shoulders and gives me a squeeze. I don't dare look at him for fear I'll tear up, but I do make a promise that I'll try my best to live up to that sermon title.

When the service is over, but the postlude is still playing, his mother leans over Dr. Peterson to ask if we'd like to go get a bite of lunch with them. T.J. looks at me and asks, "Are you wanting to get home like we planned or would you like to eat before we leave?"

"I think we should have lunch before we leave. That way, I won't have to listen to your stomach growl all the way home." I look at his expression and can't stop my giggle.

With his arm still around my shoulders, he smiles as he asks, "Would you like for me to spank you right here in the church for that remark?"

"Be careful, Doctor, you'd better remember my talents."

His dad and mom are both chuckling and shaking their heads as we stand and head for the exit. "Oh, to be young again," his dad remarks.

When we reach the pastor, he smiles as he shakes our hands. "I'm hoping that my sermon put those smiles on your faces, but I think there may be a more personal reason for them today. It's good to see you looking so happy, T.J., and I assume this young lady has something to do with that."

"You are so right, Pastor. This is Jill Hale and she's keeping my life very exciting although exasperating at times and humbling, too. Jill, Sweetie, this is Pastor Lindsey who has been our pastor since I was a little boy. He knows my history so, of course, he can see the change in me, especially today."

I extend my hand. "It's so nice to meet you, Pastor Lindsey. This is my second visit to the church and I've enjoyed your services very much. Thank you for caring about T.J. and his family. My sister is at the beach teaching pre-school and dating C.J. so we'll try to keep them both under control and smiling."

He's still holding my hand as he looks at T.J. with a gentle smile. "T.J., you've chosen well. This one can give your life meaning that you've never experienced before. I suggest you hold onto her." He pats my hand tenderly before letting it go and then smiles directly at me with the most expressive eyes. I feel he's reading my utmost thoughts and knows exactly how I feel toward the one he has watched over all these years.

We go to a cafe for lunch which is a small out-of-the-way place that I love at first sight. It's so homey and the server has a wonderful smile which would lift your spirits even if you were having a bad day. Their specials are Meat Loaf with mashed potatoes and green beans, or Fried Chicken, potato salad and candied carrots. A nice crisp toss salad is also included.

"I can't decide which I want because I'd like a little of both," I complain. T.J. gives me that understanding smile of his and proceeds to order a plate of each.

"We'll share so you can have some of each, but you don't get any of my salad," he smirks.

"Anyone watching would definitely think you two are married," his dad laughs. "We used to share like that, but Jeannette finally decided I ate more than my share, so she started ordering her own dinner and not letting me touch it. I miss getting a taste of twice as many items." He reaches over to pat her cheek and she looks at him with a love I hope someday to see on my husband's face.

She then smiles at me. "I wish you lived closer, Jill. Maybe I could convince you to come work for me. You mentioned you would like to someday own a Real Estate office, but I wonder if helping people furnish their homes would appeal to you at all. I go into many homes to give advice about furniture, wall colors, window treatments, and, of course, measure to see if an item they like will fit. I've even helped a few decide on a renovation job, and it was rather exciting. Right now, of course, I need a bookkeeper," she laughs, "but I'd love to have someone who would work with me on other projects, too. If you ever wish to change jobs, let me know, will you?"

"I most certainly will. I've been thinking about the bookkeeping, and if you want to just stack the invoices on the desk, I'll be happy to bring you up to date each time your son invites me to come for a weekend." I grin at T.J. who, with his dad, had been sitting very quietly listening to the conversation between Mrs. Peterson and me. As I think of that very interesting antique store, I can't help but wish I could stay and become an intrinsic part of that unique operation.

After enjoying the delicious meal, which again T.J. ate about two-thirds to my one-third, Mrs. Peterson and I decide we have to have some dessert. The men look us up and down to see where we could put it, but we assure them that we'll work it off. Since we decide to have their home-made pie ala mode, the guys decide they'll have some, too. We discuss the game a little, the sermon a little, our drive to Sanford, and if T.J. is going to drop by his parents' home when he gets back.

When we finish all that, we head for the cars. After transferring my suitcase from his folk's car into T.J.'s, it was a thrill to see Mrs. Peterson extend her arms toward me for a hug goodbye. "It's such a delight getting to know you, Jill, and we'll look forward to the next time you're invited to come to Chapel Hill." She gives a 'you heard me' look to T.J. and then smiles at me. "I think the game is out of town next weekend, but the following one's at home although I don't know the day or time. I'll keep you both in my prayers."

T.J. opens the car door for me, gives his mother a look that I don't quite understand, but then he kisses her on the cheek. We're soon on our way to his condo for the rest of my clothes although he keeps telling me he's going to keep something. When we pull into the garage, he asks where my perfume is as he opens the trunk.

"What do you want with my perfume?"

He doesn't answer as he now has my suitcase open and holds up my small make-up case. "Is it in here?"

"Yes, T.J., it's in there, but why is it so important to you?"

With that big smile on his face, he shuts the trunk, takes my hand, and leads me to the elevator. We're soon on 4th floor and in his condo. "If I let you have this, will you get your perfume out for me?" he asks as he holds the case way over his head.

Well, it finally dawns on me why he wants my perfume. That's the item he plans to keep. I'm flattered that he wants something to remind him of me when we're apart, but I hate to let go of my favorite perfume which was a birthday gift from Jodi and Richard.

"What am I going to wear if you keep the only bottle I have of that? It was a gift for my birthday and I wear it almost every day."

"You can use something else until you see me again, can't you, Sweetie? I'll let you have your clothes if you'll let me have your perfume so I can feel close to you while I'm in bed. Please, Jill, will you do this for me? I slept so well last night."

"All right," I sigh and sling my hands out hopelessly. "If you feel so strongly about it, how can I refuse you?" He hands me the case, I find the bottle and give it to him. "Just don't use over a tiny drop or you'll run yourself right out of your room. It is perfume and it is strong."

"Thanks, Sweetie. Shall we find your clothes and get on our way or would you like to stay here and romp and play for awhile until it gets cooler." He's chuckling as he flutters his eyelashes and squeezes my chin with his thumb and forefinger.

I slap his hand away. "We still have a serious topic of discussion to iron out so we'd better get in the car where you can't create a distraction."

"Aw shucks, Cutie Pie, I was hoping I could show you how comfortable my bed is again and how our 'more than friends' situation might work." The bright ray of sun coming through the windows is dancing in his eyes and his smile is so mischievously darling but also daring that it's hard for me to believe that he's never been in bed with a woman before.

"You aren't very convincing, T.J., when you say things like you just did. Are you sure you've always remembered your pledge of abstinence until marriage?"

"I'm sorry, Jill," he chuckles. "You bring out all the desires that a normal man could possibly have, but I respect you too much to follow through on any of my feelings or the teasing that you've put up with. Let's find your clothes and be on our way."

CHAPTER TWENTY

T.J. is seriously concentrating on his driving which makes me slightly suspicious of his intentions to avoid the conversation we're going to have, one way or another, about his 'more than friends' remark. I guess I'll have to get it started, so here goes, "T.J., we have to finish our discussion about your remark last night before I can answer your question. Since it isn't raining, it isn't foggy, and it definitely isn't snowing here in North Carolina, I'd think you could relax your staring at the highway and let's get this ironed out."

"Oh, but I think I remember you telling me Friday evening when we were coming up to Chapel Hill to keep my eyes on the road and my hands on the wheel." He looks over at me with that innocent grin, but somehow he can't keep from laughing. "Okay, Sweetie, let's talk. I'm sure that statement sounded way out of line to you, and maybe it was when I made it after the game and dinner Saturday night. I've tried to think of how to express my thoughts to you, with no success; but what I really want with you, Jill, is much more than a mere platonic friendship because I need to be able to touch, hold, and kiss you without feeling any guilt or upsetting you. I want you to be someone I can rely on and know you'll always be there for me, like a steady girlfriend would be in High School, maybe a fiancee' if I could get my feelings under control on that score, or even a wife to which I'm definitely not ready to commit.

I'm so confused, Jill, because in my heart I actually feel I do know what I want right now, but I just can't make myself take the step to the future because of the short time we've known each other, and it's driving me crazy. I keep thinking that if I could be sure you'd always be there for me, maybe I could finally put the past behind me. I didn't mean, when I made that remark about being more than friends, that I wanted a real intimate involvement because neither of us would go for that. Would you please tell me how you feel about my dilemma?"

I ponder my answer for several minutes because I know it'll probably determine for sure whether we can continue seeing each other or not. "I wish there was a magic wand to tell us if this special friendship could have a favorable outcome, because I do understand how badly you were hurt. My only concern, since it's been so long now since Adele left and you haven't been able to forget, is just how long it's going to take for you to get rid of all the guilt and pain. How do I know what I'm going to be facing if, after spending whatever time you need to get your head on straight, you decide I'm not the one you want after all? I have my future to consider, too."

"I'm sorry, Jill. I shouldn't ask you to make a commitment that I'm not able to do myself. What if I were to promise I'll make a decision right after the holidays? Could you put up with me for that long as a 'stand by your man' date? That doesn't sound like a very favorable deal for you either, does it?" he moans.

"Maybe I could act as your convenient fiancee with only us knowing differently. If you have someplace you want me to go with you, I have a real pretty zircon ring I could wear if you'd like a fiancee on your arm." I smile as I wait for his reply.

"I think you have something there, Jill. I have two friends who are always trying to set me up with blind dates, especially for this Charity Banquet we all attend every year in early November. They're both married and seem to think they're missing out on all the fun of being single, but if I have a fiancee, they'll have to leave me alone, won't they?"

"I guess we can fool them if they're not diamond experts."

"I don't think we need to worry about that, but I just thought it might cause some other difficulties if they start pushing for a wedding date, bridal showers, etc. I do want to talk to you about going to this banquet, though, and also a golf tournament. I promised I'd check to see about one, but with all the blunders I've made the last two months, it's getting a little late for any of the big ones. With the football and basketball games coming up, I could only find three tournaments that might be of interest. There's one in Mississippi, but it happens to be the same weekend as our next home football game so we'd have to decide between the two if we wanted to go to that one. The next one is a Texas Open in early October and one in Arizona a little later in October. I haven't checked the football schedule for October, but if you'd like to go to one of those golf tournaments, we can certainly miss one football game."

"I...ah...I didn't think they'd be so far away from home. I thought maybe there'd be one at Pinehurst or even Hilton Head. With the UNC games starting, I'm really partial to the games, but if you're anxious to see a tournament this year, I guess I could go with you."

"Thanks for being honest with me, Jill. None of the three stood out as one I couldn't miss so I'm rather glad you feel the way you do. I'd much rather follow our teams and help them with fan support. I don't have the date or any information about the Charity Banquet, either, so I'll have to advise you later about that, but will you be willing to attend with me?"

"I'll keep the first part of November open just for you. Is it usually on a weekend or will we have to make other arrangements?"

"It's usually on either a Friday or Saturday night, but if you should seriously think about going to work for Mom, there'd be no problem." He looks over at me and grins. "I probably won't get an answer to that because I'm afraid we've gotten you home."

"It's only about 4 o'clock, T.J., so I was wondering if you'd like to get some exercise before you start back. It's probably too late to get a time on the golf course, but we have a nice putting green and even a miniature golf course in our little town. Just a thought," I giggle.

"It really sounds like fun, Jill, but I do have some patients' files I need to look over tonight so I'd better take a rain check. Would there be any chance you could get a time slot next weekend, like late Saturday or Sunday afternoon, when we could play?"

"I can check and let you know if you'll give me your cell phone number. I promise I won't call during office hours unless there's an emergency."

"I have a card in my wallet that I'll give you which has both the office number and my cell on it. I'm sorry I haven't given it to you before now."

"Can you come in for something to drink before you have to leave? Mom and Dad will be terribly disappointed if they don't get to see you this time."

"Didn't think you'd ever ask," he chuckles as he gets out to come around to open my door. "I guess we should get your luggage, too, unless you've decided to let me have all of your things to keep me company when I'm all by myself and so very lonely."

"You're crazy, T.J.," I laugh. "I need those things so I'm not about to let you have all of them. Do you want me to carry something?"

"Not unless you want to cut your suitcase in two pieces. You're wearing the one outfit that we carried on a hanger. I can't remember telling you how nice you looked today, but you always look beautiful to me, and I mean that with all my heart. Did you happen to pack the padded hanger you had it hanging on?"

"No, it's still in the closet at your folks. I'll get it the next time I stay there."

We've almost reached the door when he stops and sets the suitcase down. "I need my goodnight kiss before we go inside, Sweetie."

"It's still light, T.J. At least come into the foyer so the whole neighborhood doesn't get to watch. Most of them think I'm going to be an old maid so I'd really hate to disappoint them by being kissed in the front yard."

"Jill Marie Hale, you don't believe that for one minute. If I thought you did, I'd be holding you in my arms and kissing you over and over again until I was sure everyone in the neighborhood got to see us."

"Whatever, but let's go in," I scoff at his unreasonable remark. The house seems a little quiet, but after a fabulous kiss in the foyer, we go to find my folks, but instead we find only a note. "Jill, we've gone to Jodi and Richard's for dinner. We plan to be home around 8 o'clock. Come on over if you'd like. Love, Mom."

"Well, so much for getting to see my folks. Would you like something to eat with the drink before you start back? We have soft drinks or I could make some coffee, and I'll check the fridge to see what we might have to eat."

"Would you mind making coffee, Jill? It might help me stay awake on the way home when I won't have anyone to argue with, ogle at, or try to touch," he grinned.

"Are you really tired, T.J.? I don't want you driving out on the highway if you're apt to fall asleep. You can take a nap before you start home, if you'd like."

"No, Sweetie, I'm not tired. It's just a little boring to drive by oneself without anyone to talk to, but I'll turn the music on and sing along. I wouldn't have to do this if you'd come to Chapel Hill and work for Mom," he chuckles.

"Are you a job recruiter for your mother or is it that you don't like driving down here to get me so you're trying to push me off on your poor mom?"

"Hey, she was the one who brought up the possibility of you working for her, and I think I heard an almost urgent plea from her that she needed someone like you."

"Well, I'll give it a lot of thought in the next few days because it sounds so exciting and definitely different from my job at the bank."

The coffee is done and I'd looked in the fridge and found some roast that Mom had apparently fixed for lunch, and also a yummy vegetable salad. I set the salad on the table, warmed the meat in the microwave and then asked, "Do you want it in a sandwich or just on a plate?"

"If you have some ketchup, I'll take it on the plate, please."

Deciding to join him, it tasted good to me, even the hot coffee, and T.J. seemed to enjoy eating again, too. Of course, that didn't surprise me.

"Seriously, Jill, have you given any more thought to the conversation you and Mom had while we were eating with them this noon? She's very impressed with you and your interest in the store, and I know she's wanted to hire someone she could trust for some time now. With all your knowledge in bookkeeping, you'd make an ideal partner for her, and with you in town, we'd get to see each other a lot more often, too. Would that be a plus or a minus for you?" he rather seriously asks.

"I've been giving some thought to it although I haven't had much time yet when the afternoon has been taken up with our situation. The store is so unique and I think I'd like to help people like your mom does. The bookkeeping would be easy to handle, but would you really want me to be that much closer? It might be easier for you if I stayed farther away. You have your problems to work out and I wouldn't want to interfere with that."

"The more I see you, Sweetie, the easier it's going to be to forget, or at least accept, the past. It has really helped being with you, and like I said earlier, I really want you to be someone I can depend on to be there for me. That way,

I can learn more about you, your likes and dislikes, and the dedication we can promote toward one another. I dated Adele for two years and apparently didn't know her at all, so I need to be with you as much as possible."

"I'll emphasize the one fact that I can promise you right now, T.J., and that is I'm nothing like the Adele I've heard about from you or what Jessica has told me that she's been told by Emily and C.J. It's such a tragedy when someone loses a loved one like C.J. did, but it has to be an even deeper scar that has to heal when you've faced a deception like you did. I'll promise to stand beside you, as you asked, until after the Christmas holidays, and then we'll re-evaluate our situation to see if things have changed enough in your eyes to make a difference in our relationship. Is that sufficient enough for you to put your faith in me for the time being?"

"I couldn't be more pleased. I wish I'd met you twelve years ago instead of Adele, but you would've been so young, only a little fourteen year old, I probably wouldn't have noticed you. That's a shame because I'll bet you were a real cutie back then, too. Are you sure you're comfortable dating a guy almost seven years older than you? I guess I hadn't even thought about that before because you and Jessica are so mature and in control."

"Our age difference is no problem, T.J., because my dad is six years older than my mom, Richard is three years older than Jodi, and C.J. is five or six years older than Jessica. I guess it just runs in my family to fall for you older men." Of course, I can't stop the silly giggle.

"It's a pleasure to be so lucky, Miss Jill Marie, but I suppose I'd better be getting back to the statistics on those files I need to study. Thanks for the wonderful food, and I'll call you or you call me about playing some golf next weekend." He pulls me into his arms and just holds me for what seems like several minutes. He's really smiling as he stares into my eyes and then his lips slowly reach mine. I melt against him as my arms go around his waist. I don't know how long that kiss lasted, but finally he separates us with a moan. "I've got to go, Sweetie, before I kidnap you and take you back home with me."

So, I get one more peck on the cheek before he's out the door. With a little toot of the horn and a wave, he's gone.

I realize that I'm rather tired so I decide to go to my room instead of driving over to Jodi and Richard's. Even though it's still fairly early, I change into my pajamas and robe, curl up on the chaise lounge and open my Bible. I haven't finished one chapter of Acts when my eyes become so heavy I have to close them. I awake when I hear Mom and Dad come in the door just below my bedroom and realize they'll see my luggage and know that I'm home. I'd neglected to bring it up with me, but I expect Mom will be bringing it up shortly to check on me and about the weekend. The lounge is so comfortable that my eyes close again and I'm off to dreamland. This lounge has been used so many times as a bed when we'd invite girls over to spend the night, but I'm still surprised when the next time I wake, it's morning.

CHAPTER TWENTY-ONE

*A*fter I shower and get dressed for work, I find Dad in the kitchen having his cereal, orange juice and coffee. "Hi, Dad," I greet him as I sit down with my cup of coffee.

"Good morning, Sweetheart, you must've had an exhausting weekend to fall asleep so soundly on the chaise last night. Your mother came back down without waking you after there was no response when she softly called your name."

"It was quite different, I must admit. I don't have time to tell you all about it now, but I'll tell you and Mom tonight so I don't have to tell it twice. Right now, Dad, I have a question for you. What do you think the chances would be of me getting a tee time next Saturday or Sunday afternoon so T.J. and I could play some golf?"

"Well, the way it's been the last few weeks, I'd have to say it would be pretty slim, Jill. About what time were you wanting to play?"

"Since they have office hours on Saturday morning and he'd probably go to church and then drive down here after lunch on Sunday, I'd say anytime after 2 or 2:30."

"My tee time with Carl is at 2:45 on Sunday, and I know he'd be thrilled to include you if you'd like to play a foursome with two old men. He's been telling me lately that it's been rather boring with only the two of us and that we need a new challenge."

"Are you sure, Dad? I'm positive T.J. would love to have more competition than I'll be able to give him."

"Well then, let's plan on that, Sweetheart. You check with T.J. and if it's all right with him, we'll make it a foursome."

"That's so cool. Thank you so very, very much." I give him a big hug and then go to fix a piece of toast and jelly for my breakfast.

"No problem. I'm really looking forward to it. T.J. will probably whip the pants off all of us, but it'll be fun. Maybe Carl will be content with me as his golfing partner after he gets through trying to keep up with T.J." He's still having quite a laugh as he picks up the day's newspaper to read the latest news in our paper which probably contains the news of about two days ago.

❧

I'm so anxious to call T.J. that the day doesn't seem to ever end. I'd decided to wait until after dinner because I didn't want to cause any problems at the office. It's a little after 6:30 when I get to my room and dial T.J.'s cell phone number. After six rings, the forward to voice mail comes on asking me to leave a message, but I hang up.

Why don't you have your cell phone with you, T.J.? The very first time I try to call you, you don't answer. Did you look to see who was calling and then ignore it because it was me, or are you with someone else and don't want to be disturbed? No, No, I'm not going there and get all upset until I know why you didn't answer. After all, we were just together the whole weekend, and I made a promise to be there for you until after the holidays. What did you promise, T.J., except to make a decision by that time, too. What does that give you permission to do while trying to work on that decision? Oh, here I go again! I never dreamed I could be so suspicious, or jealous, or the green-eyed monster. T.J. hasn't given me a single reason to doubt him so I just have to trust him. He'll probably have a very good excuse.

About twenty minutes later, I hear the phone ringing downstairs, but I'm a little surprised when Dad calls to let me know it's for me. "Hello, this is Jill," I answer as I definitely wasn't expecting it to be the voice I hear on the other end of the line.

"Sweetie, I'm sorry, but I was in the shower when you called. I had a rather slow afternoon so I went and played nine holes of golf which made it a little late when I got home.

I'll have to get in a lot of practice this week so I can keep up with you. Were you able to get a tee time for us to play on Saturday or Sunday?"

"That's why I called. I talked to Dad this morning and he felt I'd have a pretty slim chance of getting a time because it's been so busy the last few weeks, but he offered a nice alternative. He said that he and his partner, Carl, would be happy to play a foursome with us if you'd like to do that. Apparently Carl has been telling Dad that it's getting a little boring with just the two of them playing and they need a new challenge. Would you like to give them that challenge or would you rather it be just the two of us if I can get a tee time?"

"How do you feel about it, Jill? It's fine with me either way, but I don't want you to be disappointed by having to play a foursome with three guys."

"I think it'll be fun, and I know you'll like more competition than I can give you, so I'll tell Dad that we'll definitely plan to join them Sunday at 2:45. Is that time all right with you?"

"It's perfect. My only problem right now is that my stomach is growling because I haven't eaten since noon. I guess I need someone who would have my meals all ready for me when I come home. Would you like to volunteer for that job, Sweetie?"

"Not with our situation as it is right now. I'll try to be someone you can depend on, but I'm not going to be your slave, Dr. Peterson. You're on your own until you get your feelings where you want them---then I'll figure out if I fit in your life the way I'd like to."

"My, but aren't we a little touchy tonight? I meant that as a joke, Jill, but I see that you're taking me quite seriously tonight. Have I done something again that has you upset?"

"No, T.J., and I'm sorry. I guess I'm rather sensitive to anything lately that appears a little different than I expect. You didn't answer your phone when I called so my mind went off imagining all sorts of reasons why. I don't want to be a person who can't trust a friend, so it has me a little upset with myself. It'll be easier when I know exactly where I stand with you."

"You stand very well with me, Jill, and you don't need to worry that I'm up to any deceitfulness when you can't reach me. I'm sorry I have to put you through this trial of sorts while I try to clear my mind about whether I can trust any woman again. It isn't fair to you and I hate myself for making you suffer because of my problem. If you think it would be easier for you if we didn't see each other for awhile, please let me know. I won't like it, but I'll definitely do it if that's the way you want to proceed."

"No, T.J., that's not what I want. When you made the remark that you wanted to be a little more than friends, I guess I was expecting, or maybe hoping, you were a little closer to being free of your doubts. However, let's continue to be friends so we can get to know each other a lot better and see where that takes us. I'll look forward to seeing you Sunday afternoon for a round of golf."

"Jill, you're upset with me again, aren't you? May I come down Wednesday night and take you to dinner so we can talk face to face? I really need to see you."

"I'm not upset with you, T.J. I'm more upset with myself for all these drives you have to make down here to see me and try to reassure me. Maybe we'll have to find a place about halfway between the two towns to meet."

"You are so considerate of everyone, Jill, and I love you for it, but I don't mind the drive down when I know you're going to be there when I arrive. Of course, there's always the other option that's waiting your decision so we could be closer. Sorry, Sweetie, that was out of line. I'll plan to see you around 6 o'clock if that fits your plans."

"That's fine, I'll see you then. Thanks for calling back, T.J."

"Thank you for being you, Sweetie. Until Wednesday, I'll be seeing you, holding you and kissing you in my dreams. Your perfume really works wonders, by the way." He's chuckling as he says in a sexy voice, "Goodnight, Jill."

As I click off, I still have to wonder just how much or how often he actually thinks of me when we're apart. Are all of his endearing words just words to keep me dangling on a string, or could he really be trying to get over his fear of another Adele?

Oh, what is wrong with me? My very first relationship is unbelievable, filled with fun and surprises as well as some tender moments that are wonderful, but I seem to be doing my best to lose it. I know we had some upsetting times, too, but we got through those with no ill effects. So, come on, do what you need to do to conquer life and love.

Glancing at the clock, I realize it's not too late yet, so I pick up the phone again and dial Jessica's number. Talking to my little sister always seems to put my doubts to rest.

CHAPTER TWENTY-TWO

I'm not surprised at all when he pulls into the drive at 5:59 p.m. Wednesday. I've come to the conclusion that he'd much rather be early than late, especially after the time I was a nervous wreck when he'd been called to help with the car accident victims. This time he gets to see both of my parents before we head for the restaurant. Dad, of course, assures him that it's really great about the golf game and that Carl is especially looking forward to some new competition. "I hope you can make him apologize to me for saying I'm getting boring," he laughs.

"I'm not so sure that I'm the golfer you expect me to be, Mr. Hale, but I'll do my best to test his skills. I didn't get to play a lot of golf during my medical training, but C.J. and I did play a lot as teenagers and during my early college years, so we'll see what can happen. I understand Jill has remembered her training quite well, too, so I may be the underdog here," he chuckles.

"Well, I don't think it'll take too much to put Carl in his place, but we're both sure looking forward to the match on Sunday."

"Yes, it should be fun. Are you ready to go, Jill?"

"Anytime you are, so would you like to be on our way?"

"I'm ready." Turning to my folks he said, "It's nice to get to see you both, Mr. and Mrs. Hale, and I'm looking forward to seeing you both again Sunday. Goodbye for now."

It was a rather short evening, but he was very attentive and upbeat. He shared some jokes one of his patients had told him, he asked a few questions about the golf course, and then invited me to go to the football game with him the following weekend. "Mom is very anxious for you to come because she says her desk is getting covered with invoices again, statements to be sent out, and a few orders she'd like you to help her with. Think you'll be up to that? Of course, she feels she's taking advantage of your generous offer to help."

"Of course, I'll be up to that and she insists on paying me. Do you think there's anything that needs to be done before next weekend? I could drive up after the bank closes Saturday, stay overnight and then follow you back down Sunday to play golf."

"I don't think it's that serious, but she did wonder if you'd be able to enter all the necessary programs and show her what she'd need to know and do if she and Dad were to buy a computer for the store."

"Yes, I could do that, T.J., but will you tell her not to be in a big hurry to buy one because I think it might be easier to finish the year as the books are set up now. We could, before the end of the year, get the computer ready to enter the year-end figures. Starting the New Year on the computer, without a lot of closing entries to be entered, would save both time and space or bites."

"Are you saying a computer bites?" he laughs.

"Just stupid computer talk."

"I've heard the girls talking in the office occasionally, and it's certainly all Greek to me, but I'm so glad you're willing to help the folks with this."

"It's a pleasure."

Hesitating for a minute or two, T.J. was seriously studying my face which made me very self-conscience. "Do I have something on my face?" I ask as I use my napkin.

Shaking his head and smiling, he said, "No, Sweetie, you're beautiful as usual. I'm just concerned that I'm making you uncomfortable with my inability to make a decision on my future. I get down on myself and then it carries over to the way I treat you. I just want you to know that I adore you, I don't want to hurt you in any way, but I'm wondering if you can tolerate my behavior for another three months."

"I promised I would give you until the first of the year, and I'll do that. It's a little hard at times, especially when you seem to ignore me like you did in July and August, but I'll try my best to give you time to work things out."

"That's all I can ask, Jill. Shall we go?"

When we got back in the car, he leaned over to give me a short simple kiss. "I have something I want to give you tonight, Sweetie." He opens the little storage unit between the seats and brings out a very pretty package.

"What is this for? It's no special occasion that I know of."

"Just open it and then you'll understand."

My hands are shaking as I try to get the ribbon and paper off this small box. It's not the shape of a ring box but I can dream, can't I? I finally get it unwrapped and then start to laugh as I realize it's a new bottle of the perfume he'd kept. "You haven't used the whole bottle already, have you?"

"Oh, no, but I didn't want you to be without your favorite perfume, either. I've been sleeping like a baby, Jill, since I've had your scent near me every night. That should make me realize something, shouldn't it?"

"Are you saying that you might be taking a step in the right direction to putting the past behind you?"

"I'd love to honestly say that, Sweetie, but it just seems that my heart continuously says one thing while my mind says another. I'd better take you home now."

⮟

Sunday's golf game is hilarious. Carl starts out with so much confidence and he's actually doing well on the first two holes, getting pars on both. T.J. pars the first hole but birdies the second, Dad pars the first but bogies the second, and I'm not even going to say what I did. Except for T.J., everything went down hill from there and after nine holes we were all ready to call it quits. You can't really play golf too well when you're laughing so hard your eyes are watering, you can't see your ball, and you finally don't even have the strength to swing the club. "We'll have to try this again sometime when we're a little more in control," Dad remarks as we head for our cars. "I can imagine how happy that group was behind us when we left the course."

"I'll be happy to try again. It was certainly a different type of golf game from any I've played before, but I really did enjoy it," T.J. chuckles.

There was some sort of a grunt from Carl who then said, "I'll talk to you one of these days, Stuart, and I'm sorry we wasted a good afternoon for you, Dr. Peterson. I've never had such a bad game in my life, but I certainly enjoyed meeting you."

"I don't feel the afternoon was wasted, Carl. If nothing else, we all probably lost a pound or two from all the laughing and hunting for balls, and I met another friend."

When we reach the cars, T.J. asks if I'll go for a ride with him. I nod and watch as he puts my clubs in his car along with his own. He drives out of the Club and soon turns south onto Route 15-501. "Where are we going, T.J.?"

"For a little ride," he says as he reaches over and takes my hand in his. "Just a little ride," he whispers against my palm and then kisses it tenderly.

He continues to follow 15-501 which, of course, I know will take us to Pinehurst.

"T.J., you don't have a pass for Pinehurst, do you? If I couldn't get a tee time on our little course, surely you don't think you can play this one. Jessica and I got to play it once when we were on the golf team in high school. It had been a two-day tournament of players from six schools around the area. They were wonderful to us, we had a lot of fun and it's such a beautiful place to get to visit."

"I have a friend who lives here and this is about the time of day he and his wife play a round of golf. If we can catch them, we just might be able to join them since he's been bugging me for years to drop in and play a round with them."

"I don't believe you. You don't just drop in expecting to play golf on a course like Pinehurst."

"We'll see. Maybe we'll just have a cocktail with them." He pulls into the driveway of a very pretty house. "I'll see if they're home." I watch as he rings the bell and just stands there quietly waiting. I think he's crazy, but then the door opens and a guy about T.J.'s age smiles and throws his arm around T.J.'s shoulder and pats his back. They both look toward the car. I wish I could hide, but T.J. is on his way over to my side. "Come on, Sweetie, both of them are home and they want us to come in."

Jeff and Diane are a darling couple and so easy to talk to. We find out that they had played golf earlier today because they have a party to attend at 8 o'clock, but they are really thrilled that we dropped by. "Now, tell us T.J., where did you find this lovely lady who has your eyes sparkling and your smile including that sweet dimple again?" Diane asks as she sits beside me on the couch.

"That's quite a story, Diane, but I have to give C.J. the credit for rescuing both of us from our doldrums, although we both feel it was actually an act of God that gave us our lives back. Jill's sister was down on the beach near C.J.'s resort when she became faint, and just as he reached her, she collapsed into his arms. She was on spring break from UNC and was in need of a rescue from a boyfriend who thought he was going to have his way with her. He'd decided to break promises he'd apparently made only to convince her to come to the beach with him. Well, the relationship grew between C.J. and Jessica, he came to her graduation, and our folks invited her and her family to our house for dinner the night before the ceremony.

Of course, my curiosity made me be there, and when I saw this sweetie come in the door alone, I at once put on my best behavior and became her escort. She's truly captivated me, but as much as I've tried, I still can't bring myself to fully trust anyone since Adele's stunt. Jill has been wonderful, and even promised to put up with me for awhile as I try to rid myself of this baggage I carry."

"It has certainly been a long time coming, T.J., and we hope you can finally accept the fact that there are very few Adeles out there compared with the number of real down to earth girls who only want the best for you," Jeff remarks.

"This one has certainly proved that, especially since I haven't been able to leave her alone and she very politely puts me in my place." He looks over at me and grins.

"Ah, a lady with not only beauty, but also morals and dedication, it seems. That *is* quite a catch, My Friend."

After a drink and a few snacks, we decide it's time to be on our way and let them get ready for the party they're attending.

"Please come back anytime, you two, and if you can let us know you're coming, all the better. Don't let that stop you from just dropping in, though." During the visit, they'd been told about the golf game and why he was down this way. Jeff walks us to the car, and after I'm inside, he and T.J. walk around the back of the car with Jeff's hand on T.J.'s arm while he's whispering something in his ear. They're both laughing when they reach the driver's door of the car, and Jeff stoops down to look in at me and say Goodbye once again. They both slap the other's shoulder and then wave goodbye. Those three must've been very close at one time since they both knew about Adele.

On our way back to Sanford, T.J. tells me a little about Jeff and Diane, how they'd met in college and then married about three years after graduation. He kept my hand in his as he drove along, kissing it occasionally, and then looking over at me with that special smile with the dimple that I now know disappeared because of Adele.

"Diane mentioned that it was nice to see the dimple back in your cheek. Did you lose it after Adele disappeared?"

"Not exactly. I didn't pay much attention to a dimple, but Diane loved to make a fuss over it after we'd known each other for awhile. She was already dating Jeff when we met, but when I started dating Adele, she made it a point to remind me quite often that she missed seeing my dimple on the rare occasions I smiled anymore. We had a class together that one term, and I was pretty upset with her by the time the year ended. I'd felt she was trying to drive a wedge between Adele and me so I ignored her as much as possible. It really wasn't too hard since she'd made it clear she didn't approve of my choice of Adele as a girlfriend. Jeff and I had a couple of classes together so our friendship continued."

It's rather dark by the time we reach my home so I'm in his arms as soon as he gets around the car and opens my door. "I wish I had you at the condo," he chuckles as his lips smother mine and he has me in a bear hug. "I'd better be getting on home, though, after I tell your parents goodbye and thank them for having such a wonderful daughter."

CHAPTER TWENTY-THREE

*T*he following weekend is the beginning of October, and I'm again in Chapel Hill working at the Antique Store on Saturday morning before going to the game this afternoon. Mrs. Peterson and I talk quite a bit about setting up a computer to handle all the financial entries, including the inventory of all items in the store, the purchases and sales, etc. We actually go to Best Buy to see if they'll have the programs we'll need to get this done.

"Are you any closer, Jill, to considering coming here and working with me? If not, I'm a little hesitant about getting into all this technical stuff that I don't understand at all."

"I've been giving it a lot of thought, Mrs. Peterson, and if you're sure you want me to work with you and stay in your home for awhile without any definite plans between T.J.

and me, then I'm ready to start taking the necessary steps for changing jobs."

"Oh, Jill, that's wonderful. That son of mine had better get his head on straight, like C.J. has, but I can't make him do something that he's not ready to do."

"I understand. He's asked and I've given him until after the holidays to work on his problem, so we'll see how that goes. My concern is whether you'll still want me in your employ and in your home if things don't work out between T.J. and me."

"That would *not* change my need for you in the store, Jill, so we'll worry about all that when the time comes, but I'll pray extra hard that things work out for all of us."

"I've been thinking I'd give the bank two weeks' notice on the 16th of October, and then take a few days vacation when I'm through there. I hope I'll be asked to come to the game on November 10th and I'll then plan to stay if that fits everyone's schedule. That will give me plenty of time to get everything in place to start the New Year on the computer. I'd like to try to keep it a secret from Jessica until I see her in person, but it might not be possible. She says she and C.J. and Emily are all planning to come home for Thanksgiving so I'll try to figure out something that gets her to come here first before going to our folks'."

"You'll figure out something, Jill, and I'll make sure I keep my mouth shut when I'm talking to C.J.," she laughs.

"I may have to recruit his help which means I may need your help, too. If I were to call and talk to C.J., it might cause Jessica to think something is up, but if you talk to C.J., there would be no reason for her to suspect anything."

"Oh, you're so clever, Jill, and tricky. Do you have something up your sleeve right now that might work?"

"I've been thinking about something, but I don't have all the details worked out yet. I'll get your opinion before I set anything into motion," I grin. "I'll probably have to talk to my folks, too, so they'll know what going on."

"Just let me know when you need my help." She was smiling as she walked away to help a customer who had just entered the store.

I'm surprised when T.J. and his dad walk in about 2 o'clock. I'd thought we'd meet the men at Dr. and Mrs. Peterson's home and leave a couple of the cars there. T.J. hadn't come after me last night because a group of my friends were hosting a birthday bash with a night out on the town for three who were turning 25 just days apart. I'd then come directly to the store when I'd driven up early this morning.

Now, however, T.J. doesn't waste any time coming to the desk, giving me a nice kiss and running his fingers through my hair. "I thought you might have a little hang-over today, but you look as bright and chipper as usual," he remarks with a chuckle.

"A big night out for our group doesn't mean getting ourselves drunk, T.J.," but his lips back on mine prevented me from saying anymore.

"Hey, you're not supposed to make advances toward the help," his mother orders as she comes laughing and patting him on the back.

"OK, I'll just kiss the boss, then." He turns and gives her a kiss on the cheek as he picks her up and twirls her around a couple of times. "Is there anything you need us big, strong, handsome men to do before we go to the game?" he asks as he sets her back down.

"Speak for yourself, T.J., because your old dad is really tired from picking up all the youngsters who came in for shots this morning. I thought they were supposed to have all their shots before school started."

"Those who came in this morning are the ones who, because of financial problems, had failed to get them, and they wouldn't be able to attend school any longer if we hadn't given them their shots today."

"How did we get involved in that humanitarian situation?" he chuckled.

"I volunteered our services at that meeting you asked me to attend. You know I can't turn away a child's need. Of course, I don't think you can either."

"Yea, I know. That's why I sent you. I thought it was about time for us to volunteer our services again, and I wanted you to experience the thrill that I always have when I offer to get the little ones ready for school. God Bless You, Son."

"Well, there's nothing around here to do to further hurt your tired old back, Dear, so let's close up, take some cars home, and go to the game." Mrs. Peterson stands on tiptoe to give her husband a kiss and then we all head for the door.

❧

After all the food we devour at the game, which UNC won, we go without dinner and just watch a movie with his folks. We do have cake and coffee, however, before T.J. leaves. We go to church Sunday morning and then have lunch, but my agenda for moving is now set and approved. I'm so excited about my future that I plan to start checking my clothes and doing some packing as soon as I get home this afternoon. I politely excuse myself, explaining that I do want to head home. T.J. wants to follow me, but I jokingly say that I don't have a tire with a slow leak or a gun-toting ex-boyfriend to fear so I see no reason for him to make that trip. I guess my rather strong independent nature is showing, but I'm soon on my way home alone.

What I hadn't anticipated, though, was a crazy driver coming north toward me in the southbound lane and weaving back and forth across the road. I laid on the horn thinking it'd alert him to the danger, but he just keeps coming and weaving too often for me to know where he'll be when he reaches me. I slow down, and finally, at the last minute, I swerve to try to miss him, but he catches my back fender and bumper which twirls me around and I land in a shallow ditch just off the road. I'm stunned as the air bag opens, but otherwise I think I'm unhurt.

The doors of the car open very quickly on both sides as people have stopped to see if they can help, but the one who hit me has continued on his way. I heard that someone had gotten his license number and called 9-1-1, so he'll probably be caught soon. I just hope no one gets badly hurt before he's stopped.

My purse had apparently catapulted into the back seat, but someone retrieves it for me. I get my cell phone and call Dad. I'm told by an off-duty EMT, who has stopped and helped move the air bag off of me, that I need to sit still in the car until the ambulance and police arrive. He doesn't want to take any chances of moving me in case I've been hurt and don't realize it.

I guess I'm closer to Chapel Hill than Sanford because the ambulance comes from there shortly after the State Troopers arrive. I'm really surprised, though, when I see this car that looks exactly like T.J.'s pull up. I watch but can't believe my eyes when it *is* T.J. running up to the car.

"I'm Dr. Peterson," he tells the troopers, "and I know this young lady very well. Do you think I could examine her before she's moved?"

"Of course, Dr. Peterson, I remember you from a three-car pile up not too long ago. Please be careful, especially where the seat belt goes across her body."

He checks my eyes and whispers, "Why didn't you call me, Jill?"

"I haven't memorized your cell phone number yet, but how did you find out about it so soon?"

"Your dad called because he thought I'd be closer than he was, and I am a doctor, you know. Do you have any pain anywhere?" He touches my shoulder, my chest and my stomach where the seat belt had been, but there was no pain. "Do you feel any pain or any numbness in your arms or legs?" he asks as he starts examining my arms.

"My right leg feels a little funny but it's probably just from sitting here waiting for all of you to show up," I smile as I continue, "but I sort of like all the attention I'm getting from the attending physician."

Of course, he's all business and immediately reaches down to touch my leg and I let out a little scream. "Oh, Jill, I'm so sorry." He motions to the ambulance personnel and they are there immediately. He tries to talk softly to them but I hear him say, "Her leg is sensitive to the touch and there's a possible knee injury. Let's get her to the hospital so we can better examine her for injuries. There may not be anything broken, but there is blood on her slacks, and she is in pain when it's touched.

About that time, Dad and Mom come to the side of the car looking like they're about ready to faint. "T.J.," I whisper, "please check Mom and Dad and make sure they're all right to continue driving to the hospital. They look like they're in shock."

He backs away to let the EMT and other attendant from the ambulance get to me and start the process of getting me out of the car. I can hear a young man talking to T.J. now and he's saying that he had been out riding with a friend so he would be free and willing to drive my parents to the hospital if that would help. T.J. has the police check his driver's license and ask some other questions, but he's taking him over to Dad and Mom now.

It seems like hours, but I'm finally in the ambulance and Mom is going to ride with me. Dad is going to let the young man drive him to the hospital in our van. After they'd gotten me out of the car and onto the gurney, T.J. examines my right thigh, which is definitely bleeding, and also checked my knee more closely. He then instructed them to apply a splint so it wouldn't move, put a cold compress on, and to give me something for the pain I'll most likely experience before we get to the hospital.

I smile as I'm wondering how the EMT is taking all those instructions from T.J. since he's most likely trained to do all those things at an accident scene.

I try to tell Mom what happened because I don't want her to think I'd been driving recklessly, but she assures me they didn't think that at all. They'd heard most of the details from ones who had witnessed the crazy driver and the result. My knee is hurting a little more now and I can tell that it has swollen. It must be from the shot they gave me that my eyelids are getting heavy, but as I drift into dreamland, I have the comfort of my hand being held so tenderly by my wonderful mother.

Chapter Twenty-Four

The x-rays show that I have a cracked kneecap, and the nasty gash in my thigh will require a few stitches. T.J. explains that I'll most likely be in a cast for about three weeks and then a knee brace for maybe a couple more. "It's not splintered or anything," he says with a smile, "so I think the healing time may be shortened if you're a good patient and will follow all the directions given you by the surgeon."

"Why don't you just change places with me, Dr. Peterson, so you can follow all the directions from the surgeon?" I smirk. "You doctors think it's so easy to be obedient when your leg is itching like crazy inside a cast, you're hopping around on crutches, and you're having a very hard time getting upstairs to your bedroom."

"Aha, it sounds like you've been through something like this before. Is there a story behind it that I'd like to hear?"

"Nothing that would give me a movie contract. When I was in ninth grade, I was trying to slide into home plate during a game with a nearby town, but the big husky catcher had her leg in the way and I hit pretty hard against the leg protector she was wearing. I cracked a bone in my leg, but I wasn't the only one hurt. She'd tried to tag me without her glove on and broke two fingers. We spent hours together in the emergency room getting our casts put on. Of course, we didn't like each other because we were from different schools, so it wasn't the most pleasant experience to go through. I guess they thought we were buddies or you'd think they would've put a curtain between us at least. And, you get that grin off your face, T.J., before I use my good leg on you!"

"Oh, Jill, you are really a joy to get to know. On top of everything else I've learned about you, now I find that you were, and maybe still are, a tomboy. What makes it even more amusing is the fact that you don't look like a tomboy at all, but a feminine little thing who almost anyone would want to protect and care for."

"And that 'almost anyone' gives you the excuse, I presume, to let me know that you might be the exception, the one who wouldn't want to protect and care for me, right?"

"No, Jill, that is absolutely not the case. If I felt that way, why would I have been at the scene of the accident, come to the hospital to see that you are taken care of properly, or still be here, for that matter?"

"Because you're a doctor, I'm a friend, and you feel a little guilty because you let me go home alone? I'm sorry, T.J., I guess I'm filled with self pity right now because I don't want to be in this hospital. I don't want to wear a cast for the next three weeks, and I don't want to think about how this is going to affect my plans for the future." Of course, I can't keep the tears from running down my cheeks, and I try to wipe them away quickly with my hand. I look at him still standing right beside my bed, and he actually looks concerned, but he wasn't fooled by my actions. Did I really expect him to be?

He takes me in his arms, wipes the tears away with a tissue, and then tenderly kisses my cheek. "Jill, you have every right to feel upset after being in a very scary accident and suffering a break most likely requiring a cast. They're going to be ready for you in a few minutes now so I'd better let your parents come in and be with you. I'll stay around and be there while the stitches are put in and the cast is put on. Please don't worry about your future--everything will work out fine."

"Do you like me in my pretty non-fitting hospital gown?" I smile as I sniff and then reach for a tissue to really blow my nose.

"You look darling in anything you have on, Sweetie, and I can't wait until I---ah--- oh, forget it, I'll get your parents."

Did he almost run out that door? I do believe this friendship thing is getting a bit hard on both of us.

Not only Mom and Dad, but also Dr. and Mrs. Peterson come into the examining room. The doctor speaks up first as he kisses my hand and then my cheek. "We're not going to stay long, Jill, but we just wanted you to know that we're here for you and also our prayers will be heading upward on your behalf. We're so upset that this had to happen to you, but you'll heal fast and be as good as new." He backs away and Mrs. Peterson comes and gives me a big hug.

"Please don't worry about anything, Dear. Just take your time and get completely healed before trying to do anymore about moving. My concern is about you climbing the stairs to the bedroom, and your mother mentioned that your room at home is upstairs, too. We were discussing the possibility of your staying at T.J.'s where there would be no steps to worry about. Would you like us to ask T.J. about that possibility?"

"Absolutely not! I'm going home and I'm sleeping in my own bed! I'm sorry if I'm sounding ungrateful, but staying at T.J.'s is completely out of the question. He has his own problems to deal with, and I want to be home with my folks. I also have to give my notice to the bank and work my two weeks before I can come here to stay."

Mom comes to the side of the bed and takes my hand. "Don't get upset, Jill. We're just trying to find someway to make it easier for you. You were quite a bit younger, you know, when you broke your leg and bump, bump, bumped down the stairs every day and then waited for your dad to carry you back up." She's laughing as she remembers my determination to eat and spend time with the family during those other horrible weeks that I spent in a cast.

"I need to apologize to all of you. I'm just not myself right now and I've already hit T.J. with a self-pity outburst that I'm ashamed of. Let's see how everything goes in surgery and what the instructions are from the surgeon. Will that be OK?"

"Of course, Honey, we didn't mean for you to make those decisions tonight."

It wasn't long until Dad reported that the gurney was coming now to take me to surgery. "We'll be waiting when you're all patched up," he said.

I get a kiss from Mom, and then Dad comes to pat my cheek as he always had whenever one of his girls was hurting. His smile is so comforting as he reminds me that God will be there with me, and I'm suddenly ready to get this ordeal over with.

I see T.J. standing at the door as they wheel me past him. He touches my cheek and gives me a big smile as he whispers, "I'll be there when you're back in your room."

I don't know how much time passes, but I'm finally back with Mom, Dad, and T.J. all smiling as I open my eyes. "Do I still have my leg?" I ask as I slowly take in my new surroundings.

"Yes, Jill, you're a very lucky girl," T.J. answers. "The crack was so slight that they put you right into a knee brace instead of a cast. It won't be high enough to irritate your stitches and also shouldn't make you itch." He's smiling as he's proven that he remembered what I'd said to him earlier about the itching during the healing in a cast. "You'll have to be extra careful, though, because it could worsen if it gets bumped or twisted in the first few days."

"Are those your instructions, Dr. Peterson, or do they come directly from the one in authority around here?"

"From both, actually. The surgeon wants to see you again Tuesday so your mom and dad are going to stay with you at the folks' until then, and we'll see that you're carried up to your room and that your prescription is filled. There cannot be any bumping down the stairs, either. Is that understood?"

"Yes, T.J., I understand and I appreciate everything you're doing for me, but does all this mean I'm ready to leave? I can't go in this gown and I doubt I can get my slacks back on, so what am I going to wear? I see that smile on your face, Dr. Peterson, but don't even think about it."

"Mom brought one of her smaller skirts which has an elastic waist. She thinks that you can possibly wear it to their house, at least. You may have to use a safety pin to keep it from falling off, but you'll be covered. I did rescue your suitcase from the car before they came to tow it to Sanford, but I thought you'd only had slacks with you this weekend. I'm sorry to say that the slacks you were wearing are no longer wearable since there was a tear where the car keys apparently dug into your leg, and then they continued the mutilation when they cut them off here at the hospital."

"Did they ever catch the crazy guy who ruined my new pant suit?" I moan. "I guess I should've changed back into my jeans."

"Yes, they did. He was high on drugs so he won't be driving for some time."

That's good. If you and Dad will leave now, Mom can help me get into the clothes I'll be wearing out of here."

"Aw, shucks, Jill, you aren't any fun at all. Don't you think you might need us men to help in some small way?"

"Out the door with both of you!" I say it in a demanding voice but also with a grin on my face. They are both laughing as they shuffle out of the room.

Just as Mom had finished folding and pinning the skirt so it would stay up, a nice looking young man in a white coat walks into the room. "Jill, I'm Dr. Calvin Hall, and I just wanted you to know who you'd be seeing Tuesday when you come for your post surgery appointment. I've set it for 10 o'clock which I hope will be convenient for you." With a big smile, he says, "I see you found something to wear home although I doubt it's from your regular wardrobe. It's a shame we ruined the slacks you were wearing, but it's standard procedure so we don't harm the injured area anymore than necessary."

"I understand, Dr. Hall, and this is something that was available for me to wear so I don't have to otherwise embarrass myself walking through the halls of the hospital. I'm sure I can't get into any of the clothes I brought with me for the weekend so I'll be happy to get home and see what will fit over this brace." I can't stop the giggle. "I'll be here Tuesday and thanks for coming by so I know who to look for. Are there any more instructions other than what Dr. Peterson has told me?"

"Dr. Peterson, is it? When he couldn't let you out of his sight, it looked to me like there was a closer relationship between the two of you than the formal Dr. Peterson and Ms. Hale. I was hoping that T.J. had found someone to give his life real meaning again. He is certainly deserving of a true love to bring him the happiness that has been missing way too long. I'm sorry, I'm probably out of line. I'll see you Tuesday and the instructions T.J. gave you are complete. The only correction I'd make is your remark about walking through the hospital halls would be that you'll be in a wheelchair until you reach the car you'll be riding in. By the way, where is home?"

"Sanford. How I got to know T.J. and why I'm here for the weekend is a long story, so I'll just say Thank you, Dr. Hall. I might also add for your ears only, that T.J. and I are a work in progress, and I'm hoping he'll soon find the answers he needs that will give me a chance to bring him the happiness we both crave."

"Well, that sounds promising and I'll be praying for its fruition. Until Tuesday, Jill, take care of that knee." His smile is very genuine, and I feel that God is really here beside me and has given me a wonderful doctor to look after me.

Mom had slipped out of the room when Dr. Hall had come in, so I'm relieved that no one heard that conversation except the doctor and me.

CHAPTER TWENTY-FIVE

*W*hen my folks and I arrive at the Peterson's, T.J. is waiting to carry me into the house where there's a wonderful aroma coming from the kitchen. Mom and Dad head in that direction to see if they can help with anything, and T.J. asks if I'd like to eat with the rest of them or go directly to my room.

"I want to be with everyone, and I can't turn down whatever that is that smells so good. If you're not going to put me down, please carry me to where we're going to eat, Muscle Man."

"I'm not going to put you down, Ms. Hale, until you've been off that leg for at least 12 hours. I'd get you some crutches, but I don't think keeping the knee bent all the time is the right thing to do, either."

"Didn't you get all the instructions from Dr. Hall? He said you'd know what to do with me."

"Oh, I know what I'd like to do with you, all right, but this isn't the time or place to discuss that line of action." His smile spreads across his face as his lips are finding mine for just a short kiss. "You are such a wonderful breath of fresh air, Jill, and I wish I had the courage to--ah--er, let's go see what there is to eat."

"With all those other thoughts in your head, Dr. Peterson, I think eating sounds like a splendid idea."

Dr. and Mrs. Peterson had stopped and bought some pizzas when they'd left the hospital, and she is now warming them in the oven. They smell so good and when they're on the table, I'm afraid I stuff myself. "Thank you so much for the pizza. I didn't realize I was so hungry."

It wasn't long until T.J. stands up and informs everyone, "It's been a long afternoon and evening for all of us, and I think it's time now for the injured lady to be taken to her room. Are you ready to be carried upstairs to the nice comfortable bed that's waiting, Jill Marie?" I was in his arms before I got a word out of my mouth.

Someone had turned my bed down, and T.J. lowered me from his arms so gently onto the welcoming softness. I wasn't expecting him to stay and sit on the edge of the bed, but I was glad he didn't just dump me and leave.

"I'm so sorry this had to happen to you, Sweetie, but I'll pray that you'll heal real fast. Will you try to memorize my cell phone number so you can call me whenever you want or need to? I don't want to hear about another accident, but I would love to hear your voice anytime you're thinking of me."

Of course, I start to giggle. He must not realize that he'd never be off his cell phone if I were to call every time I thought of him. Noting the perplexed look on his face, I reach my hand over to pat his cheek. "T.J., that's awfully sweet, but you wouldn't be able to take care of your patients very well if I called you each time I thought of you."

"Is that really true, Jill? From some of your latest actions and remarks, I haven't been able to tell exactly how much time you spend thinking of me. I love your spunky personality and wouldn't want to change you, but it's hard for me, at times, to understand how you really do feel about me or our relationship."

Luckily, at that precise moment, Mrs. Peterson and Mom walk into the room. "We hope we're not interrupting a sweet romantic scene, but we think it's time for Jill to shed her misfit clothes and get some rest," Mrs. Peterson jokingly remarks. "Would you please help and bring in her suitcase, T.J., so she can slip into her gown?"

"I'm on my way, Mother Dear, but you did interrupt a very important conversation and now I'll never know the answer I was trying so hard to ascertain." He looks at me and grins, pats his mother's cheek and slips out of the room. I breathe a sigh of relief.

≼

The next morning, after a very restful night, I'm feeling ready to tackle the world until I try to move my leg. I suddenly realize that I'm not quite as limber as I'd like, so I slowly work my leg to the edge of the bed until I can sit up on the edge. I take a look at the bandage and the brace and find that the bandaged area is throbbing and hurting much more than the knee. Unless there's an infection there, I'm glad it's that way because it means the knee is going to be back to normal first and then the stitches won't interfere with my trying to walk.

I notice the door opening slightly and a familiar head peeking in. "Come on in, Dad, I'm awake and need company."

"I didn't want to bother you if you were still sleeping, but I have your medication if you're ready to take it. It says to take it with some food, so I brought a piece of toast and some orange juice along with a cup of coffee."

"You're so thoughtful, Dad, and I love you. I think I can eat that, but I want to have my coffee first. I wish you had a cup to drink with me," but just then I notice two cups and a thermos on the tray. "Someone is really reading my mind."

He just chuckles as he sets the tray on the nightstand and pulls a chair over close to the bed. "I guess I made a remark to your mother that I'd love to spend some time with you this morning, and she and Jeannette took it from there. How are you really feeling, Honey? I was so scared when you called to tell us you'd had an accident. I could imagine all kinds of things even though you tried to assure me you weren't hurt."

"I wasn't feeling any pain so I really didn't think I'd been hurt."

"I knew your mom would want to let Jodi and Jess know, so I called T.J. real quick so she could have the phone. Of course, she didn't talk long and we were on our way. We did let them know later what had actually happened and that you were still the survivor you always had been."

"Thanks for everything, Dad. You can't imagine how surprised I was when I saw a car that looked just like T.J.'s pull off the road and then I got to watch him come running up to the troopers. He was a little upset because I hadn't called him, but I couldn't remember his cell number. I'm glad I'd given it to you."

"I am, too. He knew exactly what to do, and that young man who drove my van to the hospital was just what I needed. He's a junior at UNC this year and he'd been down to Pinehurst with a friend. They were on their way back to school when they saw that crazy driver ahead of them. They watched as he crossed over into the south lane and then clipped you even though you'd tried to swerve out of the way. They got his license number so they called 9-1-1. I got his name and address so we can write a thank you note."

"That's great, Dad. I'll do that in a day or two unless you want to take care of that. One thing's for sure. I wouldn't want to go through either of my accidents again, but I'm glad I survived both and had a lot of help getting through them. Where the stitches are in my thigh hurts the most this morning, but the medication will probably help with that. I suppose I should take it before my orange juice is all gone," I giggle. "Is Mom downstairs with Mrs. Peterson?"

"Jeannette was going to the store this morning and asked if we would like to see where you'll be working. I told your mother to go and I'd stay with you because she hasn't been able to talk about much else. I'll see it sometime before we leave tomorrow if the doctor says you can travel."

"Have you talked to Gary about fixing the car or was it too badly damaged?"

"I called the body shop, but Gary was out on a call. His assistant did say that the car had been delivered and they didn't think it looked too bad from the initial appraisal. I'll find out more when we get home."

We talk about several other things and it's fun to have Dad all to myself. All too soon, though, there's a knock on the door, then it opens and Mom and Mrs. Peterson are walking in. I can't believe it's lunchtime already and here I sit still in my gown.

Shortly there are heavy footsteps running up the stairs and T.J. comes bounding in. "How's my injured little sweetheart today?" he asks as he slips by the others rather quickly and is now sitting on the bed beside me. He proceeds to raise my gown above my knee so he can look at the bandaged stitches.

I try to push my gown back down as I'm almost shouting at him. "T.J., this is not your office and I'm not even your patient, so what do you think you're doing?" I quickly notice that everyone else is quietly leaving the room. "Hey, you guys, don't leave me with this out of control maniac!" I can't say anything more, though, because he's picked me up in his arms and his lips are trying to reach mine. I push his face away as I finally mumble, "I haven't even brushed my teeth yet." He gently lays me back down on the bed.

"You've been sitting up long enough with your knee bent, Jill, and you need to have it straight for awhile. As for your teeth being brushed, you smell and taste like coffee, and that's not all bad. I'll have to try harder to remember that you want and need your coffee before any kissing is done in the mornings," he chuckles.

"What are you doing here on your lunch hour, anyway?"

"I came over to carry you down to lunch, have a bite to eat myself, and also to bring you something."

"You know the twelve hours are up and I can stand on my leg now."

He just smiles, kisses me quickly and then pushes himself up off the bed and heads for the hall. He comes back carrying the most beautiful vase of pink roses and puts them on the table by the window. "A poor little injured girl has to have flowers to make her feel better," he sort of drawls it out slowly as he again sits on the edge of the bed and just looks at me.

"What are you thinking?" I ask.

"Just wondering what I did for entertainment before I met you."

"Is that all I am to you, Entertainment?"

"There I go again, letting my big mouth get me into trouble. Jill, you're definitely entertaining, but there's so much more about you to be admired, adored, and treasured. You're amusing, frustrating, amazing, intelligent, aggravating, and yes, even lovable. I know I've never said the word love to you, Jill, but I want to be absolutely sure before I make a commitment."

"Because I know the reason behind it, I've been able to accept your decisions, T.J., but you did call me 'My Love' when you said goodbye the night I called you from this very room." I give him a mischievous smile. "Actually, I think it's wise that we get to know each other real well. There are certainly things about you that I need to understand so time is the best way to solve both of our problems."

"If I did that, it must've just slipped out unconsciously because I was so surprised that you called." He lets out a big chuckle, pats my cheek, and then continues, "I hope I can call you My Love very often and very soon, Sweetie, but do you really think there are some problems with our relationship, or is it just my past that's the big culprit?"

"I hate to answer that, T.J., but I guess your past is the largest problem that we're facing. I've also noticed that you have a tendency to be a little too possessive which might be a problem if it were to get out of hand."

"I'm sorry, Sweetie, but I think that has to do with my being so unsure of whether I can truly trust a woman again. However, I want you to know that with every day that goes by, I'm feeling so much more confident about my feelings toward you; and my mistrust of women is fading in droves as you show me your dedication over and over again. I'd better get you downstairs, though, so you can have some lunch, and I can get back to the office."

"Thanks, T.J., for this wonderful time together. I love the roses and won't mind if I have to stay in this room when I have them to admire and get to inhale the aroma."

After a fabulous kiss, he carries me to the bathroom so I can brush my teeth, wash my face, and brush my hair. There's another kiss and his sly comment that it had made a little difference, and then he carries me down the stairs to where the others are eating.

I'd had him get my sweater out of the suitcase so I was a little more covered than just my gown. After half a sandwich, some chips and a few red grapes, T.J. carries me back to my room with some of my drink still in my glass. I ask very sweetly if he'll bring me my purse because there's a book I've been reading in it, and then he's gone.

I take a glance at the roses and smile. *It's the second bouquet of roses I've gotten from just a friend, or so he wants me to believe. What was it he said about me being not only entertaining but one to be adored, treasured, admired, and even lovable? He still can't say he loves me, but I do feel he's trying. Will he continue to show all this concern when I'm back on my feet? Of course, I'm probably going home tomorrow so he won't be close enough to do what he's doing here. I almost wish I could stay here, but I definitely have things to get done at home.*

❧

A little later I hear the doorbell and wonder if anyone is still downstairs, but then I hear Mom say, "Thank you so much, they're beautiful." Soon I hear her light steps coming up the stairs, the knock on the door, and a bouquet coming in ahead of her.

"Who in the world are they from?" I ask as she sets them down on the night stand.

"I don't know, Honey, but there's a card."

When I get the card from the envelope, I have to smile. "Of course, my two sisters had to send me flowers. Aren't they pretty?" A full and tight short bouquet included a bunch of short mini roses, light greenish button mums, a few orchids as well as a few other flowers all in a pretty square ceramic bowl together with white accents.

Mom was examining all the different flowers and then remarked, "It's certainly a lovely combination. The different shades of roses combined with all the other flowers and then accented with the white bring them all together. That's also a beautiful ribbon and so clever how they made it so much a part of the whole bouquet." Turning back to look at me, she remarked, "I see you've been reading, Jill. Are you going to rest for awhile now or do you need anything that I can get you?"

"No, Mom, I'm fine. I think I'll read for a little while longer and then I'll get up and see what I can do about getting washed and dressed. I'm trying to think what I have to put on so I'll look a little more presentable this evening. I just brought slacks, though, and I doubt if any of those tight fitting ones will go over the knee brace."

"Well, you rest now and we'll try to figure something out before dinnertime."

Leave it to my mother---she makes Dad go with her to find a store that carries the small junior apparel and proceeds to buy me the cutest chocolate colored outfit with wide cuffed legs on the pants and a tunic with a boat neckline, ¾ sleeves, and a belt that drops below the waist in front. She even buys me another pair of wide legged pants because she knew I had a sweater or two with me, new underclothes and a pair of pajamas, so I feel like Cinderella getting all dressed up for the Ball.

No doubt about it, T.J. is impressed. When he walks into my room, he just stands there and stares. "You look adorable, Jill, and I smell the same wonderful aroma I have in my bed at night. I'm sure you didn't go out and buy that outfit yourself, so your mother has very good taste in clothes for you. I wish I'd thought about buying you a new outfit."

"That isn't your responsibility, T.J., and Mom has been buying clothes for us girls for quite a few years. We've always loved her selections."

∽

I wear the same outfit, of course, when Mom and Dad drive me to see Dr. Hall on Tuesday, and he also makes a remark about it. "Now, that looks more like clothes that were made for a beautiful lady of 26. Oops, sorry, I guess I shouldn't mention a lady's age, but it's just between you, me and the record sheet, right?" he chuckles.

"I have wonderful parents who went and bought me this outfit so I didn't have to come see you in my gown or pajamas."

"I can see they love you a lot, but let's take a look at your thigh and knee, shall we?" It wasn't long until he was putting a smaller bandage on my leg, and giving me a few more of his suggestions on how to exercise the knee. "I suggest you see your doctor in a few days, Jill, if you aren't going to be around here, but I'll be happy to see you anytime if you do one day settle around here and I can be of help or you'd just like to talk." His smile makes a person feel so special, but then he adds, "The talks would be free because I'm very interested in you and my friend's future, but I'm not anticipating any other need of my services for many years."

"I'm moving up here in a few weeks to work with Mrs. Peterson at the antique store, so you never know; I may take you up on that, Dr. Hall. I won't be acquainted with many people and it's rather hard to talk about a family member with a family member, especially a parent. Mrs. Peterson has been wonderful, though."

"You have really put yourself in a rather perplexing situation, but I agree with you that the one and only Jeannette Peterson is hard to beat as a boss or as a friend." He then stands and says, "All right, Jill, we may or may not see each other again, but I'll continue to remember you in my prayers, and I'm sure you'll be as good as new very soon.

"Thank you so much, Dr. Hall. Just for your information, that I again ask you to keep to yourself, T.J. has asked for some time to try to solve his problems which you seem to be familiar with. He says he'll make a decision about us by the first of the year. So, I really do appreciate your offer of prayers."

"You've got them, Jill. You're quite a trooper and may God be with you and give you success and happiness in the near future."

CHAPTER TWENTY-SIX

*T*ime has seemed to pass quickly since I came home three weeks ago on the Friday following my appointment with Dr. Hall. My knee is back to normal, almost, the stitches were removed from my leg that first week home, and it is healing well.

T.J. didn't come down that first weekend because his dad had supposedly asked if he would attend a medical meeting in his place. He'd said he'd drive down on Wednesday instead, but then he'd had to have an emergency dental appointment which resulted in a root canal. He finally drove down on Sunday afternoon, took me for a drive and then we stopped for an ice cream cone and a drink, but he didn't stay very long.

I'd gone back to the bank that next day, turned in my resignation and started my two last weeks of work. I insisted that T.J. come get me that Friday night so I could spend some time at the store Saturday morning and then go to the game that afternoon if he was going. He did seem a little more subdued than usual, but I decided to ignore it. I did have a pleasant surprise at the store, though, when I mentioned to Mrs. Peterson that we'd most likely have to take an up-to-date inventory before I started to enter data on the computer.

She'd quickly pulled a thick folder from a desk drawer to show me. "This is our typewritten list, area by area, that was made the first of the year," she explained. "By taking the previous year's list, which had the items we'd sold marked off with a yellow highlighter pen and all purchases added in black pen, we then went through the store to check that all the items that should be here were still here. We tagged each item so we could also see if there were any pieces in the store that were not on the list. Then this new list was typed, and that was our starting inventory for this year. You can see the items that are highlighted and added so far this year. It has been done like this since the store opened."

"It's certainly a unique way to keep an inventory, and I think it would be great to continue keeping track of things that way. Although they'll be on the computer, it'll be an excellent way to cross check. Also, for those who don't want to use the computer, it'll still be an up-to-date record."

The doctors came after their office hours were over, we went for lunch at a nearby cafe, and then stopped at the grocery for a few items. By the time we got them home and put away, it was time to head to the game, which was exciting as usual, but UNC lost. I want to spend as much time as possible with my family now so T.J. took me home right after the game. I'd talked to Mom so they planned to have dinner after we arrived. Steaks were put on the grill when we got there, but potato salad, sliced tomatoes, a veggie salad and fresh-baked brownies were ready. Jodi and Richard joined us for dinner so they could see T.J. once again. I then spent most of Sunday relaxing for the week ahead.

෯

Now there's only the one more week of work at the bank, and I'm a little sad that my days there are going to be finished soon. Several of the girls took me to lunch on Wednesday and gave me an encased $1.00 bill to remember them by. It was so sweet, and they wished me luck with T.J., too. The bank president even came to my desk and gave me a bonus check that I would've normally received at the end of the year. He also wished me well and said they would miss me. Just three more days to go.

Mom and Dad are really happy for me, but the thought of an empty nest has them a little depressed, I'm afraid. Of course, Jodi's baby is due in December, and with Jessica's recent engagement to C.J., I imagine they'll soon have a wedding to look forward to, too. Of course, I'm not leaving quite yet, but it's just a short vacation before I start work at the Antique Store.

It's now Saturday afternoon, my work at the bank is finished, and I'm all packed and waiting for T.J. to pick me up for another football game tonight. So what's new? The phone rings. A young patient has been taken to the hospital whom T.J. is quite worried about, so he's not coming--again. He is always so apologetic when he calls, but I wonder if this has anything to do with trying to get his feelings under control. Maybe he's trying to pull away from me slowly, thinking it won't hurt me as bad when he gives me his decision that I'm not the one he can trust either.

I was really looking forward to the basketball season because I've always liked to watch basketball better than football, so I hope I'm wrong about T.J.'s recent actions and that his final decision will be in my favor, if and when he decides he can trust again. Then maybe I can go to some basketball games with him. Ha. Ha. Aren't we funny tonight? I think I'll call Jessica and see if I can talk to my best friend before she goes out with C.J.

I'm in luck. Halloween is coming up next week and she's trying to think of some new games to play and how to decorate the pre-school room. "What's up with you?" she asks. "T.J. has called several times lately and talked to C.J. From what he tells me, the guy thinks he is finally getting over his fear of trusting a woman, and it's all because of you. You must be doing something right, Sis."

"I wouldn't really know because he keeps making excuses for not coming down and seeing me. I've only seen him one weekend since I came home three weeks ago except for a rather brief visit that one Sunday. Maybe his excuses are legit, but it's certainly hard on my peace of mind. I see the doctor Monday and should get to take the brace off for good, so I'm hoping I'll get to do things again."

"Are you still helping Mrs. Peterson with the books or has the family found a good bookkeeper to take over? I hear you suggested a computer and would be willing to help get it set up for them. That's awfully nice of you, Jill."

"Yeah, nice old Jill. I've fallen in love with that antique store, though, and Jeannette Peterson is so wonderful to work with."

"Maybe you should apply for the job. It would get you closer to T.J. and then he wouldn't have an excuse not to see you," she laughed.

"What would the bank do without me? I feel like I've become a permanent fixture in that establishment." (I wish I could tell you the truth, Jess, but I want it to be a surprise when you come for Thanksgiving. Five weeks is a long time, however, to keep something from my best friend. We have shared so much.)

"You seem to be hesitating about saying something, Jill. Is there more to this call than just a little chat?"

"No, Jess, I'm just a little down tonight with another cancelled date, and I thought if I could talk to you, it would help. I'd better let you go, though, so you can work on your

THE LUCK OF A SISTER

spooky decorations. I may call someone and go to a movie. Tell C.J. and Emily I said Hi."

"Will do. Keep your chin up, Sis. You know things will work out as God has them planned. Remember what happened to me, and I couldn't be happier. Bye, now."

A few minutes later, my cell phone starts ringing. It must be a wrong number since Dad had gotten them for the three of us girls only if we promised to use them sparingly and for emergencies. "Hey, this is Jill Hale."

"This is an emergency, Ms. Hale." I hear a familiar chuckle but why is he calling again? The date has already been cancelled. I then hear him say, "I'm so lonely I don't know what to do. Have you planned anything else for tonight?"

"My first date sort of fizzled out, because duty called, so I talked to my sister and I think I'll go see a handsome movie star to spend the evening with. What's up with you?"

"Just wishing you were with me so I could see the sparkle in your eyes, enjoy the smell of your shampoo and perfume, have my arms around you and maybe see what kind of mischief I could get into with my lips and fingers. Would you like to see me, Jill?"

My heart is pounding just thinking about the scene he's described, but how do I answer his question when he's 35 miles away? "I guess I'll just have to imagine that you're next to me in the movie and trying to be a little too romantic."

"I found a doctor to stand in for me tonight, so I'm hoping I can still come see you."

"It's too late to go to the game, T.J., so what's your plan?"

"Wel-l-l...I was thinking if you haven't unpacked, we'd drive back to Chapel Hill, maybe watch a movie in my cozy den and then scan the sky to see if Orion might show his hunter's belt and sword. Also, there's going to be a Choral Concert at our church tomorrow afternoon that I thought you'd enjoy. You've mentioned the possibility of getting rid of the brace Monday, so I'd take you home after the concert and maybe we could get something to eat before I start home. Does that appeal to you at all?"

"Are your folks aware that I might be coming?"

"Ah,....would you mind staying with me again, Jill? Mom and Dad are taking a weekend trip together to celebrate their 35th anniversary."

"And you're talking about getting into mischief?"

"Honey," he chuckles, "I promise I won't do anything I haven't done before."

"That's enough to make me hesitate agreeing to this plan of yours, Dr. Peterson. As much as I'd love to go to the concert tomorrow and even try to find Orion tonight, I'm a bit concerned about you and your mischievous actions."

"I sincerely promise and cross my heart, Sweetie, I won't be a bad boy."

"Well, with your promise and my new defense talent, I guess I might chance some time with you. If you misbehave, I may have to steal your car and drive myself home."

"Are you as agile with your left knee as you were with your right one? You must remember not to re-injure your right knee," he chuckles.

"What time are you planning to be here? It's 7:30 already."

"How about 7:35? I'm just pulling into town. I've been driving while talking."

"You know Dad wouldn't like that. He thinks it should be a crime to talk and drive, but I'll go check myself in the mirror, get my suitcase, and be waiting."

"Thanks, Jill. You're truly a dream come true."

"Sometimes a dream doesn't turn out to be what you want, though, does it?"

"We'll discuss that later. I'm almost to your street. Are you going to be ready?"

Our trip back to Chapel Hill is full of jokes, some sarcasm, and a lot of laughs. He seems to be in a wonderful mood tonight, so could he actually be getting closer to realizing he can put Adele out of his thoughts and into his past where she belongs?

CHAPTER TWENTY-SEVEN

*W*e pop some popcorn, fill our glasses with a cold drink, and then sit down in his office-den to watch Three Coins in a Fountain. "You really dug way back, T.J., to come up with this one. I've heard of it but have never seen it. Where'd you get it anyway?"

"My grandparents gave it to me when I moved in here," he chuckles. "They thought I needed a little bit of true romantic training if I ever wanted to find a decent girl to marry. I guess Cary Grant was the tops in romance back in their day."

"He certainly was handsome, but I'd heard that Tyrone Power was the heart throb of that generation. He wasn't around as long as Cary Grant, though, so maybe that made a big difference."

As soon as he finishes his popcorn, he takes my dish away from me, too. He then lifts my legs onto the couch and after he sits back down beside me, his hands are on my shoulders and he pulls me back against his chest. He's sitting at the end of the couch and is turned slightly toward me. He's nuzzling his face in my hair and one finger is slowly making its way down my cheek, across my lips and up the other cheek. His lips are soon on my forehead, then the tip of my nose and onto my lips. "I can't watch the movie with all that going on," I moan as the kiss ends. I try to push him away, but he seems determined to pester me.

"That's really too bad, Cutie Pie. Isn't it more fun to be in the action than to just sit and watch others having all the fun?" He turns me just a little so I'm now lying across his lap with my head resting on his arm. It does make my legs a little straighter on the couch. Lifting my head with his arm, his head quickly comes forward, his lips are again on mine, and he is so masterful with those kisses.

He becomes interested in the fountain that they're tossing coins into, and I'm again sitting up with my back against his chest watching the movie. His arms are around my waist, but that is all the attention I get for at least 20 minutes. I wonder if I'll see a picture of this fountain in his collection of paintings one day.

When the movie is over, we head for the roof-top garden to watch the stars and try to find Orion. I hope we do because it sounds fascinating. He leaves just the corner lamps on tonight because the stars aren't as bright and the twinkling lights might draw away from the phenomenon of stars above us. I get to see another shooting star, but Orion will not appear. It's almost 1 o'clock when we go down to bed.

Now comes the big test. Will he act like he did last time and refuse to leave my bedroom, or will he kiss me goodnight without any of the other antics. "Would you like something to take to your room, Jill, or maybe you'd like a little dish of ice cream before we call it a night? That popcorn wasn't a start to what we would've eaten at the game."

"A little ice cream sounds pretty good. May I help dish it up?"

"Sure. There are some small dishes that you can get out while I get the ice cream out of the freezer. They're over there in that second cupboard." When he gets to the freezer, I am sure I hear him whisper, "Oh, no, I'm in trouble again." He then turns and says to me, "Jill, I only have two flavors, Chocolate or Chocolate Fudge Nut Sundae. Do you still want ice cream?"

"I'd certainly be in trouble if I didn't like chocolate, wouldn't I? But since I love it, I'll try the Fudge Nut Sundae one."

"We're getting to be more compatible all the time, Jill, and you have no idea how much that means to me. When I realized I only had the two flavors, I almost panicked as I remembered that Mom had to always have Butter Pecan or French Vanilla for you know who. I'm sorry that I even bring her name up anymore."

"That's no problem, T.J., because I understand she was a big part of your life and it left a deep impression on you. I just hope it's getting easier for you to leave that part of your life behind, though, so you can look forward to the future."

"With you in my life, Jill, I feel so sure that I can do it." We finish our ice cream, rinse the dishes and put them in the dishwasher. "Well, I can't think of anything else to do that'll keep you with me just a little while longer, so I guess we'd better say goodnight and go to bed. May I have a parting kiss to hold me until morning?"

"Let's have it here in the kitchen or in the hallway this time, Dr. Peterson, so you're not tempted to help me undress."

"How about here *and* in the hallway, My Little Sweetie Pie?" he chuckles as his arms encircle my waist from the back and his hands start moving up my sides. I slap them hard, but he only chuckles as he drops them to my waist and turns me around. His lips are so soft and warm, and I think he's now trying to drain every ounce of defense from me, so I push away and hobble as fast as I can toward the guest room. "I still get another kiss in the hallway," he's saying as he catches up to me long before I can reach the safety of my room.

"Please, T.J., don't act like you did last time because I'm tired, my knee is aching a little, and I forgot to take my medicine. I'll need a glass for water."

"O.K., Sweetheart." I receive just a peck on the cheek and he returns shortly with a glass filled with ice cubes, holds my chin in his hand for just a second, and then gives me that great dazzling smile. I'm amazed when he guides me into my room and then he's on down the hall.

It's not as exciting or terrifying as it was before, but I decide it's much better on my nerves. I take my medicine, get into my new pajamas, and crawl into the waiting bed.

When I awake in the morning and am lazily stretching after a wonderful night's rest, I'm suddenly aware that T.J. is standing in the doorway leaning against the jamb. And, of course, he has a big grin on his face which makes me realize I hadn't locked the door last night. "And just what right do you think you have standing there watching me sleep?"

"I was gonna knock, Ma'am, but the door moved a little and just came open all by itself, so what was a fella to do but take a peek?" He moves on into the room and sits down on the edge of the bed. "It's almost 9 o'clock, Miss Sleepy Head, so if we're going to church I guess you need to be getting up pretty soon."

"I slept that late? I'll get up and get dressed as soon as you leave."

"I wanna see your new pajamies," he sort of whispers as he pulls the covers off of me and then whistles. "Dey sure are purty, Ms. Hale, but I's sorta partial to those gowns you been wearin' lately."

"Did you play character parts somewhere in your past, Dr. Peterson? Maybe you should've gone into the movies.

Oh, I know, this is something you do to help your little patients try to forget about the big bad needle that's coming at them, right? Whatever, I'm not a little kid, and I'm not going to be fooled by your silliness and what you may be thinking about doing next. I want you out of this room right now so I can get up."

"Yes, Ma'am, but don't get up quite yet. I'll be right back." Those long legs of his make short work of the distance between the kitchen and this room, and he's back with two cups of coffee on a small tray. "I remember my little lady likes her coffee in the morning before any romance can take place." He puts the tray on the table by the rocker and comes to stack the pillows behind my back so I'm sitting up. He then hands me a China cup of the wonderful smelling brew and he sits down over in the rocker.

"This is awfully nice of you, T.J., but aren't we wasting a lot of time that I should be using to get dressed? You aren't planning to skip church this morning, are you?"

"Nope, as soon as you finish your coffee, I'll get my good morning kiss, and then I'll leave you so you can make yourself even more beautiful and we can go to church."

I almost gulp my coffee because I know time's slipping away. I hand him my empty cup and motion for him to leave, but I'm soon reminded that a morning kiss is now required before he'll obey that command.

He's sitting on the bed beside me again, his arm goes around my back and pulls me toward him so his lips can take full advantage of the situation. His other hand is running fingers through my hair while the thumb is caressing my cheek, but his fingers are soon on my neck and starting to creep down toward the front of my pajama top. I grab his hand and try to remove it, but he lifts his lips from mine and whispers, "Just one touch, Sweetie, and then I'll go."

I get my hands on his chest and give him a big shove which almost sends him onto the floor. "No, T.J., you promised to behave. Now go!"

He kisses my cheek and then stands up. "You're so precious, Jill, and I still don't know where all that strength comes from." He meanders out of the room, but I notice that mischievous smile on his face. What is he up to now, I wonder?

I follow him as quickly as I can and lock the door, but then I remember the bath-room is available from his den, too. I wish my knee was working a little better as I hobble in and lock that door, too, but then decide to take a quick look at my watch to see exactly how much time I have to get dressed. I almost scream and just wish I could get my hands on that prankster. It's only 8:30 now. He'd known there was plenty of time for all his goofing around but he made me sweat through it all. It's going to take some deep thought, but I *will* make him pay.

He has a wonderful breakfast ready after I'm finally dressed in one of the new pairs of slacks that Mom and I bought to go over the knee brace. They're a soft dressy fabric of gabardine and wool in chocolate brown with which I'm wearing a long-sleeved belted tunic sweater in pale yellow.

I decide to wear my hair pulled back in a big comb-style barrette but let a few tendrils fall at the sides. I get the desired whistle, but also a fabulous kiss as he pulls the chair out for me at the table.

"Am I ever going to get to sit at the counter and eat?" I ask but then see the lovely bouquet of fall flowers on the table. "The flowers are beautiful, T.J., but where did you get them so early on a Sunday morning?"

"I'm a doctor, Jill, so I made my rounds at the hospital and then stopped at the store to pick up a few items including the flowers. I'm glad you like them. To answer your other question, though, don't you remember sitting at the counter when we ate our ice cream last night? You won't be sitting there, however, whenever you look as lovely as you do now."

"You've been to the hospital already? You let me sleep until 8 o'clock, just in case your watch isn't working correctly, while you were out watching after the sick? I can see I've got a lot to learn about the medical field. Aren't you tired since we didn't get to bed until 1:30 or later?"

"I guess that's why they make us work such long hours during our medical training. We doctors can get by on very little sleep when need be."

"I admire you all for the dedication you give to your profession. I guess I've taken my doctors for granted over a good number of years, and I need to change that pronto."

"Doctors could all use an encouraging word now and then, but some of our greatest satisfactions come by seeing a patient recover from a serious illness or surgery, or keeping

SALLY M. RUSSELL

a person from having a serious problem by discovering the cause before it becomes a real danger. One of our greatest disappointments is when a person has put off coming to see a doctor for a check-up until it's too late."

❧

It's another very touching church service including the hymns How Great Thou Art and Amazing Grace. The sermon titled "Just Four Little Words" stresses how many times in each of our lives we can experience God's Most Amazing Love.

The concert doesn't start until 3 o'clock so we go for a leisurely lunch and then take a drive out around Jordon Lake. The deciduous trees are turning to their vivid fall colors of red, rust, orange, and yellow which make for a beautiful ride. We stop and take a nice walk along the lake before returning to the church. Of course, we're holding hands and also get to share a wonderful kiss or two.

The all-male choral group is outstanding as they feature a barber-shop quartet and a sextet as well as the entire group of twenty-five which almost takes my breath away. The renditions of the hymns and old-time spirituals are absolutely amazing, and they end their program by asking all of us to sing along with them on the two final selections.

While driving back home, we found ourselves singing several of the familiar hymns and discovering that our harmonizing wasn't too bad at all. "They could probably use us in the church choir when you get moved up here, Jill. Would you like to do that?"

"It might be fun if you can get to practice every week. Are you called in the evening very often?"

"Not too often. I make my rounds in the evenings, if I have patients in the hospital, but I can fit them in before or after practice."

"Let's keep the choir in our plans then. I'd really enjoy doing that together."

Mom and Dad were just getting ready to have some appetizers when we arrived, so we enjoyed a cold drink and some delicious stuffed mushrooms that Mom had just taken from the oven as well as some tortilla chips and her special guacamole dip. Of course, they then persuaded T.J. to stay for hot dogs, baked beans and a wonderful green salad before he headed back home.

CHAPTER TWENTY-EIGHT

*W*hat a way to start my vacation, but it couldn't have been any more exciting than spending a weekend with T.J. I started today with a doctor's appointment, and my hope was fulfilled when I got to throw the brace away. I'm ready now for the freedom of moving my knee without the restraint of that leather.

I remember how Jessica struggled as she tried to decide what she wanted to take to the beach, and now I'm in the same place she was as I start the sorting and packing of what I want to take with me to start my new job and adventure. I also have a small bag to pack for next weekend and I'm getting so excited.

T.J. had suggested, when he brought me home Sunday evening, that we run down to the beach to see Jessica and

C.J. before I start work at the Antique Store. "Did you have anything else you were planning to do during your short time of freedom?" he'd chuckled. "I promised to take you down there when I tried to change your plans one other weekend, so I'd like to keep my promise to you, get to see my brother, and let you see your sister. I'll get Dad to be at the Clinic Saturday morning so we can leave no later than 4:30 or 5 o'clock Friday evening, and I'll schedule my appointments on Monday afternoon so we can come back that morning."

"Are you sure, T.J.?" I'd asked. "I'd thought about driving down myself, but it'd be a lot more fun if there were the four of us."

"It's a date, Sweetie," he'd grinned as he patted my head.

Now it's Friday afternoon, I have most of my packing done and also have a small bag packed for this weekend. I'm so excited I can hardly wait and it's almost time for him to be here. "Please, God, don't let anything happen to prevent our going." I just finish my prayer when I see his car turn into the drive. I'm ready to run out to meet him, but I know he'll want to see Mom and Dad before we leave, so I make myself wait for him to get to the door. Luckily, he doesn't tarry long or I may have dragged him out of that house.

Before he starts the car, however, he has to have a kiss and I could've slapped him instead of kissing him because I'm so anxious to get going so I can see my sister. The kiss does the trick, as he most likely knew it would, since it puts me in a dreamy mood and we are soon on our way. "That's more like it," he whispers as he pats my hand which he then holds most of the way. We stop at a drive-thru and get some food when we realize it will be far past the dinner hour when we get there.

Of course, C.J. and Jessica are there to welcome us, and it is a wonderful weekend except for the difficulty for three out of the four trying to keep a secret from Jessica about my new job. Her school is getting decorated for Thanksgiving and looks so festive, and she's looking extremely happy as everything seems to be going so well. The hours fly by as we do so many things, see much more of the beach than when we were here before and Jessica and I both found outfits on sale that we can put back for next summer.

She asks the guys if the two of us can be excused fairly early Sunday night, and she proceeds to hand me a pair of brand new scissors to help her cut out some of the cute Pilgrim collars and caps that will be used at Thanksgiving time. She hints that she'll get C.J. to help her with the Indian headbands, but she really appreciates my help with the Pilgrim outfits. I wonder if this time of separation was planned by her and C.J. so the guys could also have a heart to heart talk. We certainly take the opportunity to have one of our sister talks, but these days they are mostly about two handsome brothers.

❦

We watch with C.J. as the little ones arrive Monday morning, like my family had done in September, and now we're on our way back to Sanford. "She is such a great gal for that brother of mine," T.J. sighs as we drive along. I'm not sure just how to take the sigh, but decide not to ask. He soon continues, "I want to be as happy as C.J. is, Jill, and when I'm with you I feel like I am. It's only when I'm alone and start thinking about all the things that can go wrong in a relationship that I get back into my doubting mood. It's not as often, though, and I think this weekend has helped a lot, especially after the private talk I had with C.J. last night when you girls deserted us. Are you still willing to give me the little more time we agreed on since you most likely had a sister to sister talk with Jessica, too?"

"I promised I would be there for you until after the Christmas holidays, T.J., so I'll be around as much as you want me to be for the remaining two months. When I get moved to Chapel Hill, we can be together more often, if you'd like, and we'll see if that helps or hinders your situation."

"It certainly can't hurt, Sweetie, because I feel so content when I'm with you. It's like you're a balm to my heart and soul. By the way, there are two things I need to talk to you about. I just glanced at the invitation to the Charity dinner and dance that came in the mail Friday and it's going to be on Saturday, November 11th. It's a rather fancy dress-up occasion, so are you all right with that just after we've been to the beach?"

"Since I have the brace off my knee, I'm ready for anything, but does a fancy dress-up occasion mean any length dress, or should it be an ankle length formal?"

"You'll see all lengths that night, but I'd just as soon see you in a somewhat shorter dress so you're not fighting all that extra material and I can see those beautiful legs." Of course, his lashes are fluttering, his eyebrows are arching, and that mischievous grin is on his face.

"I think I'd better check out my big assortment of long formals," I smirk. "What's the other thing you wanted to talk to me about?"

"What are your plans for getting things up to the folks' and starting your work at the store? Will it be before the 11th and do you want me to help in any way?"

"Thank goodness, all that I'm bringing with me right now will fit in my car. I had planned to drive up Friday, get it unloaded and then try to get you to take me to the game. Now, of course, we may have to miss the game because of the Charity dinner Saturday night. I was probably being a little too presumptuous anyway."

"Of course you were, Ms. Hale, because I was all set to take a special friend to that game, but I luckily hadn't gotten around to asking yet. I don't know what I should do about the game or the dinner now. What do you think I should do about my situation?"

"Maybe you'll have to disappoint both of us. It'd probably be for the best because you wouldn't want to be going with either one if it'd make you feel bad about cancelling the other date,. I wouldn't think you'd want one to feel like a discarded or unwanted friend, would you?"

"Heaven forbid that should happen, but I think I'll plan on taking both of you to the game Friday night, which should prove to be a barrel of fun," he chuckles. "You will be willing to sit on my lap, won't you, since there is only one extra seat?"

"T.J., be serious for a minute. Is there someone else you were going to ask to go to the game with you? I'm sorry I made that comment because I really shouldn't assume that I get to go to all the games."

He's really laughing by the time he turns into the driveway at my folks. "I do love teasing you, Jill, but you are the only 'two' I want to take to the game. I guess, if you're moving up on Friday, I won't be driving down to get you since I assume you'll want your car up there now that it's all fixed after the accident."

"Yes, I'll want my car, and I was thinking about getting there Friday afternoon so I could go to the store with your mother on Saturday morning. It will be over three weeks since I've been there, though, so maybe I should come early Friday morning and get all the end of October entries done. That way, I can get started on November Saturday morning and be ready to start work on the computer by the middle of next week. I'll try to talk to your mother later today or tomorrow."

"You're so dedicated to a project when you take one on, and I love that special way you seem to dig in to do the things you want to accomplish. The bank is going to miss you. You are everything I've looked for in my special someone, and I really need to get my head on straight. I'll come over to the house Friday after office hours and see what the situation is. I can hardly wait for the Charity Dinner this year."

He walks me to the door, kisses my forehead and then my lips. "I'd better be on my way because I do have appointments this afternoon. I'll see you Friday. Have fun for these few days you have left of your short vacation, and I'll probably pester you with phone calls. I hope you enjoyed the weekend."

"Thank you so much, T.J., I really did enjoy the trip. Please drive carefully now and may God keep you safe. Bye, now." I watch as he does his usual toot and wave when he reaches the street, and then he's on his way to those lucky patients. No one is home so I go upstairs to my room, recheck my moving items and reminisce about the weekend.

What a wonderful time we'd had at the beach, and I can hardly wait for this next weekend when I'll become a part of his family, in a way, since I'll be living in his parents' home, and I'll hopefully get to be with T.J. more often. What my future is really going to be like, I don't know yet, but I feel that God is leading and I'm ready to follow wherever it may take me. I wonder if T.J. has prayed about his situation over the years, or if he's ever thought about putting it completely in God's hands.

After talking to Mrs. Peterson, I make a list of the things I'd like to do the next three days. I'm going shopping tomorrow morning to see if I can find a suitable dress and shoes for this dressy affair that we'll be attending. I want to go to my golf lesson tomorrow after-noon so I can see Ellie and Penny one more time. I'm going to call some friends and throw a nice going-away party Wednesday night and then have a family get-together on Thursday night. I think that should keep me busy and having fun for three days. Of course, the most exciting will be Friday when I get to see T.J. again, start working at that amazing antique store, and then going to the Charity dinner that has me a little apprehensive.

Well, it's Thursday already and everything has gone well except I haven't been pestered with calls from T.J. like he hinted I would be, and that bothers me a little. Did he think I needed some time with the family like when Jessica was leaving, or is he the one wanting the time to ponder his own next steps? This uncertainty is hard to deal with, and I'm beginning to wonder if it's a trait that would always be there to confront us if we were to ever marry. Maybe he has lived with this fear of being the victim of women far too long, and I'm wasting my time with any dreams I'm having of a future with him. As we'd talked in one of our earlier conversations, maybe all he does want is a convenient companion to spend time with. Well, I'm going to enjoy it while it lasts, and I'll let God make the final decision because that will be the right one for both of us.

The family dinner is great, but Jodi is tiring more easily now since she's already in her seventh month of pregnancy, so she and Richard are getting ready to leave. There are hugs, tears, more hugs, best wishes for the future, and then more hugs, but everyone is so happy that I'm getting a chance to do something that will be close to what I'd dreamed about for such a long time. To learn from the very competent Mrs. Peterson on how to work in different type homes and around the beautiful furniture gives me a thrill that is hard to describe.

I'm up quite early Friday morning to have breakfast with Mom and Dad, and since I'd packed the car yesterday, I'm ready to leave. Of course, there's more tears and hugs, but I'm soon on my way and actually get to the Peterson home before Mrs. Peterson leaves for the store. She helps me carry the hanging clothes in, so I show her the dress that Mom and I had selected for the Charity dinner tomorrow night. I had looked, modeled, and looked some more but couldn't decide from the three or four that I liked. I'd finally called my own trusted clothes expert and asked that she make the final selection. She'd immediately given the clerk back two that were pretty but not the color for a first appearance with T.J.'s group of doctors, etc. That left the two black ones and after I'd modeled them for her, she'd also picked the one that I was hoping she would.

"It's absolutely gorgeous, Jill, and you'll look stunning in it," Mrs. Peterson was quickly remarking. "I hope T.J. can see that you're a wonderfully considerate, beautiful Christian girl, and he would be a fool to let you get away," she chuckles. "I'll run along now, but you take your time and get settled before you come to the store."

It doesn't take long to put my things in the drawers of the unique antique dresser that I've admired each time I've stayed here. I arrange my hanging clothes a little better in the closet, and then arrive at the store a little after ten-thirty and begin to tackle the stack of papers waiting for me on the desk.

Mrs. Peterson, of course, apologizes for the backlog, but I remind her that I'm the one who hasn't been here for about three weeks, and actually, it really isn't that bad. There are no interruptions, except for a sandwich at lunch that we have delivered, so by 4 o'clock I have all the month's invoices entered, the checks written and the statements ready to mail. It'll be easy to take a trial balance tomorrow morning and then possibly enter the first nine or ten days of November. Mrs. Peterson sees me closing the book and only then does she come to stand beside me.

"I don't know how you do all that, Jill, and in such a short time. Why don't you run on home now, because T.J. told me he's coming over to see you after office hours today? I certainly wouldn't want him accusing me of working you too hard or keeping him from seeing you," she laughs.

"Thanks, Mrs. Peterson, I do need to stretch my back and legs so I'll scoot now and see what your son has on his mind."

"Most likely a game. I believe there's a basketball game here tonight so I hope you like basketball. I think T.J. enjoys the basketball season more than he does football. Brian and I won't be able to attend this one because we have another commitment."

"He did mention a game when he was telling me about the Charity dinner tomorrow night. I love basketball so I hope he's planning to go. I'll see you later."

CHAPTER TWENTY-NINE

*W*e did get to the exciting basketball game which UNC won easily. T.J. seemed to be one excited guy watching the game and didn't hesitate to yell when he didn't like a call, or cheer when the ball went in the basket. Now, it's Saturday evening and I can hardly believe I've spent almost two full days here already. It's time to get ready for the Charity dinner.

The weather is perfect for all the people who will be dressed in their finest, and I think T.J. is almost spellbound when I come into the living room. My dress has a strapless bodice in a rich black polyester with tiny stitches of silver thread scattered here and there which makes it almost shimmer. A matching tight fitting short jacket that features a small lapel and tiny black buttons down the front is the only wrap I'll need. The slightly flared skirt falls just an inch below the knee and I'm wearing black high-heeled sandals that are barely there. I have my hair pulled back with a silver barrette holding it high on my head and little wisps falling around my face and neck. I'm wearing a silver choker that forms a solid Y in front which has tiny crystal chips sparkling like diamonds, and my fairly small diamond earrings go well with my outfit.

"Wow," is all he can say but he has that approving smile on his face that I've seen a few other times. Of course, I'm a little captivated myself as he stands there in a Tux and looks better than any dreamboat I've ever seen in a movie.

"You look mighty handsome tonight, T.J., so are we ready to go and see how many we can give something to talk about? I have the ring in my purse if you decide you'd like me to wear it."

"I don't think we'll need to make false claims tonight, Jill. Just having you with me looking like a beautiful angel will be enough to turn quite a few heads."

There are four sitting at the round table for eight when we arrive, and I'm surprised to see that Dr. Hall and his wife are one of the couples. Although he had talked to me as if he knew T.J. pretty well, I guess I wasn't expecting to see him socially.

"Well, Jill, it's good to see you all healed up and ready to party," he chuckles. "I'd like you to meet my wife, Debra. Honey, this is Jill Hale, the one I told you about who had a cracked kneecap in that accident. She's been dating T.J. for a few months now."

Turning toward T.J., he continues, "How's it feel, My Friend, having a lovely lady by your side to admire, dance with, and of course, cuddle up close to?"

"It's pretty nice to have a close friend you can trust and confide in, David, but don't be getting any other ideas in that head of yours."

Dr. Hall glances at me but I can only smile, squint my eyes a little, and barely do a shake of my head to let him know the situation hasn't changed much since we'd had our talk in his office. He puts his arm across T.J.'s shoulders and they walk a little ways from the table. I just hope he doesn't do anything to make matters worse between T.J. and me.

Debra introduces me to the other couple and they immediately make me feel at ease. It's another doctor and his wife, and the fourth couple arrives as Dr. Hall and T.J. return to the table. After those introductions, he takes me to the dance floor for two or three dances. "Don't let them bother you with all their questions and insinuations, Sweetie. Just tell them we're friends and it's too soon for them to be drawing any conclusions."

Actually, they aren't bothering me, but they do try to tease T.J. and get him to admit how I'm fitting into his life. He's decisively quiet and just keeps taking me to the dance floor instead of giving them any answers. I can see the smiles and maybe hopes on their faces, though, as their chairs have been turned to watch the dance floor.

When they finally get a chance to ask me about my work, I excitedly tell them that I'm coming to the Antique Store to set up the new computer with all the financial needs, and also the plans for me to learn all the facets of the business from Mrs. Peterson. I notice that the wives are all smiling now as if they'd just received some hot news off the press and I suddenly realize how my remarks must've sounded. My face is turning hot and red, I'm afraid, as I struggle to explain that T.J. and I are just friends. They just continue to smile and graciously agree that they'll probably see me at the store, especially with Christmas so close now. They just love to shop for those special and unusual presents that the Antique Store carries for the holidays.

I timidly glance at T.J. to see how much steam or smoke is rising above his head, or shooting out of his eyes, but he is only looking at me with that mischievous smile that has the dimple very prominent in his cheek. He puts his arm across my shoulders, pulls me to him so he can kiss my cheek, and then whispers, "Let's dance, Sweetie."

T.J. holds me so tenderly, kisses the top of my head, and squeezes my hand, but all I can think about is my stupid mistake of talking when I should've kept quiet. I know I'm shaking and there's nothing I can do about it. When is he going to tell me it's over and he wants nothing more to do with me?

We finally return to the table, the music stops, and someone has gotten up to speak. He congratulates the doctors for raising the largest amount of money for this year's charity, plus two or three other groups for their efforts. He then announces the total amount which has been raised. Of course, that brings a big round of applause. It's an enormous amount in my eyes, but everyone else at our table seems to accept it as rather normal.

Glasses have been filled with champagne at each plate, we are asked to stand, and the evening ends with a toast.

"It may have cooled off a little by now, Jill, so you'd better put your jacket on," T.J. says as he holds it very politely for me. As I'm buttoning it, I'm afraid to look at him for fear I'll see the anger that I know must be there in his eyes. He turns toward the others and does the usual goodnights and it's been nice seeing all of you. He then turns back to me, takes me by the elbow and guides me toward the door. I hear "Goodnight, Jill, we've all enjoyed meeting you," but I have my eyes staring at the floor as I try to make my feet keep pace with his long strides. Dr. Hall catches up with us when we reach the door and tries to whisper to T.J. "We're so sorry, T.J. The girls didn't mean to upset her. They don't know all the circumstances."

"Don't worry, David. She was only trying to follow my instructions which were impossible with your lovely wives around. It's my job to console her," T.J. softly replies.

I don't hear any more of it, because I'm trying to brace myself for whatever may be coming, but I never would have been ready for what happens when we reach the car.

He turns so that his back is against the door of the car and then pulls me to him. He lifts my chin and I finally see that the smile and dimple are still there. "You were the most beautiful person there tonight, Jill, and I was never so proud of anyone in my life. You are so sweet, so adorable, so soft and huggable, so honest and genuine, even though a little too naive at times, that everyone, especially at our table, wanted to wrap their arms around you so they could protect you from themselves.

I tried to shelter you by keeping you on the dance floor as much as possible, but I knew deep down that they'd get the information they wanted sooner or later. I also knew, when it happened and you saw their smiles, that you'd realized very quickly what they'd probably assumed from your words, and I could only smile and love you for it.

The only thing I didn't expect was that you would be so afraid of what I might do or say. You were shaking so hard that I knew I had to get you out of there so I could reassure you. You are special to me, Jill Marie Hale, and I'm so sorry if I've given you any cause to be afraid of me." He is just bending down to kiss me when sounds of people approaching the parking lot are heard. He opens the door for me and then goes around to get in on the driver's side.

I'm not sure where he's going, but I know it isn't toward his parents. I soon see that he's turning in at his condo and I'm not sure this is a good idea after the speech he has just made about his feelings and such. "T.J., I don't think we should stop at your condo tonight. It might not be the right time after such an emotional evening. Don't you think you should take me on to your parents?"

"Please give me just a few minutes, Jill, to be with you alone and give you a proper romantic kiss. You know, you've been here for two whole days and I haven't had you to myself except to walk you to the door after the game last night. I just want a chance now to hold you in that beautiful dress and kiss you with a little more meaning than a mere friend. Do you remember that Jesus commanded His disciples to love one another and for all of us to love our neighbors as ourselves," he chuckles. "If I love a neighbor as much as I do myself, just think how much I should love a friend."

"You are impossible, T.J., but I guess I can give you a few minutes if you'll put some coffee on. I need to get rid of that champagne, but there's no use you trying to smooth over the actions of those ladies tonight. I'm not sure they'll ever be my friend."

When the coffee is ready, we sit in the den and start to watch some late news. It's not at all what we want, so he turns to the movie channel and we start watching "One Flew Over The Cuckoo's Nest."

Of course, I'm not quite through with my coffee when he takes my cup and sets it, along with his, on the coffee table. Immediately he pulls me into his arms and I receive the long awaited romantic kiss, but now he's unbuttoning my jacket. "Isn't that a little warm to have on in here with my arms around you? You didn't wear it at the dinner." He slides it off my shoulders and carefully lays it on one of the chairs. He had taken his tux jacket, vest and tie off as soon as we'd stepped inside the door, and now he's slipped off his shoes and unbuttoned the top three or four buttons of his shirt.

"You did say just a few minutes, T.J., so let's not get so relaxed that you won't want to take me home."

"O.K." he chuckles as he's sitting sideways with one foot on the floor and the other knee bent and lying on the couch. His arms are sort of stretched out holding my shoulders, and he's just looking me over from my head to my toes. Of course, I'd kicked off my new sandals just inside the front door so I'm somewhat curled up on the couch. "How do you girls keep those pretty strapless dresses from slipping down?" he asks so innocently as he gives it a little tug at the waist.

"Just never you mind, Dr. Peterson, about how these dresses stay up. That is for the girls to know and for the guys to never find out," I chuckle.

"Oh, I wouldn't bet on that, Ms. Hale." he whispers as he changes his position, his arms enfold me and he quickly finds the zipper down the back of the dress. In seconds, he has it unzipped and I'm holding it up as best I can. He's smiling as he takes my hands and pulls them away so the bodice drops to my waist. "Wow, Sweetie, what kind of a new idea have they come up with now? It's awful pretty, but do I get to take if off of you tonight?"

"No, T.J., the few minutes are up and you're going to take me home." I try to stand, but his hands are on my waist and then I'm on his lap. "My dress is going to be ruined and that's a lot of money to spend on a dress to wear only one night. Let me up and then you take me home. You promised, T.J. Otherwise, I'll call a cab."

"Why don't you take the dress completely off and let me hold you while we watch the rest of the movie? I need to study this new garment of yours because doctors need to keep up with new things in case they confront them in an emergency. What kind of a name did they put on it anyway?" he chuckles.

"I'm not sure. It's supposed to eliminate the possible bulges between the bra and panty and keep everything smooth under a rather tight fitting dress. Now, come on and take me home. I hope this isn't the way you act whenever you've had a glass or two of wine."

"No, Sweetie, but you are so beautiful tonight and you have me in a very unfamiliar mood that I don't want to stop. It's not right but I just wish I could keep you all night."

I try to get up but he pulls me back so I'm lying on his left arm while the other is getting ready to examine my clothes which he must think is a new plaything for him. He isn't watching too closely because my left hand comes up and slaps his face pretty hard. I hope he's not black and blue tomorrow, but he's got to learn that I'm not a complete push over for his playful mood.

"I want to go home, T.J., and I want to go now. Are you going to take me, or do I call a cab?"

He looks a little shocked as he helps me to my feet. "I'm sorry, Jill, I don't know what came over me. I've never acted like this before but you have made me feel like I've never felt before. I'll take you home. Just let me zip the dress back up for you."

"I'll zip it myself, thank you." I stomp through the bathroom into the guest room and I'm trying to hold the dress up as I move away from him. I know zipping it back up isn't the easiest thing to do, but I got it done earlier and I can do it again. I'm angry, I'm hurt, I'm confused, and I'm just a little sorry because I've probably lost him, but I can't go on like this any longer.

The next and the last words that are spoken tonight are mine. "I'm ready to go."

CHAPTER THIRTY

My eyes are pretty puffy Sunday morning after all the crying I'd done last night. T.J. had walked me to the door, held it open until I was inside, and then had left without saying one word. The ride home had been silent, too, but I'd been determined I wasn't going to be the one to start a conversation with an apology like I'd done a few times before. I'm just hoping a cool shower will help now and maybe some of my eye cream will soothe and make me appear a little more rested.

I go to church with his parents but T.J. isn't there. They don't seem to be concerned so I assume T.J. must've talked to them this morning and they're planning to stay out of the situation. I can't say that I blame them--this is definitely between T.J. and me. Whatever side they might choose to favor could create a difficult problem. I don't think I hear much of the sermon, but I'm there and the music does wonders for me.

I decide to scan the Classified section of the paper in the afternoon to see if I can find an apartment. I don't feel right putting Dr. and Mrs. Peterson in this predicament so I'll try to find another place to live. I go to my room under the pretense of reading, but I search the ads for at least two hours. Most are for multiple renters since it's a college town, and they are much more expensive than I can afford on my own. I'll just have to keep looking.

The Petersons had gone to visit her parents so I decide to go for a ride and stop at a shopping center that is having a pre-holiday sale. I enjoy browsing through a few stores and find a nice pair of slacks and a sweater for a great price which raises my spirits a little. I remember to buy a few needed cosmetics, and then get a cool drink and sandwich before returning home. No one is home so I go to my room and put my purchases away. I then read the devotion and Bible verses for the day from a book my parents had given me way back on my 21st birthday. I don my pajamas and apparently fall asleep.

᷍

I've been working with the technician all week now getting the programs entered and set up. By mid-afternoon on Friday, he finally feels he's gotten all the unneeded programs removed and it's ready for me to start entering the names of accounts, both Accounts Payable and Accounts Receivable, Payroll, etc. As he heads for the door, he gives me a big smile and says to call him if I have any problems. I know what I'd like to call him since he's been another egotistical guy and a pain to work with, but I give him a quick half smile and say, "I hope you have a nice Thanksgiving." I feel it's too late to start anything on the computer today so I get the regular posting arranged and start to catch up on some of that and I'll finish up tomorrow morning. The computer can wait until Monday.

About 3 o'clock I hear Mrs. Peterson talking and laughing with someone who has just entered the store. Shortly, she and this casually dressed handsome hunk of a guy are standing beside my desk. "Jill, I'd like you to meet my very good right arm and leg, Isaac Stormison. Isaac is a scout, of sorts, who travels a lot in his other job and keeps his eyes and ears open for good deals in antiques. He's found some great items for me the last few years. Isaac, this is my new financial whiz, Jill Hale, who is finally putting the store on a computer and maybe changing my entire life."

"Hi, Jill," he chuckles, "I must say you're a big improvement over the other book-keeper who wasn't going to let a computer come through the doors of this store no matter what." He picks up my left hand, which is the closest to him. "I see you're not wearing a ring so I assume you're neither engaged nor married. Maybe I can persuade you to have lunch with me when I come by after Thanksgiving. Could that be a possibility?"

"Not at the moment, Isaac, but who knows what might happen in the future?"

Luckily, Mrs. Peterson had gone to help another customer so I didn't have to worry about that remark. T.J. has not bothered to call, drop by, or even send a note via his dad since the Charity dinner, so I have no idea what is going on in his head or what his plans are. If he's talked to his dad about the problem, I have heard nothing about it, so how am I to know what to do or think? Of course, he could be thinking the same thing, couldn't he? After all, I was the one who slapped his face and demanded to be taken home. Oh, shucks, why is it always me who feels guilty and has to give in?

"From your expression, Jill, I think your thoughts are many miles away from here, possibly thinking about someone who is on your black list at the moment. You know you love the guy but something a little unusual has happened and you don't want to be the one to apologize. Am I anywhere close to what you're facing right now?"

I just stare at this guy who doesn't even know me, but still has put his finger on the problem I'm facing. "How did you do that? I didn't say anything except who knows what might happen in the future."

"That's enough for a guy to understand that you have a problem with another love so you're just cracking the door a little for self preservation. I'll be watching you closely, Jill, because you seem to be someone I'd very much like to get acquainted with. You have to be an outstanding person if

Mrs. Peterson wants you to work for her in this capacity, and I can see that you like what you're doing here. I enjoyed meeting you, I hope you have a nice Thanksgiving, and that things work out well with this lucky guy, but only if it's God's will."

"Thanks, Isaac, I appreciate that. Do you have a family you're going to be with on Thanksgiving? I'd hate to think that you're going to be alone or traveling."

"My parents are expecting me in Charleston, but there're also siblings and in-laws, plus nieces and nephews. I'm the youngest of the siblings and the only one unmarried, but I have two brothers and a sister, three in-laws, four active nephews and two very sweet nieces. I'm really looking forward to seeing all of them, but I'll be back to see you soon." He turns and heads for the door after saying goodbye to Mrs. Peterson.

I smile as I close the books. For some reason, my mind isn't on invoices or checks.

Dr. and Mrs. Peterson have plans for tonight so I stop and pick up a deli sandwich and a drink on my way home. I go to my room and plop down on the edge of the bed and start staring at the phone. I'm wondering if I really want to bare my soul again to a guy who keeps making me doubt his sincerity. The remark that Isaac made about my being in love with someone but didn't want to be the first to apologize, though, keeps reminding me that I don't want to lose him. I know I apparently have to make an attempt to save that love if it's possible to do so. His pride may be getting in his way.

I check my watch to make sure he would've had time to get home, and again I look at the phone. "The worst thing you can do is refuse to talk to me, T.J., so I guess I'll give you that chance. You've got me talking to myself now, so a talk should let me see just how sincere all your sweet and admiring remarks have been these past few months, and then I'll determine if there is really a future for us." I try to dial rather slowly, but he answers on the second ring. "Hey, T.J., this is Jill."

"I'd know your voice anywhere, Jill. What can I do for you this evening?"

He sounds a little sad but also a bit reserved and maybe uninterested. "Would you like to talk to me, or would you rather I hang up? I think it's time for us to make a decision one way or another on whether we're going to be friends or not."

"I'd love to talk to you, Jill, if you're sure you want to talk to me. I've been told that it would serve me right if you never spoke to me again. I don't know how to say it, Jill, but it's really hard for me to admit that I'm a failure. I guess, like Romans 7:15 says, 'I do not understand what I do. For what I want to do I do not do, but what I hate I do.' It certainly describes me when it comes to matters of the heart."

"Would it be easier for you to continue this conversation on the phone, T.J., or is there a chance you'd like to talk face to face?"

"May I take you to dinner?"

"I'll be waiting. I even have a new outfit I'm dying to wear and get your opinion."

He must've exceeded the speed limit because he's here really fast and it turns out to be a wonderful evening. I order a salad and he orders a bowl of soup; we then just look at each other and start laughing. Neither of us had wanted to mention that we had already eaten. We actually discuss a lot of things, including the Thanksgiving plans, our feelings for one another, his terrible week, my progress at work, and last but not least I tell him about Isaac and how he read my mind.

"Didn't Mom tell you that he graduated about four years ago from a theological seminary and is right now filling interim positions around the country? I understand that he is very good with young people and usually fills the youth minister's position. He'd love to have his own church someday, but he's also interested in doing some foreign missionary work if the opportunity arises. I think he speaks three or four languages. Mom thinks the world of him, and he's found some outstanding antiques for her in his travels."

"Wow, that *is* amazing. I'll have to remember to treat him with greater respect when he comes back and wants to take me to lunch after Thanksgiving." I can't hold back a giggle when I see the surprised expression on T.J.'s face.

"He wants to take you to lunch, does he? Would you like to be a minister's wife or a missionary in a faraway country?"

"It sounds like quite an adventure, but I think I'm pretty satisfied with my life as it is right now." My mind, however, is desperately trying to recall a conversation I'd had with Sara during a lunch break recently.

"I'm really glad to hear that," he whispers as he's studying my face expression.

Conversation continues to flow freely and easily, but when he finally gets me back home, he walks me to the door with his arm across my shoulders. He slowly turns me toward him and asks, "May I have just a little goodnight kiss, Jill?"

"I can't think of anyone's kiss that I'd rather have, T.J." He very lightly touches my lips with his, but my arms go around his neck and I'm determined to have a kiss that both of us will remember as we fall asleep tonight. "I'm sorry, T.J., but it's been so long since I've had one of your kisses, I just couldn't help myself." I couldn't hide my satisfied smile.

"Don't apologize, Jill. I'm just so afraid of doing something wrong again that I'm thrilled you took the initiative. By the way, is this the new outfit you wanted to show me?" He holds me at arm's length as his eyes travel from my eyes to my feet. "The color of the sweater looks great on you; it brings out the sparkle in your eyes and it feels so soft, it has to be cashmere." He now has that mischievous look in his eyes that I've seen before, and his hands are moving up and down my arms for a few seconds, but then he backs away. "I'd better go before I get myself into trouble again by not being able to keep my hands off you. Goodnight, Sweetheart."

"Goodnight, T.J. Thanks for a great evening." As I climb the stairs to my room, I'm expecting to have wonderful dreams tonight, but I can't wait to see Sara tomorrow.

I'm able to get all the posting done Saturday morning and I take Sara out for lunch. She's working with Jane this afternoon but Jane is having lunch with her big handsome husband. I was able to confirm that Sara is thinking about joining the Peace Corps and does speak three languages. We also have time to browse through some different stores and I'm really thrilled when I find a darling coat that is 60% off. The check I received from the bank has come in pretty handy for getting some new clothes that were greatly reduced. I notice Sara going back to look at a sweater two or three times so I add it to my coat sale and then present it to her.

"Jill, you can't do that," she protested, but I told her about the check and that I'd consider it a getting acquainted present. I know how little money students have even when they work and I was elated to see that smile as she let the clerk put it in a separate bag.

No one is home when I get there, so I go up to my room to hang up my new coat. My cell phone starts ringing and I again smile as I wonder if Dad will cancel it if it's used for non-emergency calls.

"Is this an emergency?" I ask and then hear chuckling on the other end. "T.J., what are you up to now? I just got home from another shopping spree and I hope you'll really be happy with my purchase."

"I'm sure I will be, but I also have a surprise. Mom and Dad can't go to the game again tonight, so I was wondering if you'd mind if I let Dr. Hall and Debra use the tickets. They haven't been able to get season tickets since moving here, but Mom and Dad have given them their tickets before and they've enjoyed the games. They're on a waiting list so maybe they'll have their own next year."

"I didn't know that you were going to a game tonight, T.J., but since I won't be there, it doesn't matter to me if you give them the tickets or not."

"Why won't you be there, Jill? I thought you loved basketball."

"I do, but I don't remember being asked."

"Oops, another mark against me. Sweetheart, will you please go to the game with me tonight? I just took it for granted, I guess, that you'd go whenever I go. I'm so sorry."

"Well, your convenient companion has been a little upset with the doctor lately, and I'm afraid I need some proper treatment for you to get back in my good graces."

"Do you want me to come over right now and try to get myself back in your good graces, Ms. Hale, or could it be before, during, and after the game tonight?"

"You have an answer for everything, don't you? I'll be ready to go to the game, Dr. Peterson, but don't expect me to be putty in your hands tonight."

"Thank you, Sweetie. I'll see you at 6:00. Bye, now."

I still don't know why I put up with him, my mind keeps asking, but my heart is overjoyed that I have my exasperating friend back again.

CHAPTER THIRTY-ONE

*T*hanksgiving is tomorrow and I'm watching out the window so I won't miss C.J. and Jessica pulling into the drive. I'm wondering what she'll think when she sees my car sitting there. Well, I won't have long to wait now because I can look across one of the greens on the golf course and see his old Caddy coming down the main street before it'll make a turn and go around a curve before it reaches our driveway.

As soon as the car stops, I'm out the door and have my sister in my arms. Of course, her first question is, "What are you doing here?"

"That's a story I'm dying to tell you," and I'm dragging her into the house as I see T.J.'s car pull into the drive. Through tears and smiles, I tell her a short version of how I now have a new job, but not exactly certain about my future with T.J. The plans for her riding with me tomorrow and the guys coming down on Friday are included, and then we hear a knock on the door. The guys are standing there with Jessica's suitcase and also an invitation for some appetizers in the den. The rest of the evening is almost as if we were a family gathered to celebrate the Thanksgiving holiday and hear the plans for a wedding coming up soon. Of course, no one had seen the ring, which is beautiful, so there are a few oohs and aahs, and the obvious question of when is the wedding.

"I'm hoping to see my pastor while I'm home and then I'll be able to answer more of your questions with positive dates, times, and places," Jessica graciously replied.

The ride to Sanford Thursday morning is filled with plans for the weekend, and we are so lucky when everything falls into place. Thanksgiving dinner with the family is great, as usual, and then Jess and I unexpectedly run into Pastor Steve while we're out walking. By Friday afternoon, the arrangements at the church have been made, we find both her gown and my Maid of Honor dress, and talk with Mom about the reception and decorating the church. The flowers are to be her responsibility, too, although Jess and I decide which flowers we want for our bouquets.

The guys arrive a little later than they'd planned because of a sick child that T.J. had to admit to the hospital, but it all works out fine. We eat pizza, Jess and C.J. go to have the conference with the pastor, and then the four of us take in a movie. Saturday, for sure, is a day of saying goodbyes again and packing a few more things into the trunk of my car, but T.J. and I are finally on our way back to Chapel Hill by mid-afternoon.

"How about going by the riding stable and see if we can rent a couple of horses?" he asks when we reach the city limits.

We'd used the walking trails a few times, but there had never been any horses available. "I can imagine, on a holiday weekend, they'll all be taken again, but it's worth a try," I reply. I haven't told T.J. that Jess and I did quite a bit of riding before we went off to college. I've let him assume that I would be a beginner so I can surprise him when we do get to ride.

To our delight, there are two in the corral, but then we're told they are a little frisky so only the staff has ridden them so far. T.J. is ready to say we'd better not chance it when I speak up, "I'm willing to try riding them if you are."

"Are you sure?" He glances at me unbelievingly, and then I see the lights go on in his eyes when he realizes that I've been on horses before. "You've been holding out on me, Ms. Hale, but if you're game, I certainly am."

Holly and Pepper are two wonderful yearlings, who are eager to get right out and start trotting, but I reach out and pat Holly's neck and talk softly to her and she very quickly slows to a gentle walk since we're still on the narrow trail. T.J. must've done the same but he comes along side me when we reach the wider track. "If we take the turn-off up ahead, we can soon be in the meadow area. Not too many riders get off the regular trail so we can let them trot or maybe even gallop if you're familiar with that."

I know he's watching to see what my reaction will be so I just give him a smug grin.

"O.K., Smartie, so you've galloped before, but I do think you'll enjoy feeling the wind blowing through your hair and getting to smell the freshness of all these wonderful meadow grasses. This is what's so great about living in this part of the country. You get to enjoy the pleasant weather almost all year. Here's the turn so are you ready to go?"

"I'm right with you." We ride for almost two hours before we reluctantly return to the stables. There had been a pond where we'd stopped and let the horses drink and rest for a few minutes, but they seemed to enjoy the chance we gave them to really run. It had been invigorating, but since it has been a few years since I've ridden, I'm afraid I'll be a little sore in the morning.

"Do you think we'll be able to walk into church tomorrow and fool everyone about being on these horses?" I laugh.

"Speak for yourself, Ms. Hale. This cowboy never gets sore," he chuckles as he pretends to hobble on to the car. On the way to his folks, he remarks, "I suppose I'd better head home and get cleaned up since I'll have to make a trip to the hospital. Dad checked on my patient last night and this morning, but I need to see him tonight."

"Will I see you in church tomorrow?"

"I'm definitely planning to go so save me a seat, or I'll save you one if I happen to get there first. You know, the choir might be getting ready to start the practices for their Christmas cantata, so we should be joining if we still want to do that. We can talk about it and decide what we want to do tomorrow. Right now, if you're willing, I need a kiss to hold me until I can find a time and place to kiss you tomorrow."

He walks me to the door, gets a gentle kiss, and then quickly heads to his car that has been in the family garage while we were in Sanford. I visit with his parents for a few minutes and then go to my room. I must admit that I'm rather tired and realize that I haven't eaten since lunch, but I really want sleep more than I do food. After I shower, I drink a large glass of water and get into my pajamas. I then curl up in bed with my Bible, but I've only read for a few minutes and I know it's only about 8 o'clock, but my eyes close and I awake Sunday morning with my Bible still open beside me.

≋

With our work, choir practice, basketball games, and even some more riding, the days are flying by. I do get to talk to Sara some more about her plans for the future, and I had remembered correctly that she'd told me about taking a Christian Bible study class, she wants to join the Peace Corps and work with the needy in some foreign country.

Sara is working more, now that the Christmas shopping has started and classes are dismissed for the holidays, so when Isaac shows up on Friday, the 1st of December, I'm so excited. Mrs. Peterson has gone to an estate sale, Sara is dusting on the far side of the store, and Jane is helping a customer. Jake, our muscles, whom we can call if needed, is in the storeroom. Isaac comes directly back to my desk with a big smile and a greeting. "Jill Marie Hale, as if I could forget such a pretty girl or her name. I feel like my return has taken forever, but I'm here now to ask if you'll go to lunch with me."

"I'm sorry, Isaac, but the someone I was upset with has been apologized to and we are an item again, sort of, but I have someone I'd love for you to meet. Sara is graduating mid-term and has been taking a Bible study class, speaks three languages besides English, and is thinking about joining the Peace Corps. Her favorite foreign language is Spanish but she can also speak French and Italian. She's over there dusting, so take a look and see if you'd be interested in meeting her."

"You've got to be kidding, Jill, she's beautiful! You'll always hold a special spot in my heart, but when do I get to talk to Sara?" He sort of gasps, but then turns back to look at me. "And who told you about me? Mrs. Peterson promised never to disclose my real work until I was ready to have it known."

"If you remember, Isaac, it didn't take you very long to read my mind and decide an apology had to be taken care of. Well, I took your advice and the apology was to Dr. T.J. Peterson. When I told him you'd invited me to lunch, he couldn't wait to tell me all about you," I chuckled. "Are you ready now to let me introduce you to Sara? I'll keep your work a secret."

"Thanks, Jill, and I'm glad you made that decision to apologize. You're a special lady, and I'm so happy for T.J. He's suffered way too long for something he had no part in creating. I'll keep you both in my prayers, and I hope you'll keep me in yours. And yes, let's go and see if my special personal charm is still working today." As he takes my hand and pulls me out of my chair, he's stammering, "Wha-what di-did you sa-say her na-name wa-was?' but then he starts chuckling as we walk across the store.

"Sara Elaine Tallison, you--you character with a 'no loss for words' vocabulary," I smirk but can't keep from laughing at his uncontrolled or put-on excitement.

After the introductions are taken care of, I leave them to get acquainted, and I return to my desk to finish my posting. I'd thought I'd do that before taking a break to eat the plain unappetizing bagel I'd brought with me this morning. I'm just so glad it won't be long now until I can do it all on the computer which is just waiting to be used.

Jane has made a nice sale and is marking the inventory accordingly when I hear the bell on the front door jingle again. I look up and can hardly believe my eyes when I see T.J. coming toward us with a smile on his face and two sacks from a fast food restaurant in his hand. "Hey, Everybody, I knew Mom was gone today and you might be having trouble figuring out what to do for lunch, so I brought enough for all of you." He quickly glances around the store until his eyes focus in on Isaac and Sara. "Isaac, it's good to see you. It's been a while. There's enough food for you, too, if you want to join us."

I have to cover my mouth tightly to keep my laughter from being heard or seen, and when I look over at Isaac, his eyes are sparkling and I can tell he knows exactly why T.J. is here with lunch items.

"It's so good to see you again, T.J." Isaac is grinning as he extends his hand when he and Sara get to my desk. "However, I have already asked one of these lovely ladies to have lunch with me outside the confines of this outstanding establishment. So, if you don't mind, I think I'll take her to one of the nice restaurants down the street."

Only then, as T.J. is about to open his mouth in protest, does Isaac lift up Sara's hand and turn toward the front door. He pats T.J. on the arm as he walks by chuckling. "Enjoy your lunch with that very special and pretty lady, T.J. and be sure to thank God every day that he's brought her into that otherwise lonely and miserable life of yours."

They'd been gone only minutes when the bell jingles and Jane excuses herself to help a customer, although it proves not to be a customer. It's Mrs. Peterson coming back from the sale. "Did we have a problem, Jill, that caused you to call T.J.?" She'd apparently seen his car outside, but then she notices the food sacks and a smile is quickly on her face. "Just being protective, I see, while your mother is away, or could it be that you thought Isaac might drop by today? Did he come today?" she asks as she glances around the store. "I was hoping he might have found something special this trip for us to sell with Christmas coming so soon.."

"I don't believe he brought anything in, Mrs. Peterson, but he's in town and he has taken Sara to lunch," I reply.

"Oh, my, it appears you made all this fuss for nothing, Dear," she giggled as she patted T.J.'s arm.

"You don't need to rub it in, Mother Dear. I just thought it might be a little difficult for the girls to get away for lunch, but apparently they had it covered pretty well. Have you eaten or would you like to join Jill and me? It's going to be cold if it's not eaten soon.

"I'm a little hungry, and since the whole store smells like a hamburger joint, I'll be happy to help you dispose of this very large lunch you've brought. Where did Jane go? Maybe we'd better see if Jake has eaten yet--he can usually eat anything at anytime of the day, so he can help us out." She pushes the buzzer which tells Jake he's needed.

"Jane is around here somewhere, but I think she brought something she's going to heat in the microwave. She's watching her calories again. Sara going off with Isaac seems to have surprised T.J. a little." I give him one of my sweetest smiles, but I only get a quick wrinkled up nose in return. "However, I'm really starved so shall we see what kind of yummy things he brought for us to share, Mrs. Peterson. It has to be better than the plain bagel I brought with me this morning. You do trust his selections, don't you?" I giggle.

"You two are going to pay for this teasing--someway, sometime, somehow, just you wait and see." He tries to put a stern determined look on his face but it doesn't work as his mother reaches up and pats his cheek.

"We love you, Dear, and you were very chivalrous by trying to take care of the girls while I was gone. Let's have a bite to eat."

Mrs. Peterson tells about the three items she found at the sale, and she'd arranged for them to be delivered this afternoon. Jake is finally answering the buzzer and is sniffing the smell of food as he joins us. "Oh, Jake, please help us eat some of this food that T.J. brought for lunch. I also have a delivery coming this afternoon that you may need help with." She looks toward T.J. and asks, "Would you be available, T.J.?"

"I'd love to help, Mom, but I have four or five patients coming in this afternoon so I should be heading back to the office. Maybe Isaac will stay and help if he ever decides to bring Sara back."

"Don't worry, Mrs. Peterson. If I see I can't handle the items and the delivery guys can't help, I'll call my son who's on vacation this week," Jake remarks.

Before he leaves, T.J. bends down to whisper in my ear, "I'll call, Pretty Lady. There must be a story that goes along with that earlier remark by Isaac."

"Not really, but thanks, T.J., for bringing the food. I really did enjoy it," I whisper back.

CHAPTER THIRTY-TWO

*T.*J. calls about 6 o'clock and asks if I'd like to go to a movie or maybe watch one at his place. "I have one whose title fits what Isaac remarked that you were, but the movie may be about a girl who is nothing like you. I haven't seen it, but would you like to come and see what it's about? It's cool enough that maybe Orion might show up, too."

"How can we watch the movie if we're on the roof looking for Orion?"

"Magic, Sweetie, magic," he chuckles. "Actually, there's a TV and a DVD in one of the cabinets right at the top of the stairs. I guess we never got around to watching a movie up there."

I'd really like to see Orion up there in the sky, but I'm wondering if T.J. will behave himself or try to cause problems again. He must be ready to get his face slapped again if he's inviting me over. "T.J., you remember what happened the last time I was there, don't you? I certainly do, and I haven't been back."

"I remember very well, Jill, and there won't be any repeat performance. Shall I pick you up or do you want to drive over so you can leave whenever you want?"

"It would save you making two trips if I drive over, and we both have to work tomorrow morning. I'll see you about 7:30." After we eat, I pull on a sweat suit for the warmth that I'll need on the roof. It feels so good, and I guess I'm now ready for another adventure.

"Before we go to the roof, T.J., I have to tell you about the items Isaac had in his car for your mother when he and Sara got back not long after you'd left. The heavy one she'd mentioned was an unusual antique chest with unique carvings and handles. There were also two beautiful glass items--a punch bowl with 12 cups and a matching pair of candlesticks that were outstanding. The other was a beautiful bowl in perfect shape that dated back to 1846. I even got a little kiss before he left--a 'good luck kiss' he said. It was nothing like yours, T.J. Your mother got a big hug, and Sara walked Isaac out to his car which I'm sure ended in a nice kiss."

"He's certainly trying to be a lady's man, isn't he? I wonder how many more sweet ladies he has across the country. I guess it's a good thing he works with youth and not all sweet ladies."

"T.J. that's a horrible thing to say. You've known him for several years and I doubt that you've heard anything bad about him. He acts and thinks like a pastor, at least the ones I've known. **Your** pastor even kissed my hand, when he was talking to us that one Sunday, and he hardly knew me."

"I'm sorry, I shouldn't have said that. Isaac is a wonderful guy and it's just my own insecurities showing up again. It's probably his age being so close to yours that made me cringe when you said he'd kissed you. I'm trying, Jill, really I am. I don't want to be like this. Shall we go up to the roof now?"

The movie is "Pretty Woman" which was filmed in 1990. It's funny, touching, and very good. We also luck out and see Orion, which is a thrill, and I have to sit and enjoy the sight for at least 20 minutes. He did put his arm around me during the movie, but nothing else happened. We go downstairs to have a cup of coffee and some brownies which he says he baked himself. I must admit that the condo smelled like something chocolate had been baking when I arrived.

During our snack, we decide that we'll try to go shopping together for a little while tomorrow afternoon. Christmas is coming so quickly, the store has really been busy, the calendar is filling up with activities, and Jessica and C.J.'s wedding is going to be here before we know it.

Of course, since Isaac had a kiss, T.J. wants one before he'll let me leave. He has been so good that I can't refuse one kiss. However, that leads to his walking me down to my car where one additional kiss is required before he'll open the car door and another one before he'll close it. "Goodnight, Special Lady," he calls as I pull out of his parking garage.

Since Christmas is on Sunday this year, they have scheduled the Christmas Cantata on the 18th to accommodate all those who will be traveling. The practices are held early on Sunday mornings as well as the usual Wednesday evening rehearsals, so I've been meeting T.J. at the church. I'm amazed at how smoothly everything is going and can only guess that the director has done this many times before. At the last rehearsal on the 14th, we all feel ready for the big performance. Now, we're all here on Sunday, and it's really so thrilling to be part of a very outstanding and meaningful Sunday morning Cantata.

❧

It's unbelievable but it's only five days now before the wedding. I've talked to Jess and Mom many times during the preceding weeks, and I'm assured that everything is ready. C.J. arrives as planned on Wednesday evening, and I try to stay out of the way so he and his family can make any last minute plans that are needed. There will be four cars going on Friday although I'll be ahead of all the rest. C.J. will need his car to get them to the airport for their honeymoon trip, T.J. will drive his because I'm staying to celebrate Christmas with my family, and Dr. and Mrs. Peterson will drive down in their own car.

I get to Sanford for lunch on Friday and have to hear about all the things Mom and Jess got done on Thursday.

Later, while Jessica is getting ready, I'm sent to the church to make sure the groom has arrived. It's my turn to shower and get dressed when I get back, and we're soon ready to go to the church and get this little sister of mine married. I must say everything is beautiful, Mom has done a magnificent job, and Jess is lovely walking down the aisle on the arm of her father. Of course, I have tears in my eyes, (since I always cry at weddings), but I do my job when I'm supposed to and do it well, if I do say so myself.

The reception is quite a gathering and I get to meet many of the Peterson family. T.J. is introducing me to grandparents, uncles and aunts, cousins, and friends that I'll never be able to keep straight. It won't be hard to remember the grandparents, though, because Mr. and Mrs. Cameron are a delightful petite couple with constant smiles on their faces and ready to go onto the dance floor and dance the night away. The Petersons, on the other hand, are both quite tall, stalwart and rather reserved, but they get into the spirit of things and start celebrating after a toast or two.

It's getting rather late and Jess and C.J. have slipped away when I see T.J. coming toward me with an odd look on his face. "May I have this dance, Jill?"

"Of course, T.J." It's a slow dance and he's holding me ever so close until he has us maneuvered right off the dance floor.

"I wanted to see you, Sweetie, before you disappeared and I'd have to drive home tonight without wishing you a

Merry Christmas. When do you think you'll be coming back to Chapel Hill?"

"Since my job will be waiting for me on Monday, I'll most likely drive back before dark Sunday night. I'm sure, with the baby, Jodi and Richard won't stay long at either of the grandparents' this year."

"Would you consider coming to the condo when you get back?" he whispers. "I've got something I need to talk to you about."

"I realize that the time I promised to be your companion is running out, T.J., but you do have another week. I suppose we could negotiate for a few more days, but I'm not too crazy about continuing something indefinitely that isn't really going to benefit either of us. If you haven't made a decision by the 1st of the year, I really see no reason to keep up with the pretense."

"Just come see me, Jill. Will you please do that?" Before I can answer, he pulls me into his arms and I get one of his unforgettable kisses. He then brings his lips to my ear and whispers, "Pretty please, Sweetie?"

"All right, T.J., you win. I'll drop by when I get into town. I really need to go help Mom now, so I'll see you Sunday. Have a nice Christmas." I hope he'll be surprised when he finds the small package I'd slipped under the tree at his parents.

When we open our presents on Sunday, I'm a little disappointed when there's no gift from T.J. in the shopping bag that Mrs. Peterson had given me Friday morning before

I'd left for the wedding. No comment is made by Mom or Dad, either, so could they just be trying to spare me the pain of talking about it or could T.J. possibly be planning something special that they know about? I really don't think there's any big surprise, though, from the tone of our conversation at the reception.

֍

When I reach the condo, the door is unlocked so I step into the entrance. I was just about to call his name when I hear his voice and realize he must be talking on the phone. I can't help but hear his side of the conversation which goes something like this:

"I don't know what to do. She hasn't been very communicative the last few times I've tried to talk to her about the situation, but it's obvious that something is bothering her."

"I suppose I could use the other technique, but I've been a little hesitant to suggest it because of how she might react."

"All right, maybe I'll try that. I have to do something before it gets completely out of hand and she walks out without anything being settled concerning her future."

There's a long pause while, apparently, the other person is talking.

"Yeah, I know, and when she's with me, I'm not sure how much longer I can control my feelings. She gave me a deadline; actually I set one for myself, and that is almost up. I have come up with a plan over the last few days which

I hope she'll accept. If not, I may face something I'll regret the rest of my life."

"No, I don't feel there's any problem in that category although I was a little upset about the one situation I discussed with you the other day. I was out of line again, but my insecurities just made me act like a crazy fool.

"I'm sure now that I don't need any more time, and I'm not having second thoughts about my true feelings. Oops, I just heard the door shut so I'd better go. It's probably her and I don't want to keep her waiting."

"My life certainly isn't the way I'd like it to be right now, and there's only one way to correct it. I've decided to make a positive decision, most likely tonight."

"Just remember you were the one who pointed out to me that I'm not a kid anymore, and I finally do know what I really want. But what if she won't go along because she doesn't want me anymore?"

"You're probably right. God always knows best."

"O.K., thanks. I'll see you tomorrow."

∽

I have just finished hearing 'made me act like a crazy fool' as I go out and slam the door after me. If he feels I have something on my mind but won't talk about it, and now he's ready to try a new technique, he's got a big surprise coming. And what about the situation he's been discussing with someone else and a plan he's come up with which he hopes I'll accept? Well, T.J., my friend, I probably won't. I said Friday that I'd promise to be there for you until after the holidays, but I'm declaring that the holidays are over for us as of tonight. Your time is up, Dr. Peterson, and I'm definitely out of here. I can't take anymore of your uncertainties.

I've pushed the button for the elevator, but wouldn't you know this is the time it's taking its slow sweet time getting up here. I'm stomping my foot and pushing the button again and again when I feel his arms go around my waist.

"What are you doing standing here waiting for the elevator, Jill? I didn't know you were here until I heard the door shut. I thought you were coming in, not going out."

"Apparently, Dr. Peterson. Remove your hands from me and get your elevator up here so I can go home. Whatever your new technique is that you're thinking about using on me isn't going to work, and I'm not going to agree to any of your plans for satisfying your male ego, either. Our holidays are over and I'm not giving you anymore time."

"Jill, please come back in and let me explain the entire conversation that you must have heard only a portion of, and by the way, thank you so much for the money clip. I've wanted one of those for quite a while."

"Don't try to change the subject, T.J. I heard enough just now to decide that I'm declaring my spending time with you is over. Ja-just le-let me go-o, and I-I'll be ou-out of ya-your li-life. O-oh, why ca-can't I ke-keep fr-from sob-sobbing when it com-comes to yu-you?"

He turns me around to face him, takes his hankie and wipes my tears away, and then I'm in his arms being carried back into the condo. He sits down on the couch with me on his lap. I feel like a little kid when he does this, but it feels so good to be in his arms.

"This isn't exactly how I wanted this to happen, Jill, but I have something to say to you and I want you to listen to every word. First, about that phone conversation I was just having. Some of what you overheard was about a patient who hasn't been cooperating with us, and her health is deteriorating because of it. We're going to try a new technique.

The other part was actually about me finally making the decision that I can't live in the past any longer or without you in my life. I love you, Jill, and I probably have since the first night I saw you. While cherishing you, spending time with you, and even teasing you, my love kept growing and I have finally come to my senses and I want to know that you belong to me, as I now belong to you, heart and soul. I want to spend the rest of my life making you happy, giving you a reason each and every day to believe in me, and that you can truly trust my sincerity. So, I'm asking you to marry me. Will you, Jill, be my most precious Sweetheart and accept my proposal? I definitely know I want you to be my wife, and I want our wedding day as soon as possible I'd even go for an elopement if you'd like to marry me before the end of the year."

He is trying to smile as he waits for my reply, but I had felt the tension in his voice, and he seems extremely nervous.

"Are you really sure, T.J.? It felt like you were slipping away lately instead of getting over your insecurities. I really don't want to elope, and I don't want a guy who doesn't truly love me but will say sweet and wonderful words just to keep me dangling either."

He slowly and tenderly moves me from his lap to the space beside him on the couch. He is then quickly on the floor in front of me. "Will this convince you, Sweetie?" he whispers as he's now on his knees and opens a small jewelry box which contains a beautiful solitaire diamond ring. "I actually bought it before the Charity Ball, but that night didn't turn out the way I'd planned."

While he's slipping it on my finger, I'm saying, "Yes, T.J., that's very convincing, and as soon as my sister gets back from her honeymoon, we'll plan a wedding." He then seals it with a wonderful kiss. He now has that cute smile on his face and that definitive dimple is also there telling me all is well.

ABOUT THE AUTHOR

As the youngest of three girls in her family, Sally has always felt she'd been the luckiest growing up. The middle sister, Mary, was her teacher; she came home from school each day and taught her practically all she had learned. She remarked often as the years passed that Sally was ready for third grade when she started in the first grade.

Mary was also the one who taught her how to climb trees, race their stick cars around a big tree in the side yard, and play catch with the only kid in their neighborhood—a boy who lived two houses away. Mary had never wanted to play with dolls but begrudgingly gave in to Sally at times, so maybe Sally was her teacher in that respect because she became a wonderful mother.

Later, Mary taught her a lot about cooking when Sally lived with her and her husband before she was married soon after her boyfriend returned from his army service.

The closeness of the sisters in this book reminds Sally of the many happy hours she shared with her sister. They were both amazed when, several times, one would pick up the phone to call the other and discover her already on the line without the phone ever ringing. They were able to continue sharing many secrets, dreams, hopes, and even failures in their long-distance relationship before Mary passed away at too young an age.

Printed in the United States
By Bookmasters